She wanted to kiss him.

The smoldering look in his eyes tore at her reeling senses, and she whispered, "Joe...we can't...we don't dare...."

She saw understanding come to his darkened eyes, combined with a sadness and raw desire—all there for her. "I'm sorry, I didn't mean to hurt you, Joe. But it's the past. The past..."

"I understand," he rasped. He sensed how much Annie wanted to be held—if but for a moment. If she had willingly stepped into his arms, it would have meant Annie had come to grips with the fact that loving a marine was worth more than possibly losing him.

Tears stung Annie's eyes as she stood in the opened door. She reached out, barely touching his cheek.

"Good night, Joe...." She turned away.

"Good night, Annie...." He watched her be swallowed up by the night....

Dear Reader,

Welcome to Silhouette **Special Edition** . . . welcome to romance. This month we have a wonderful selection of books for you, and reading them will be the perfect way to get into that summertime spirit!

June is the month of brides, so this month's THAT SPECIAL WOMAN! selection is right in tune with the times. *Daughter of the Bride,* by Christine Flynn, is a poignant, warm family tale that you won't want to miss.

We've also got the action-packed *Countdown*— Lindsay McKenna's next installment of the thrilling MEN OF COURAGE series. And you won't want to miss *Always,* by Ginna Gray. This tender story is another book in Ginna's wonderful series, THE BLAINES AND THE McCALLS OF CROCKETT, TEXAS.

June also brings us more books by favorite authors— Marie Ferrarella, Pat Warren—as well as a compelling debut book by Colleen Norman.

I hope that you enjoy this book and all of the stories to come. Have a wonderful June!

Sincerely,

Tara Gavin
Senior Editor

Please address questions and book requests to:
Reader Service
U.S.: P.O. Box 1325, Buffalo, NY 14269
Canadian: P.O. Box 1050, Niagara Falls, Ont. L2E 7G7

LINDSAY McKENNA
COUNTDOWN

Silhouette®

SPECIAL EDITION®

Published by Silhouette Books
America's Publisher of Contemporary Romance

Dedicated to Claire Gerus, my "old" editor from Harlequin days; Grace Chicorel, a powerful lady in publishing, and Rosemarie Brown, an ace researcher. I salute you all!

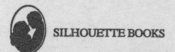 SILHOUETTE BOOKS

ISBN 0-373-09890-1

COUNTDOWN

Copyright © 1994 by Lindsay McKenna

Printed in U.S.A.

LINDSAY McKENNA

spent three years serving her country as a meteorologist in the U.S. Navy, so much of her knowledge comes from direct experience. In addition, she spends a great deal of time researching each book, whether it be at the Pentagon or at military bases, extensively interviewing key personnel.

Lindsay is also a pilot. She and her husband of fifteen years, both avid "rock hounds" and hikers, live in Arizona.

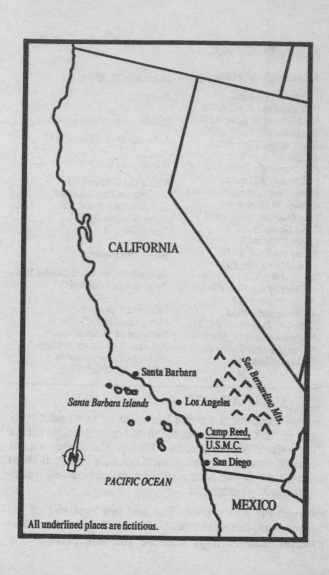

CALIFORNIA

Santa Barbara

Santa Barbara Islands

Los Angeles

San Bernardino Mts.

Camp Reed,
U.S.M.C.

San Diego

PACIFIC OCEAN

MEXICO

All underlined places are fictitious.

Chapter One

Annie Yellow Horse was nervous. As she entered the headquarters building at Camp Reed, one of the two largest Marine Corps bases in the United States, the hot California-desert wind almost grabbed the door from her hand, recalling the persistent wind where she'd grown up, on a sprawling Navajo reservation in New Mexico. Wryly, she reminded herself that she wasn't home, no matter how much she wanted to be. Annie didn't know a lot about Camp Reed, except that they'd had problems in the brig area over the years—and that Captain Ramsey asking her to transfer here meant trouble with a capital *T*.

After speaking briefly to a lieutenant in the busy personnel office, she took a seat on a bench in the hall outside and waited. The lieutenant had told her that Captain Ramsey wouldn't be meeting her after all. Instead, Sergeant Donnally, who was to be her new boss, was coming to meet her. Perhaps because she was Navajo, or a woman—or both—Annie had learned to rely strongly on her deep intuition. And if her tightened gut was any indication, she thought, this Donnally meant trouble, too.

Rubbing her damp palms on the skirt of her light green summer uniform, Annie worked to maintain her outer calm, but her stomach felt full of butterflies. Maybe it was simply because of being uprooted from Camp Lejeune in North Carolina, where she'd been stationed for the last two years, she tried to reassure herself. She had friends there and a comfortable life-style that suited her. Now she needed to find an apartment somewhere outside the gates of Camp Reed and completely reestablish herself—including making new friends.

Annie groaned. Friends. She had women friends, but none here at Reed, and it was difficult to start from scratch. Probably the only problem she had with military life was repeatedly losing the camaraderie of friends from a previous base. Hearing the door open at the end of the passageway, Annie sensed a powerful, potentially threatening presence. Narrowing her eyes, she saw a tall marine moving briskly toward her. Gulping back her initial response to panic, Annie used all her senses to decipher this dark-haired sergeant, his garrison cap gripped tightly in his left hand, his shoulders thrown back so proudly that he looked more like a furious eagle than a man.

Her Native American ancestry and reservation training had helped Annie develop an almost psychic ability to "read" people, but the approaching sergeant was projecting an unusual combination of menace and physical appeal that had her senses spinning. His square face appeared merciless, darkly tanned by the California sun and not at all softened by frosty blue eyes. His generous mouth was compressed into a single line of obvious unhappiness.

Annie tensed inwardly as he strode confidently toward her. He didn't seem to see her, his focus squarely on the Personnel sign above the open doorway next to her. Black hair sprinkled his arms and peeked out from the neck of the white T-shirt he wore beneath a tan shirt. Although he was more than six feet tall and had to be close to two hundred pounds, Annie couldn't spot an ounce of fat on his frame. If anything, he reminded her of a well-fed summer cougar, its beautifully sleek appearance masking its inherent danger.

Annie switched to her inner sensing equipment. This man was very angry. But at whom? Could this be Sergeant Donnally? Although he was still too far away for her to read the nametag above his left uniform pocket, her intuition said yes. While her head cautioned, "wait and see," Annie experienced a surprising lurch and pounding of her heart. Stunned by her unexpected response, she sat very still, attempting to integrate the unreasonable feeling. Only one man in her life had ever made her heart respond this way, and he had died in Desert Storm.

Tears leaked into Annie's eyes, and she quickly bowed her head. Marines didn't cry. Their code demanded they remain tough, not showing fear or tears or pain. To show any kind of weakness meant losing the respect of other marines, and Annie wouldn't allow that to happen. So, swallowing hard, she forced the tears away—but the memory of losing Jeff continued to ache like a wound that hadn't completely healed. Perhaps, Annie realized, as she raised her head to focus on the marine rapidly closing the distance between them, it was best that she'd been transferred here. She had met and fallen in love with Jeff at Camp Lejeune and it was still filled with memories. Yes, coming here was best. Or so she hoped.

* * *

Sergeant Joe Donnally tried to contain his fury. He was angry that his boss, Captain Ramsey, had asked him to come retrieve the world-famous brig tracker, Corporal Annie Yellow Horse. What a hell of a name. And she was probably just as different as her name sounded, he fumed inwardly. He didn't have time to be chief meeter and greeter to every new brig chaser transferred to Reed. With Ramsey turning on the heat to get the lackluster brig personnel squared away, Joe didn't need this welcoming-committee stuff. Anyway, he admitted to himself, he was angry that Ramsey felt they couldn't do without this woman brig chaser. Baloney! No one was indispensable in the corps, and they didn't need this prima donna tracker. He had plenty of men—including himself—who were decent enough trackers to hunt escaped prisoners if necessary.

Momentarily, Joe's focus shifted, and he was startled to see a young woman with copper-colored skin sitting almost at attention on a wooden bench outside the personnel office. His heart sped up, and his scowl deepened. She had huge, cinnamon-colored eyes, and her black hair was neatly coiffed in a short style that emphasized her oval face and high cheekbones. Was this Yellow Horse? No, he growled to himself. She was too pretty. He'd expected someone old and tough looking—a throwback to the old-corps days.

In spite of himself, Joe felt some of his anger dissolve as he met and held her widening gaze for a moment. Her gentle look offered him no returning challenge as he glared in her direction. Something in him told him this woman was Annie Yellow Horse, although he tried to convince himself it was a crazy idea. Whoever she was, she wasn't conventionally pretty, but had an earthy kind of unspoken beauty. She wore no makeup, yet her skin glowed, the perfect backdrop to her expressive eyes and mouth. Joe slowed his pace as his gaze settled on that mouth. He'd never seen one quite like it—full lips curving slightly upward at the corners and parted just enough to make any man groan with need.

Did she realize how damned sensuous she was? Joe wondered. He knew only that he was staring at her like a slavering wolf—a totally improper reaction to a fellow marine. Desperately gathering his strewn feelings, ignoring the blood pumping through him in response to her single, luminous look, Joe tore his gaze from hers. He was close enough now to read the nametag above the pocket of her feminine uniform: Yellow Horse. With a groan, he slowed considerably, his senses rebelling with anger and frustration.

Annie Yellow Horse wasn't anything like the image he'd invented in his mind. Captain Ramsey had spoken of her so often and in such glowing terms that Joe had automatically begun to dislike her. No one could be *that* good, he'd thought, as Ramsey extolled her capabilities as a tracker to heaven and back. After that kind of buildup, she had no right to look so young—and so damned beautiful! His gaze locked aggressively on hers, and he saw that her eyes were filled with curiosity and compassion.

If he'd expected some hardened woman corporal, he certainly didn't see one. Joe watched her slowly rise, tension evident in her tall, lithe body. He wanted to hate her. He certainly didn't need to play baby-sitter to some world-famous tracker coming into *his* section. Not right now.

Joe halted and tried to collect himself. His heart was pounding, and a strange emotion seemed to be radiating outward from it, touching him softly, subtly, throughout his body. What the hell was going on? Was Yellow Horse more than just a tracker? More than just a woman? As he drilled a merciless look into her eyes, he realized he barely needed to look down, so she must be at least five foot nine. Compressing his lips, he continued to glare at her.

"Yellow Horse?" he snarled. Joe hated himself for behaving this way, but he had to take his anger out on someone, and she was the one making his life even more complicated.

Annie felt buffeted by the marine's snarl, but she held her ground, tightened her jaw and deliberately hardened her own eyes. "I am. And who are you?" she flung back in a low, husky tone. She saw surprise in the sergeant's icy blue gaze. He was trying to tower over her, but because only three inches in height separated them, he couldn't do it, so he placed his hands imperiously on his hips to bluff her. Annie had been in the Marine Corps for six years, and she knew her place in it as a corporal. This man might be trying to threaten her with his stance, but he was only one grade above her—and he had no right to try to intimidate her this way.

Joe scowled heavily. He'd seen her eyes go hard—seen her luscious mouth thin with displeasure. And she hadn't taken a step back from him—hadn't so much as batted an eyelash. She'd held her ground and, bitterly, he had to respect her for it. "I'm your new boss, Yellow Horse. I'm Sergeant Donnally. I was sent over to baby-sit you. Captain Ramsey couldn't make it, so you've got me instead." His glance flicked to the personnel file she held tensely in her left hand. "That your orders?"

"Yes," Annie snapped back, "it is."

"Give them to me." Joe felt a little chagrined at his own rudeness. Momentarily, he saw confusion dart through Annie's beautiful eyes—the most alluring feature of her face. Her fingers accidentally grazed his as she handed over the folder, and Joe nearly jerked the file out of her grasp. He pretended to look at the paperwork, but it was a ruse. His heart was hammering so hard that he wondered wildly if this was some sort of early heart-attack warning.

As he paged through the papers in her file, Joe could feel her silent appraisal. Well, let her look, he thought, it wasn't going to do her any good. Yellow Horse meant nothing but trouble to him, arriving at a time when the office situation was still tentative and volatile. They had so many morale problems—the legacy of Jacobs, their recently departed captain—and Joe didn't want to try to integrate a new member on top of it all. Especially since, as a corporal, Yellow Horse would be looking to him for help and direction.

"Everything seems to be in order," Joe said gruffly. He glanced over—and instantly drowned in her eyes, which had again lost their hardness. He felt himself being pulled into their gold-flecked, cinnamon depths, framed by thick, black lashes. Why did she have to be so desirable? Disgusted with himself and his response to her, he added in a low snarl, "Come with me."

"Wait!" Annie tilted her head. The sergeant was obviously furious—with her?

"I don't have all day. What is it?"

She tried to let his irritability slide off her. "Sergeant Donnally, is something wrong?"

He gave her a sarcastic look. "*Everything's* wrong, Corporal."

"How so?"

Restraining his building anger, Joe drilled her with a venomous look that he hoped would put a stop to her questions. "Corporal," he announced brusquely, "you work for me. You're in my section. When I want you to know something, I'll be the first to tell you. If I don't want to talk to you about certain things, that's the way it'll be. Do we understand each other?''

Annie held his glare and felt ice pour through her veins. "I've had six years in the corps, Sergeant, and I've just taken my test to become a sergeant. In two months, I'll know if I'll be an E-5 like you. I feel a lot of resentment coming from you toward me. If there's a problem, perhaps we should work it out here and now. I don't want to start a new assignment with someone hating my guts."

Joe recoiled inwardly. Annie's soft exterior concealed a steel backbone, he realized. The look in her eyes was no longer lustrous and inviting, it was pointed and fearless. Although part of him respected her for it, a greater part disliked her for her courage. His lips lifted away from his teeth, and he put his face inches from hers, his breathing strangled as he spoke. "*Corporal,* you work for *me.* Got that? Until you get that sergeant's stripe, you'll do as I say. I'm not the kind of marine who communicates a whole lot, so you're just going to have to put up with it." His mouth twisted slightly. "Unless you want a trans-fer—which wouldn't bother me at all."

Annie swayed and caught herself, inwardly shaken by Donnally's anger. His blue eyes narrowed with such a fierce light that she knew this man was a hunter and dangerous, with a brutal side that could hurt her emotionally. "I've got it, Sergeant," she whispered tightly. But even as he pulled away and straightened, Annie knew she was in trouble. Great. Her boss hated her just for being here.

Joe tried desperately to contain his ugly, unraveling feelings. What was wrong with him? He never snarled at his people like this! Thoroughly irritated with himself, he spun on his heel. "Follow me," he snapped.

Stalking down the passageway, he tried to figure out what had happened. Yes, he was angry with Captain Ramsey for pulling him off far more important work at the brig office to come and pick up Yellow Horse. Further, he disagreed strongly with his boss about needing a world-class tracker here at Reed: no prisoners had escaped in the two years he'd been here. His conscience smarted. He'd seen his fury hurt Annie. Damn! Now he was thinking of her as Annie! *Use her last name and keep it impersonal,* he angrily instructed himself.

Scrambling internally, Joe didn't want to admit that she'd surprised him—not only with her looks, but with her courage in standing up to his blistering "welcome." Perhaps her Navajo lineage gave her a special kind of bravery, he mused. Not many marines stood toe-to-toe with him when it came down to a confrontation. Joe was a scrapper, and he was street smart. He'd grown up tough in a gang in the barrio of National City, near San Diego, and he knew how to fight—with his fists and his mouth. Although he looked like his Hispanic and Yaqui Indian mother, his father was of Irish ancestry, so except for his blue eyes, his name, Donnally, didn't fit Joe's otherwise dark looks.

As he pushed open the door, the California heat and bright sunlight struck him full force. Settling the garrison cap on his head, he glanced over his shoulder to see if Yellow Horse was coming. Disgruntled to find her near his left shoulder, he was shocked that he hadn't heard her at all. Hell! Usually he heard everything—his awareness of his surroundings was, by necessity, sharply honed. That supersensitivity to his environment had saved his life numerous times growing up in the gangs, who fought with deadly knives and pistols. Bitterness leaked through Joe at Annie's obvious abilities. This woman was going to be the number-two person in his section whether he liked it or not. And he most emphatically did not.

As they moved down the sidewalk, bracketed with recently mowed green Bermuda grass, Joe entertained the idea of telling Captain Ramsey he wanted a transfer. Again his conscience needled him—more sharply this time. Joe had a fierce loyalty to his section, to the men and women who put their lives on the line every day. No, they'd been left enough in the lurch by Jacobs, without Joe sulking and leaving them in more trouble.

"Sergeant?"

Joe started. This time he hadn't realized that Yellow Horse had come abreast of him as he strode across the asphalt parking lot. The noontime sun blasted them, and Joe began to break out in a mild sweat.

"What is it, Corporal?"

"Can you tell me what your office does?"

Having unwillingly made eye contact again, Joe tried to tear his gaze from her. She wore a bucket-style hat, her black hair as shiny as a raven's wing in the sunlight where it showed around the edges. Annie had a grace that he'd not seen in many women before—an easiness and familiarity with her body, maybe. Although Joe couldn't quite define it, the way she moved was riveting. Disgusted with himself, he snapped his head forward.

"I run Section A of three sections at the brig," he responded brusquely. "My people serve two functions: brig duty and transport of prisoners."

"How long have you been stationed here at Camp Reed?"

He knew she was testing him, trying to find out something about him—as her boss. "Two years," he replied with a glare.

"And Captain Ramsey was just assigned? I imagine that's causing you some changes?" she asked, understanding lacing her voice.

Her insight was startling, and Joe scowled again. If she could fathom that much, what else could she perceive? The thought was unsettling as hell. "Let's put it this way, Corporal—the last officer who ran the brig was a total loss. He was a screwup from the git-go, punching his ticket because he had to have this assignment look good on his personnel record so he could get early major's leaves. Otherwise, he couldn't have cared less about the brig, the prisoners, the transport of them or my people."

"So you ended up shouldering a lot of the load to protect your section?" she pressed gently.

Joe's mouth fell open. He halted and spun around, capturing her gaze. "Are you psychic or something?" he croaked. Then he caught himself and frowned in warning as he ruthlessly searched her eyes. Eyes that were wide, vulnerable and without harshness, he noted. Her lips lifted very slightly, almost into a shy smile.

"Not psychic," Annie said softly. "Being in the corps six years maybe gives me a better perspective than someone who's had less time in grade."

Disgruntled, Joe nodded. "Yeah, things got rough. I came in while Captain Jacobs was on board, and we all suffered under the bastard for two years. I saw him tear down my people because he was unhappy and didn't want to be here."

"So you ran a blocking action, took the heat and protected them?" Annie guessed. She saw the surprise in the icy depths of his light blue eyes. As growly as Donnally was, she sensed that the inner man—perhaps the *real* man beneath that armored exterior—was likable and decent. She vowed to withhold judgment until she could understand the responsibilities he carried on his broad, capable-looking shoulders.

"Yes. . . ." he admitted, hesitating.

Annie smiled a little, hoping to ease the tension between them. "And Captain Ramsey has just come on board, so you're trying to help him clean up the mess created by the previous officer?"

Joe gave a bark of laughter and dropped his hands on his hips as he studied Annie. "If I didn't know better, I'd say you were some kind of investigator from C.I.D., Criminal Investigation Division, not a brig chaser."

With an answering chuckle, Annie shrugged, noticing the way laughter changed Donnally's dark, thundercloud features, if but for a moment. "No, I'm not C.I.D., Sergeant, I'm Navajo. My grandfather was a code talker in World War II, and my mother comes from a long line of medicine women. I've lived close to the earth all my life. Six years in the corps gives me knowledge on another level. It's pretty easy to put two and two together."

Joe didn't want to like Annie, but in that moment, he liked her immensely. If he'd treated a male marine the way he had treated her so far, he knew there would be no laughter, compromise or softening between them. No, it was Annie's ability as a woman, he guessed, that had defused some of the anger he'd aimed at her. Still, he reminded himself, he couldn't afford to like her or get close to her. Not now, not *ever*.

His mouth thinning with the thought, he held her upturned gaze, which spoke eloquently of her compassion for the personal hell he'd suffered these past two years. "Your grandfather was a code talker?" he asked, with new respect for her heritage. During World War II, he knew, the Navajo code talkers had been drafted into the Marine Corps and used to convey messages in their native language to prevent the Japanese from understanding them. It had worked so successfully that Navajo men had served with great pride, helping to save hundreds, if not thousands, of lives during the war years.

Annie nodded. "My grandfather is eighty-four now, but he still has clear memories of the time he served in the Marine Corps."

"That's something to be proud of," Joe muttered. Her grandfather being a marine explained somewhat why she was in the corps. Annie was following a tradition begun over fifty years ago. Joe had to back off a little on his aggressive attitude toward her, knowing she carried such a proud history.

Standing there in the parking lot, Joe realized he was staring at her the way a biologist might stare at a bug under a microscope. But he didn't *want* to know anything else about Annie—Yellow Horse, he corrected himself savagely. "Let's take the station wagon over there," he said, pointing toward it. "I'll show you the office and then it will be chow time."

Annie knew that Donnally wanted nothing to do with her, and the knowledge hurt. She liked the proud way he held himself. She liked the rugged look of his square face. Now, in the sunlight, she noticed several small scars across his prominent chin and a more recent one across his left cheekbone. His nose appeared to have been broken several times, adding to his rough-and-ready appearance. No, Donnally certainly wasn't pretty-boy handsome. Also, despite his Irish-sounding name and blue eyes, his dark coloring spoke of a mixed heritage, probably Hispanic.

There was nothing forgiving about Donnally, either, she thought. Built tall and noble, he was medium boned and rather heavily muscled. Most brig chasers were taller and heavier than marines in other corps professions, and hauling around prisoners of all sizes and weights required top physical condition. Annie herself worked out three times a week at a gym to build and maintain upper-body strength. Her gaze ranged back to Donnally's face and especially his mouth as he turned toward the vehicle he'd indicated. He had a generous mouth, she thought, but he seemed to keep it thinned, as if he were holding back a lot, buried deep within himself.

She followed without a word to the olive green station wagon. It was a typical brig vehicle, she noted. The rear seats were separated from the front by thick, bullet-proof glass that prevented a prisoner from reaching the driver. Further, the rear doors were locked from the outside, with no inner handles, so a prisoner couldn't open a door and escape. She took in the riot gun propped in the front seat as she opened the door—and the three different types of radios installed on the dash, for communicating with various law-enforcement agencies should a brig-chaser team need help during transport.

Joe settled into the driver's seat, then glanced over at Yellow Horse. She seemed introspective, and he was relieved not to have to try to respond to small talk, appreciating her calm presence in spite of himself. Shutting the door, he inserted the key in the ignition. The station wagon purred to life, and he put the car in gear. As they drove out of the parking lot, Joe pointed out the chow hall, the hospital and, finally, the brig and brig office.

The brig sat by itself, a squat, flat-roofed, two-story stucco building that matched the color of the desert. A ten-foot-tall cyclone fence completely enclosed the area and was topped with razor-bladelike concertina wire to discourage prisoners from trying to climb up and over it to freedom. As Donnally slowed down, Annie took in the dry, barren environment surrounding the brig and the nearby office building.

"It's out in the middle of nowhere," she murmured.

"Best place for it."

Annie nodded. "A far cry from Camp Lejeune," she added with a wry smile.

"No greenery," Joe agreed. "Just a lot of sagebrush and cactus."

"It's dry, but pretty in its own way," Annie mused as the car drew to a halt.

"That's right, you come from desert country," Joe said, getting out. Damn! Why had he said that? He didn't want to talk about anything personal with her. Giving her a glare as she came around the vehicle, he said, "Follow me."

Annie frowned. Donnally's armor was back in place. With a sigh, she hoped that with time he wouldn't be so prickly about her presence. Did he feel competitive with her? she wondered. With her notoriety as a tracker, it was a possibility. Maybe Joe was the chief tracker here at Reed, and he felt demoted by Captain Ramsey bringing her here. Annie simply didn't know the lay of the land yet. She'd have to rely on her Navajo patience for now. With time, all answers came to light.

Annie's heart pounded briefly with a bit of apprehension as Donnally led her into the main brig office. She saw at least fourteen people, men and women, working diligently at their individual desks. Annie spotted two desks that were empty in one corner of the large work area. Would she have to work right next to Donnally? She hoped not.

From inside a glass-enclosed office, a heavy-set civilian woman looked up. "Joe, is this our world-famous tracker?" she called.

Annie stopped and watched the large woman, who wore a bright red skirt and white blouse, come hurrying out of her office. She took an immediate liking to her. Despite her weight, she moved with delicate grace, and the smile of welcome on her face was like sunshine to Annie.

"Yeah, this is Corporal Yellow Horse." Joe glanced at Annie. "This is Rose, Captain Ramsey's civil-service secretary. Rose has been here for ten years and knows everything about our office."

"Hi there," Rose gushed, coming to a stop and pumping Annie's long, slender hand. "I'm Rose. You must be Annie. You don't mind if I call you by your first name, do you? I hate the way the military refers to everyone by their last name. It's too impersonal. We're really excited about you being here. Welcome!"

Annie returned the shorter woman's enthusiastic handshake and smiled warmly. "Hi, Rose. It's nice to meet you. And no, I don't mind if you call me Annie."

"Such a pretty name!" Rose gave Donnally a sweet smile, then devoted her attention to the newcomer. "I don't know what I expected when they said you were being transferred to us, but golly, you are a pretty thing. Isn't she, Joe?"

Annie almost had to laugh at Joe Donnally's instant scowl. Trying to extricate her hand from Rose's, she said, "Marines don't look at each other that way, Rose."

"Oh, pshaw!" Rose said with a good-natured chuckle. "Marines think they're perfect. Well, they almost are, in my book, but they keep forgetting they're human, too." She looked at her watch. "It's noon. How about we go over to the enlisted men's club and grab a bite to eat? I'm dying to talk with you, and maybe I can fill you in on what we do around here to help ease you into your job."

Annie could have kissed her in gratitude at that point. She glanced up at her superior. "Sergeant Donnally?"

"You do what you want," he growled. "Just be back at 1300, and I'll get you squared away with a desk assignment and your duties."

His coldness hit Annie like a slap after Rose's gushing warmth, but she merely nodded, suppressing her feelings. When Donnally turned and stalked back to his desk, Annie devoted her attention to Rose.

"I'd love to have lunch with you. Any help you can give me will be great."

"Oh, wonderful!" The secretary clapped her hands together and grinned. "You don't know how much I've heard about you, Annie! Your ability to track is legendary. You're famous!"

"I just want to fit in here, Rose, and get along with everyone—despite my skills." With a grimace, she glanced around, catching quick, curious looks from other brig chasers in the office, feeling their perusal of her. Her reputation generally preceded her, and Annie had gotten used to being minutely inspected. Too many times in the past she had met male marines with their noses out of joint, unwilling to believe a woman could be a tracker.

"Well, I'm gonna grab my purse, then I'll drive you over to the club," Rose continued excitedly. "They've got great hamburgers over there. Come on! I've got lots to tell you. I want you to know," she said as she gestured for Annie to follow her into her office, "that you've got one of the finest officers in the world to work for. Captain Ramsey is such a sweet man."

Annie waited in Rose's office doorway, her hands clasped in front of her. *Sweet* wasn't a word she'd use for any Marine Corps officer! But Rose obviously was an ebullient, vital force in this office, and Annie knew she worked directly with Ramsey. Glancing over her shoulder, she stole a look in Donnally's direction. He was sitting at his desk, scowling as usual, the telephone receiver pressed to his ear with one hand, a stack of phone messages in the other.

It struck her that despite Donnally's bulk and height, he had artistic-looking hands that spoke of a different side to his character. Was he an artist of some sort? she wondered. Perhaps he played a musical instrument? Painted? She tore her gaze from Donnally's rugged profile and smiled to herself. Somehow, she couldn't picture Joe as a painter—although he'd certainly displayed an artist's stereotypical volatile temperament so far with her.

"You ready?" Rose asked, coming around her desk with her white purse slung over her shoulder.

Annie smiled and stepped aside. "Yes, ma'am."

"Ma'am? Pshaw!" Rose wagged her finger in Annie's face. "Young lady, you call me Rose or nothing at all! I don't want any of that military jargon used on me! I'm a civilian, remember?"

With a laugh, Annie agreed, feeling welcomed, if only by the lone civilian in the office, to her new home for the next three years. The single fly in the ointment—and it was a considerable one—was the scowling Joe Donnally, who made it more than obvious that she wasn't welcome at all on his turf.

Chapter Two

EM Clubs traditionally were noisy and crowded at noontime, and Annie was grateful when Rose decided to drive over to the base cafeteria instead. Once they'd selected their lunches, she found them a quiet corner.

"I think it's wonderful that Captain Ramsey got you transferred here," Rose said again as she sat down.

Annie smiled briefly and sipped her iced tea. "It's sure a change from North Carolina."

Rose waved her hand, then took a bite of her tuna sandwich. "Isn't it, though? Camp Reed has three temperatures—hot, hotter and hottest."

Laughing, Annie relaxed more. She liked Rose's easygoing nature. "I think I'll adjust. I was born in the New Mexico desert."

Her eyes twinkling, Rose said, "That's right—the captain mentioned that you were Navajo. I haven't met too many Native American marines. What prompted you to enlist?''

"My grandfather was a code talker in World War II. He saw that I was restless, that I wanted to see more of the world than the reservation I grew up on.''

"So he figured a hitch in the corps would cure you?''

With a grin, Annie nodded. "Yes.''

"And it didn't?''

"No. I signed up for a second one. I've been in six years.''

"Do you plan to get your twenty in and retire?''

"I hope to,'' Annie agreed.

"Did you have to leave someone special behind at Camp Lejeune?''

For a moment, pain flitted across Annie's heart, but she knew Rose was being kindly, not nosy. "Well...there was someone...but he died in Desert Storm.''

"Oh, dear,'' Rose murmured, and reached out to touch Annie's arm. "I'm so very sorry. Were you in Desert Storm, too?''

"Yes. We need provost-marshal and brig people in a wartime situation, too, I'm afraid.''

Frowning, Rose took a few stabs at her salad with her fork. "Were you married?''

"No, engaged. Jeff and I decided to wait until Storm was over to get married.'' Annie shrugged, feeling the residual loss and pain filtering through her. "I guess it was the best decision. I don't know....''

"My grandma always told me it was better to have loved and lost than never to have loved.''

"Your grandmother was a wise woman.''

Rose smiled a little. "Well, who knows? Maybe you'll meet someone here at Camp Reed.''

"No," Annie murmured. "I made myself a promise never to get involved with another marine. I think a civilian man will be safer in the long run."

"Now you sound like Libby Tyler—she's a riding instructor here on the base. You know, I think Captain Ramsey really likes her. Joe is doing some preliminary investigating for Libby right now, as a matter of fact. She's noticed that someone's been riding five of the stable-owned horses nearly to death about once a month. She feels something fishy is going on, so Captain Ramsey sent Joe to check it out." She paused in her monologue to take a sip of cola. "Libby was married to a marine helicopter pilot," she explained, grimacing momentarily. "He died three years ago in a crash here at Reed, and since then she's sworn off marines as potential mates."

"I don't blame her," Annie said softly, feeling sympathetic pain for the unknown woman. "People in our line of work face more dangers than most."

"I don't agree," Rose countered matter-of-factly. "I mean, I could be killed in a car crash on the way to work at this base on any given day. If marines follow the proper safety procedures, they don't get hurt any more than your average human."

"Except in case of war," Annie amended wryly.

"Yes, but that's the only exception."

Annie finished her salad and started on her french fries. "Do you think our boss is serious about Ms. Tyler?" she asked, intrigued.

Rose grinned. "I think so."

"Captain Ramsey was at Camp Lejeune when I first enlisted. I liked him a lot. He was a fair man who cared for the people who worked under his command."

"Nothing's changed that I can see," Rose murmured. "But I have to tell you, the last commanding officer,

Captain Jacobs, was a stinker. I felt sorry for the enlisted people who worked under him. He was a terrible manager and the entire brig section more or less collapsed under the weight of his mismanagement. If it hadn't been for Joe Donnally, I think a lot worse could have happened."

Annie's heart raced momentarily. "Sergeant Donnally..."

"He's quite a man, isn't he?" Rose gushed.

Not sure how to answer that, Annie kept her own counsel. After a moment, she offered, "He made quite an impression on me." At least that was the truth.

"Joe's special. He's a tough sergeant and he's a fighter from the word go. I don't know how many times he squared off with Captain Jacobs. They had awful shouting matches behind Jacobs's office door. I mean, you could hear their voices clear down the passageway sometimes. Jacobs tried to get Joe transferred, but he fought that, too, and won." Rose wagged her finger at Annie. "I'm telling you, Joe Donnally single-handedly supported the brig personnel during those two years. He was more the officer than Jacobs. He got things done right and on time—and then Jacobs took all the credit. Jacobs got even by not allowing Joe to get his next sergeant's stripe. He gave him bad ratings in his personnel record. But Joe didn't care. He knew he stood between Jacobs and the welfare of his people."

"So Joe should be an E-5 instead of an E-5?" Annie asked slowly, thinking of her stupid remark to him about passing her E-5 test to become a sergeant. Perhaps that's why he had rounded on her so angrily—she'd struck an old wound.

"Yes, he should have made E-6 at least a year and a half ago. I'm sure Captain Ramsey will right the wrong as soon as he can, but the poor man's snowed under with work. Jacobs left our office in a disaster, moralewise and every other way."

No wonder Joe Donnally had been short with her, Annie ruminated, folding her hands and resting her chin against them. "Is Captain Ramsey working to create better conditions for the brig chasers?"

Chuckling, Rose wiped her mouth with a paper napkin. "Better believe it. We were four people short, and the captain already has four new people coming in, you among them. Of course, he went after you big-time when he saw the layout of Reed—all the rugged terrain and such."

"Have there been many brig breaks?"

"No, but when there have been, a tracker's been needed. We've always had to fly someone in from another base."

Annie nodded. "When I worked with Captain Ramsey at Camp Lejeune, he set up a drug program for the base. Is he doing that here?"

"Yes. Colonel Edwards was so impressed with what he did down at the Yuma Air Station in Arizona that he had him ordered up here to set up a similar program for Reed. Captain Ramsey's a real doer, but then, so is Joe Donnally." She laid her napkin aside and picked up her purse. "They're a great team. I can already see the positive effects around our office. 'Course, Captain Ramsey's still new and I'm trying to fill him in on all the stuff that concerns us here at Reed, but he's a quick study." She smiled happily. "Well, you ready to get to work? I know Captain Ramsey wanted to see you at 1300. He wasn't able to come and meet you personally, but he wants to see you as soon as possible. Joe will take you in to meet him."

Annie's heart fell. She wished she could go alone instead of under the angry, watchful eyes of Donnally. Was he always like that, or just with her? Well, she'd find out soon enough.

Joe felt their entrance into the brig office long before he heard them. He was working at his desk over a stack of paperwork, and his heart raced momentarily, puzzling him. Annie's voice had a soft, husky quality to it, surprisingly low and soothing, as she conversed with Rose. Trying to ignore her tone, Joe hastily signed his name to several pieces of paper as Rose approached with the tracker.

"She's all yours, Joe."

"Thanks, Rose." He refused to look up even though Annie stood patiently in front of his desk. Getting up, he threw the papers into his Out basket and finally nailed her with a glance. He was struck by how serene Annie appeared in the midst of the office chaos. Did anything ruffle her composure? Probably not. He'd heard that Native Americans traditionally were stoic and expressionless.

"What would you like me to do?" Annie ventured.

Joe snapped a look at her. "That file over there. Read it."

Trying not to be hurt by his gruffness, Annie reached for the file on her new desk.

"When you get done reading the report I typed up, we'll talk."

Annie quickly perused the file on the Libby Tyler investigation that Rose had mentioned at lunch. She found it interesting that Ms. Tyler had reported the horses were being ridden hard at night during the new moon—and that the stable manager, Stuart Garwood, refused to take the matter seriously. But when she saw the scribbled note recently added to the file, she turned in her chair and stared at Joe. "She was *shot* at today?"

Grimly, Joe nodded. "While you were at lunch, the captain called me. Ms. Tyler was out riding about three miles northeast of the stables when someone fired two rounds near her."

"Near or at?"

He scowled. "I don't know." With a sigh, he tossed the pen aside. "Captain Ramsey wants us to go check out the general area where it happened."

Annie's heart rose with hope. "Both of us?"

"Yes," Donnally said irritably, rising. "The captain seems to think you walk on water, so let's see if you do. Come on."

Annie could think of nothing she could say to defuse his anger. She pointed to her uniform. "Could I change into my brig uniform before we go out?"

"This isn't going to take long."

She held his stare. "If we're going to be out in the boonies of Reed, I'll change. It will only take me a minute."

Holding onto his patience, Joe knew he'd overstepped his bounds. "Yeah, go ahead. I'll meet you at the HumVee parked out front. It's the vehicle we use for base investigations."

She offered him a slight smile of thanks. "I'll be there in a minute."

Joe was surprised when Annie emerged from the main brig building much sooner than he'd expected. Sourly, he admitted he was being hard on her. He was wrestling with so many stored feelings, and he had to stop being so nasty. She had changed into typical marine utilities, with the standard webbed, olive green belt around her waist. Ordinarily, a brig marine wore a pistol when on duty, but she hadn't been issued one yet.

Annie opened the door to the HumVee and climbed in. She felt lighter and happier than she had since her arrival—at least she was getting to work on a case right away. Maybe it would help keep her mind off Donnally's angry attitude. "I'm ready," she said a little breathlessly as she shut the door.

With a grunt, Joe pulled the HumVee out of the parking spot. "Just to catch you up to speed, Libby Tyler is one of the base riding instructors, as you probably noticed in the file. According to Captain Ramsey, who had gone down to meet her for lunch, she was out riding roughly three miles northeast of the brig area when two shots were fired. Her horse reared up and she fell off, hitting her head on a rock. The captain is with her now— she's still at the hospital getting fixed up."

"Will she be okay?"

"I think so. The captain said he was going to be taking her to his apartment, because she can't stand staying in hospitals and she's in no shape to take care of herself."

"I don't blame her," Annie said wryly.

Joe gave her a questioning look.

"My mother is a medicine woman for our people. I never saw the inside of a hospital until I entered the Marine Corps." Her voice lowered and she looked away from the eaglelike intensity of his blue gaze. "I had a bad experience with a hospital recently. I can't say I like them, either."

"You were injured?"

"Uh, no...." Annie prayed that Donnally wouldn't ask any more questions. Her heart couldn't stand to open up the very painful past before his glowering dislike.

Joe turned onto a dirt road that meandered into the desert. "I'm not a great fan of hospitals, myself," he growled, and left it at that, his attention temporarily focused on driving the big, clumsy vehicle across the rolling landscape of sagebrush, sand and cactus.

The silence was a familiar friend to Annie as they bumped their way along the road's uneven surface. Donnally seemed to know every inch of Camp Reed. He followed increasingly narrow and more rugged roads deeper and deeper into the inhospitable terrain. Off to the left, Annie could see the brig growing smaller. Finally, Joe pulled the vehicle to a halt and shut off the engine.

"Well, this is roughly three miles northeast of the brig."

"What are we looking for?"

"Where the horse reared and threw Ms. Tyler. That," Joe said as he climbed out of the HumVee, "and maybe the rocks where the bullets hit."

"So we're searching for the scene of the accident?"

"Yes."

Annie climbed out and began to look around. She could feel Donnally watching her as she moved slowly around to the front of the vehicle. He had his hands on his hips, surveying the terrain with a scowl. He was handsome in a rugged kind of way, Annie thought—if only he didn't frown all the time.

"What do you want me to do?" she asked.

Joe barely glanced in Annie's direction, all too aware of her quiet, gentle presence. "You're the world-famous tracker. You tell me," he snapped.

Annie knew better than to fall into that trap. Donnally was a sergeant, she a corporal. She was below rating and, therefore, the assistant, not authorized to make command decisions. "I can't tell you anything until you give me an idea of the framework of this investigation. You're in charge," she reminded him calmly.

Joe stiffened and turned toward her. He saw that her cinnamon eyes had gone hard and challenging again, and it surprised him. But why should it? Belatedly, Joe knew he'd overstepped his bounds with her. "You're right. I want you to search this half of the area, maybe a quarter of a mile in diameter. I'll search the other half. If you come up with something, give me a holler."

Annie gave him a slight nod and pulled the brim of her soft uniform cap, traditionally called a "cover," farther down over her eyes to shade them from the intense sunlight. "Okay." She turned and began an automatic perusal of the terrain, still feeling Donnally's gaze burning into her back. Maybe he needed to be reminded that she wasn't always going to take his anger. At least he'd backed down and started behaving in a correct manner with her. As Annie moved carefully through the brush, she admitted she didn't want to fight with anyone. At heart, she considered herself a peaceful warrior, certainly not someone who relished violence.

For more than an hour they searched the area, looking for any kind of evidence of the episode. Finding nothing at all, Joe was disgusted and finally called Annie back with a wave of his hand. As he stood by the HumVee waiting for her, he tried to ignore the delicate way she made her way between the sagebrush and avoided a prickly pear cactus. She moved with such natural grace that she looked more like a deer than a woman, he thought wonderingly. Then, angry at himself for his unbidden interest, he turned away from her approach.

"I didn't find anything," Annie told him as she arrived on the road beside him.

Joe nodded and gestured to the HumVee. "Makes two of us. Get in. When I get back to the office I'll call and tell Captain Ramsey we need more specific directions. It was a wild-goose chase, anyway."

On the way back to the brig office, Annie remained silent. She wanted to like Joe Donnally—at least as her superior. True, he was gruff and abrupt, but she'd worked with marines like that before. She just hoped that his attacks would stop seeming so personal. If she could figure out why he was like this, she thought, maybe she could understand the basis of the anger aimed at her. Maybe something was causing him a lot of stress right now. She took a deep breath.

"How long have you been here at Camp Reed, Sergeant?" she asked, struggling to keep her tone conversational.

Joe shrugged. "Too long."

"Are there a lot of transition pressures on you right now?"

He stared at her momentarily, then concentrated on navigating the dirt road. Once again, her astuteness surprised him. "Why would you want to know?"

"I'm just trying to get a feel for what's going down here. A new base always has its own set of rules."

"Isn't that the truth." Joe gave her an oblique look and was struck again by Annie's earthy beauty. Her high cheekbones made her eyes look very large. And her mouth... Joe groaned inwardly. Then, disgusted by his unprofessional response to her, he gave himself an internal shake and said, "As I mentioned before, Captain Jacobs, the officer who just transferred out of here, was hell to work under."

"In what way?" Annie hoped that if she could get Joe to talk, it might ease the tension between them.

"Jacobs was a screwup, as I said. All he was interested in was punching his ticket to get the necessary provost-marshal time on his personnel record and continue his goal toward being a major someday."

"Oh, that kind of officer...."

"You got it."

She glanced at him, his profile set and his mouth a hard-looking line. Annie wondered if Joe ever smiled. Probably not often, after working under someone like Jacobs. No wonder he was sour. "A lot of problems?" she probed.

"That doesn't even begin to describe it."

"Were you badly understaffed?"

"Very. Captain Ramsey just transferred four new brig marines to our office." Joe sighed. "It's going to help. We've all been standing twelve-hour duty, five days a week. Finally, we can start getting back to eight-hour shifts."

"It must have been pretty rough on you. You're the section leader."

"I guess."

Annie decided that Joe Donnally was the master of understatement. She had been in her share of grueling, mismanaged situations, where the officers in charge were less-than-spectacular managers. "Pulling that kind of duty must have been hard on your family," she ventured softly.

"I'm not married."

"Oh...."

Joe turned onto the asphalt highway that led back to the brig office, needled by her attempt to talk to him. The last thing he wanted to do was talk to Annie. It would mean dropping his defenses, and he wasn't about to do that. No, somehow he'd have to get Captain Ramsey to put Annie into someone else's section—anyone's but his.

Joe hung up the phone unhappily. He'd just called Captain Ramsey at home, and Annie sat expectantly at her desk, looking at him. Stifling a curse, he ripped a piece of paper off the yellow legal-size pad and folded it haphazardly.

"Ms. Tyler gave the captain specific information on where the shooting occurred. We have to get back there and check it out."

"No rest for the wicked," Annie said with a slight smile, reaching for her cover.

Joe glanced at his watch. It was 1700, quitting time. "No, we'll do it tomorrow. I know you have to get moved into a new apartment, so I'm going to send you home. We'll go out at 1400 tomorrow and check out this new area. I've got a bunch of work to catch up on for the transfer of a couple of brig prisoners. That has to be gotten out of the way first."

Annie rose and picked up her purse. Since her return to the office, she'd discovered that Rose had kindly set up her desk with everything she would need. "Okay, I'll see you at 0800," she agreed.

Joe nodded and said nothing, watching her move toward the door. Why couldn't Annie be less pretty? Less graceful? Less everything? Grumpily, he turned back to the demands of the long-overdue paperwork that crowded his desk. Not only did he have to bring Captain Ramsey up to speed, but Private Shaw, a marine in his section, had been discovered to be illiterate, and Joe had been assigned to watch over him and make sure the kid learned to read. On top of everything else, he had Annie. Well, it was too much. At first opportunity, he was going to talk long and hard to Ramsey about getting rid of her. He just didn't want her around him or his section—the pain, the memories from the past that her presence called up were too great for him to deal with on top of the responsibilities he already shouldered.

* * *

The hot afternoon sun bore down on Annie as she climbed out of the HumVee. This time she had a camera slung over her shoulder, a report in hand, and she was prepared to search the area where Libby Tyler had said she'd fallen. Joe Donnally was no different, however much she'd hoped he would be. No, he was just as gruff and grumpy as ever. Compressing her lips, she moved around to the front of the HumVee where he stood, arms crossed, surveying the terrain.

"This is it," he said, discouraged by the rough rocks and sparse vegetation. How the hell were they supposed to find the exact spot where Libby Tyler had fallen? Frustrated, he looked over at Annie's clean profile. He'd thought a day would make a difference in how he felt toward her, but it hadn't. After a broken night's sleep, with memories of the past bleeding into the fabric of the present, he was in an even fouler mood than yesterday, if that was possible.

"We need to look for sagebrush or tufts of grass that have been disturbed," Annie said.

"Yeah? Well, it's like looking for a needle in a damned haystack, if you ask me."

Annie smiled a little and set the report on the hood of the HumVee. Waves of heat, like invisible curtains, shimmered in front of them. It was over a hundred degrees, the sky a bright, cloudless blue. Only the refreshing scent of the Pacific Ocean less than ten miles away offered refreshment to Annie's senses. "Maybe not." She pointed toward the left. "You see that area?"

"What, that bunch of sagebrush?"

"Yes."

"What about it?"

"I'll bet that's where the horse dumped her."

"How can you tell?" Joe looked over at her, incredulous.

"I'll show you." Annie felt good about this opportunity to demonstrate to Joe that she knew her job as a tracker. As they walked about two hundred feet into the desert, she pointed to several surrounding markers. "She said she fell in a ravine. There are rocks on both sides of this V-shaped area. And the sagebrush down there looks damaged."

"It doesn't to me," Joe said flatly.

Annie said nothing, but gingerly made her way down the steep side of the rocky ravine. Once at the bottom she knelt. Feeling Donnally's presence, she looked up at him. "The sagebrush is broken here and here. This is where she fell." Annie turned over several branches to show him they recently had been broken.

Amazed that she could be so bold and sure about her discovery, Joe snorted. "Sure, and the next thing you'll find is where the bullets hit the rocks."

Lifting her chin, Annie tried to ignore the sarcasm in his tone. "There's one," she said, pointing to a gray-and-black rock on the other side of the ravine.

His eyes widening, Joe's gaze followed her finger's path. Stepping across the ravine, he spotted the rock she'd indicated. The surface of the huge boulder had been scarred recently by a bullet. Without a word, Joe lifted the camera and took a photograph of it, as well as where the brush had been broken by Libby's tumble from the horse.

Annie rose and started a rock-by-rock search for a second bullet indentation. About five feet away, on the opposite side of the ravine, she found what she was looking for. Calling Donnally over, she pointed to the rock.

"I'll be damned," he muttered, and took another photo.

Annie felt hope soar within her. Joe's look had been one of praise, not anger. In her heart, she wanted to like him a lot. If only he would drop that angry wall he held up like a shield. *Time*, Annie cautioned herself. They needed time to adjust to each other.

"The trajectory of the bullets indicate they were fired from that direction," she told him, pointing off into the distance.

Joe straightened. "You're probably right." He frowned and looked down at the rocks. "Whoever was doing the firing hit five feet either side of that horse."

"Yes," she murmured, "the shooter knew what he was doing."

"I don't think this was an accident," Joe said quietly.

"I don't, either."

Joe wrestled with how easy it was to fall into a comfortable working relationship with Annie. She was all-business, and possessed a keen intelligence that startled him. He tried to suppress his burgeoning respect for her. "I'm going to assume the shots came from an M-16," he told her. "Ms. Tyler said she didn't see the person who fired, so it must have been long-range."

"Six hundred yards?" Annie guessed.

"Bingo."

"You think the person who fired it was more than just an expert marksman? Maybe sniper-quality shooting?"

"Yes."

Annie saw a gleam of respect in Joe's eyes—if but for a fraction of a second—and a warmth flowed through her. At last, he was thawing a little toward her—even if it was strictly business, she thought as she nodded and followed him back to the HumVee. They rode in silence, the HumVee grinding over several small, rounded hills as Joe headed in the direction from which they believed the bullets had been fired.

"Look," Annie said suddenly, excitement in her voice. "See that cluster of rocks on top of that hill?"

Joe smiled grimly. "Great place to hide a sniper, isn't it?"

Annie grinned. She liked Joe when he acted more human and less like a cornered mountain lion. Suddenly, they were a working team. She loved the natural high that came from successful investigative work, and obviously, so did Joe. The usual frostiness in his blue eyes had been replaced by an intensity that could only be translated as enjoyment.

Getting out of the HumVee, they cautiously approached the series of boulders that were stacked haphazardly to form a semicircle at the top of the hill. Her eyes scanning the ground for spent cartridge casings, Annie felt her heart pump with excitement as she neared the other side of the boulders.

"Look! Footprints!" She knelt and pointed to a partial print barely visible on the sand and rock.

Joe grunted. "Good. Keep looking."

Feeling like a bloodhound on a fresh trail, Annie scanned the ground. Sunlight was glinting off something about ten feet from her and she picked her way through the thick sagebrush. Leaning down, her fingers searching, she felt the heat of metal and quickly grasped it. Triumphantly, she turned and held the cartridge casing up for Joe to see.

"I found one!"

He turned. The glint of sunlight off metal in Annie's fingers spoke of her important find. From where he stood, he noticed a number of hoofprints. "Great! Looks like whoever fired the rifle rode a horse, too."

Annie nodded. She moved carefully around the prints and placed the shell in Joe's outstretched hand. Just that minimal contact with his hand—callused from hard, outdoor work—was unexpectedly thrilling. Trying to hide her response, she examined the hoofprints closely.

"Wait!" she whispered excitedly. "Take a look at this, will you?"

Joe hunkered down opposite Annie. He liked the husky enthusiasm in her voice as she pointed to a particular print. "What about it?" he asked, mystified by her excitement.

"The horse has a big chunk missing from the wall of its hoof. See? There's a crescent-shaped piece gone. The horse has thrown a shoe; maybe he chipped his hoof on a rock."

"Yeah?" Joe grunted.

Lifting her head, Annie met and held his blue gaze. For a moment, she felt a thrilling sense of joy move through her, hotter than the desert breeze. Joe was a powerful man, and her heightened senses were responding. He was masculine without being threatening, stimulating her in ways she'd never experienced. Mystified, Annie forced those discoveries aside and tried to explain the importance of the print.

"Horses are usually shod to protect their hooves. If they lose a shoe, they risk chipping the outer hoof wall or bruising the soft area known as the frog." She pointed to the print. "This horse lost its shoe and chipped a chunk off the outside wall of its hoof. I can take a plaster cast of this, and we can go back to the stables to see which horse this matches—just like a fingerprint or a tire tread. If we find the horse, we might find out who rode it or owns it."

Joe assimilated her explanation. If only he didn't have to look into those warm, wide eyes of hers, with so much life sparkling from their depths. Part of him wanted simply to stand and stare like a love-smitten twelve-year-old. Fighting the desire, he said, "You're assuming the horse was used by the sniper."

"Yes," Annie conceded slowly, "I am."

"But if it was just someone riding out here, it may have nothing to do with the sniper."

"Still, it's a clue," she urged. "A starting point. The sniper couldn't have driven out here, or Ms. Tyler would have seen the vehicle. The only two ways he could have gotten here are on foot or, quicker, by horseback." She twisted around and pointed to the deep ravine at the foot of the hill. "He could have hidden his mount down there and waited for her to ride by. She never would have seen the horse."

It was good, basic logic, Joe had to admit. "Okay. Take a plaster cast of the print—and any others you think might be significant," he ordered.

That done, they'd need to bring the evidence to Captain Ramsey. Glancing at his watch, Joe realized it would be nearly 1700 before they could finish here and drive over to the officer's home with their findings. He watched Annie for a moment, then forced himself to continue searching the site. But the rocky ground had destroyed any possibility of prints elsewhere. Disgusted, Joe realized they'd probably end up with only the one hoofprint. Suddenly, out of the corner of his eye, he spotted a bullet casing near the end of the boulderlike fortress. He crossed the rough terrain and picked it up.

"Bingo," he said, holding it up to show Annie. "Here's the second spent cartridge."

Annie broke out in a wide smile of appreciation. "Good work!" she praised.

Heat sheeted through Joe at her beaming smile, and he stood frozen, stunned by the glow in her eyes and the radiance in her face. Such genuine happiness shone in her gold-flecked eyes that he was helpless to combat the rampant feeling rushing through him. Was the woman part witch? Casting a spell on him? Confusing him? Angrily, he spun around and walked down into the ravine, pretending to look for more prints. If only Annie wasn't so beautiful—and in such a natural way. She looked completely at home in this arid land—a part of it rather than the stranger to it that he felt.

Disgruntled, Joe tried to shift his focus back to the investigation. No question about it. As soon as he possibly could, he would ask Captain Ramsey to put Annie in another section—permanently.

Chapter Three

Joe tried to fight the exhaustion he felt as he entered the office earlier than usual the next morning. He hadn't slept well at all, so he'd decided to come in and try to work away his restlessness. It was 0730. Unhappy with the results of their consultation with Captain Ramsey last evening, Joe knew he had to talk to him about Annie. Wiping his eyes tiredly, he raised his hand in greeting to Rose, who waved back. She was always at work by 0730. Looking around at the sound of other footsteps, he was surprised to see Annie coming down the passageway, dressed in the normal brig attire of desert-camouflage utilities. Today, she carried the mandatory holster and pistol on the web belt encircling her waist. If possible, she looked more desirable to him than ever.

Panic struck Joe, and he gave Annie a brusque nod as he walked swiftly past her and out the door, ignoring her softly spoken, "Good morning." Stepping into the passageway, he hoped that Captain Ramsey would be in his office. He knew Ramsey had been coming in every morning for about an hour before returning home, where Libby Tyler was continuing to recuperate under his care. Knocking at the officer's door, he heard Ramsey call, "Come in."

Taking a deep breath, Joe hesitated momentarily. His heart was pounding hard in his chest, and he felt a little shaky—completely unlike himself. Wiping his mouth with the back of his hand, he knew he had to go through with this desperate, last-ditch effort. He had to make a confession to Captain Ramsey, although it was the last thing he wanted to do. What he had to tell him, Joe had hoped he'd never have to tell anyone, but he was backed into a corner now, with no other option that he could see. His strong, brown fingers wrapped around the highly polished brass doorknob. Taking a deep breath, he opened the door, praying that once he heard the painful story, Ramsey would let Annie Yellow Horse be reassigned.

Joe tried to swallow the bitter taste in his mouth as he left Ramsey's office. He felt tired, beaten and disappointed. Annie Yellow Horse was his partner—whether he wanted her or not. Ramsey hadn't been moved by his tortured confession about the haunting past that walked with him every moment of every day. He stood in the passageway, feeling lost and guilt-ridden. Dammit, why did Annie Yellow Horse have to be so likable? One thing Joe knew: he couldn't go back into the office and face her right now. It wasn't her fault, even if he was just a little jealous of her tracking credentials. No, he didn't dare to get close to a woman brig chaser ever again—even on a strictly professional basis. Their line of work was too dangerous, too filled with unknowns, to risk his heart again as he had with Jenny.

Joe walked slowly back down the passageway, uncertain of his destination. He just needed time to settle his roiling emotions, raised by talking about his sordid past. Blinking back sudden, unexpected tears, Joe shoved open a door that led him outside to a small alcove of thick green grass, a few silver-barked eucalyptus trees—and some much-needed solitude. Several picnic tables and benches were scattered around the lawn beneath the shade of the huge, graceful trees, but, thankfully, no one was using them.

Sitting down on one of the benches, Joe watched without interest as several robins hunted for worms on the recently watered grass. The dry heat of the California desert ebbed and flowed around him, but he didn't really feel it. Off in the distance, he could hear a helicopter lifting off a pad at the base airport. He *loved* his life as a marine. And he liked Captain Ramsey. The man was fair, but he was blind, too. Maybe the captain's feelings for Libby Tyler interfered with his ability to see that keeping Annie and Joe together was the wrong thing to do.

What was he going to do with Annie? Joe sat for a long time, hoping that his gut would unclench, that his heart would stop aching. It was the first time he'd told anyone here about Jenny. He'd come to Camp Reed shortly after that tragic situation, and no one here knew what had happened. Joe didn't want them to know. It was too personal, too gut wrenching, to have the story talked about over lunch or at the NCO, the non-commissioned officer's, Club.

Slowly rubbing his face, Joe was startled to see Annie's features appear before him. Lowering his hands and opening his eyes, he cursed. Somehow, he was going to have to keep her at bay, keep her from ever bonding with him the way most brig partners did over time. But how the hell was he going to accomplish that? Already his protective instincts were working overtime. Annie's face was vulnerable—not the tough marine facade he had expected. How had she lasted six years in the corps? Even her voice was soft. He could see nothing hard about her; she had remained entrancingly feminine despite the responsibilities she carried on her shoulders.

Frustrated as never before, Joe slowly eased off the bench, immune to the beauty that surrounded him as he slowly trudged back into the building toward his office. He had no answers to his questions. And right now, he was angry. Angry at Annie Yellow Horse for stepping squarely and unexpectedly into the turmoil of his life. He needed her the way he needed rocks in his head, Joe thought, disgruntled.

"Sergeant Donnally?"

Annie's husky voice, low with concern, intruded on his spinning thoughts and torn emotions. He snapped a look to the left. Annie was standing there, extending his hat to him. Her face looked serene, although her eyes reflected concern—for him. Swallowing hard, Joe rasped, "What is it?"

"Captain Ramsey just ordered us to get to the stables as soon as possible." She shrugged a little and ventured a small smile. "Here's your cover. I already put everything else we'll need in the HumVee."

Taking his hat and settling it on his head, Joe stood there, filled with anguish. Somehow, he had to *ignore* Annie's ethereal beauty. Somehow. "Yeah," he croaked, "let's get going."

"Do you want me to drive?"

"No, I will." Joe saw the question in her eyes, but refused to offer an explanation. He knew by the way she was reacting to him that he must look like hell. He certainly felt like hell.

Annie tried to ignore the hurt of their confrontation yesterday at Captain Ramsey's home, when Joe had tried to discredit her hoofprint clue. Luckily, the captain, who had grown up on the same reservation she had, understood that hoofprints were as unique as fingerprints. But it had been a minor incident, so Annie let it go. As she fell into step with Donnally, she tried to ignore new hurt that sprang from her heart as they moved into the passageway. It was impossible for Donnally to disguise the fact that he didn't like her.

Casting around for some way to defuse the unhappiness radiating from him, Annie said, "I grew up on the New Mexico desert and my folks raised sheep for a living. My mother is a medicine woman, but she weaves rugs, too. I guess I was kind of a tomboy for a Navajo girl, because I liked herding the sheep better than learning to weave. One of the things I had to learn in a hurry, though, was how to track strays from the main flock. Sometimes a ewe that was ready to birth would leave the herd to have her baby. Out there, coyotes were just waiting for strays, because it meant a meal to them."

Joe opened the door that led out to the parking lot. He was trying desperately not to listen to Annie's soft, enthusiastic voice. Heat from the morning sunlight was overcoming the previous night's coolness, and he inhaled the salt-laden air deeply.

Annie hurried to keep step with Joe, determined to break the ice with him. "I had to learn to track those ewes before the coyotes got to them and their new babies. That's when I realized that no sheep's hooves were the same." She laughed a little as he slowed down to get into the waiting HumVee. "Can you imagine me, as a nine-year-old, following ten or fifteen sheep trails, trying to sort out which one belonged to the pregnant mother?"

Annie climbed in and sensed a bit of a thaw in Joe's jutting jaw. Closing the door, she continued, "No one taught me about the differences in the way a hoof looked. I just kind of learned out of desperation, if you want to know the truth. I knew if I lost a mother and baby, I'd be blamed by my family for not taking care of something more helpless than I was."

Joe turned the HumVee down the street that led to the main boulevard, which would take them to the west-gate area where the stable facility was located. The warmth of Annie's laughter, the intimacy of the way she confided in him, unstrung him. "Did you ever lose any sheep?" he found himself asking, against his will.

Thrilled, Annie tried to keep her hopes from getting too high. At least Joe was talking to her. "Almost. I must have run down about ten sets of tracks on the red desert where we lived, and all of them came back to where the flock was grazing. My brother Tom kept watching the flock, and I'd take off running again. My lungs hurt, my legs hurt, and I was crying on top of everything else. I didn't want to shame myself. You see, I'd begged my parents to let me be a herder. They told me that if I couldn't do the job my brothers did, I'd have to learn the things women are taught and stay out of a man's world."

Joe nodded, the pain around his heart miraculously easing beneath Annie's spontaneous warmth. A large part of him wanted to know about Annie—as a person as well as a marine, but it was a dangerous area to tread. The better he got to know her, the more risk there was to both of them.

The look on Joe's face encouraged Annie as they drove down the busy boulevard. The line of his mouth had eased, if only a bit, and she could feel him listening with interest to her story, so she continued. "It was near evening, and a lot of the ewes lamb at night. On about the twelfth trail, I noticed that this sheep had a chip out of the left side of one hoof. I found her at twilight." Annie smiled fondly in remembrance. "She was just birthing, and a pack of coyotes was stalking her. I ran at them, yelling and shouting to scatter them."

"You did?" Joe turned briefly. It was a mistake. The joy in Annie's eyes was his undoing. Her lips were slightly parted, as if she were breathless, and that radiance that always seemed to be in her face was pronounced, her eyes dancing with memories.

"Coyotes aren't like wolves—they run," she explained.

"What did you have to chase them off with? A gun?"

Chortling, Annie relaxed. "No, just the wooden staff all herders carry."

Shaking his head, Joe muttered, "And I thought my growing-up years in National City were dangerous."

"Where is National City?" Annie responded, praying that he'd open up to her, if just a little. Instantly, she saw his brows dip and she felt his defenses rise.

"It's a hole," he growled, making it clear he didn't want to discuss it. Ahead, he saw the road leading to the stables. "We're going to have to talk to Stuart Garwood," he continued gruffly, changing the subject. "He's the base stables manager. We'll let him know we're going to be checking the horses."

Disappointed but careful not to show it, Annie nodded. Still, as the HumVee moved down the paved road to where the stables were situated, in a pocket among four large hills, she felt hope. At least Joe had responded to her. Perhaps she'd have to open up more of herself, become more personal so he'd realize that she wasn't a threat to him. Then maybe he'd become more friendly—or, if not friendly, at least not so angry all the time.

As she climbed out of the HumVee, Annie automatically switched her internal sensing abilities to the case at hand. A man dressed in canary yellow riding breeches, highly polished black boots and a red polo shirt stood on the porch of the stables' front office, observing their approach. Instantly, Annie felt an instinctive warning that he wasn't to be trusted. She wasn't sure what was behind the subtle feeling, but it was there nonetheless. She followed Joe as he quickly climbed the steps toward the man, who remained on the porch, hands on his hips, frowning at them.

"Mr. Garwood?" Joe queried, halting before him.

"Yes?"

"Sir, we're here from the provost marshal's office. We'd like to examine the horses stabled here for a possible identification."

Garwood scowled. "What identification?"

Joe pointed to the plaster cast that Annie held. "We found hoofprints at the location of a possible sniper. We think they're from the mount of whoever fired at Ms. Tyler."

Garwood snorted violently and glared at Annie and the plaster cast. "Why, that's preposterous!"

Joe held his temper. "No, sir, it isn't. With your permission, we'll check the stable horses as well as the privately owned ones."

Though it wasn't obvious, Annie caught the flare of anger in Garwood's dark eyes and sensed a quiet fury radiating from the stable manager.

"Oh, go ahead! I think it's ridiculous, but I guess you have to justify this stupid investigation of Ms. Tyler's allegations." Garwood turned on his heel and walked back into his office.

As the door slammed behind him, Annie winced. "Ouch," she whispered to Joe. "He's a little prickly about this, don't you think?"

Joe rubbed his jaw and looked around. "I suppose. I don't know why, though. It's no skin off his nose. We're the ones who'll be looking at horses' hooves all day," he griped.

Annie smarted under his cynicism. "You think this is a wild-goose chase, too, don't you?"

"I think I made that clear yesterday at the captain's house. Come on, let's get going."

Sighing, but controlling her temper, Annie followed Joe off the porch toward the first huge corral, filled with about forty stable horses that were regularly used for trail rides. It would take both of them, working as a team, to complete the investigation, she knew. As they slipped between the pipe rails, she suggested, "I'll check the hooves if you'll hold the horses by their halters."

"Fine with me. I don't have any experience with horses," Joe said gruffly.

Annie set the plastic-wrapped plaster cast on the ground outside the fence. It would be fairly easy to lift the various hooves. If she found one with a chip out of it, she could bring the cast over for a positive identification. Inwardly, she prayed they would find that horse. Otherwise, she knew, Donnally would hold this over her head as a "waste" of his day.

As Joe grasped the first horse's halter, he glared around at their pastoral surroundings. The scent of hay and horses wafted on a warm breeze. Silver-barked eucalyptus trees encircled the stables area, making it look more like a farm than part of a Marine Corps base. He watched with a scowl as Annie quickly lifted each of the horse's feet in succession. She was fast and thorough. He moved to the next horse. And the next. After about an hour, he decided to talk.

"Garwood seemed testy."

Annie looked up from her crouched position, the raised hoof of the current horse in her grasp and nodded. Then, she straightened and brushed off her hands. Joe stood on the opposite side of the animal. "If you won't laugh at me, I'll tell you the readout I got on him," she offered.

Joe stared at her. Annie had removed her soft cover and stuck it in the rear pocket of her utilities. Her shiny black hair was gently mussed around her face, giving her the look of a woman who thoroughly relished being outdoors. If she'd been labeled a tomboy, it was only from the standpoint of the culture that had raised her. Annie loved nature, Joe realized, and she wasn't trying to imitate a man in any way. As she ran her long, expressive fingers across the sleek back of the horse, he felt his pulse leap through him, hard and strong. Everything about her was feminine and graceful. Making an effort to derail that line of thinking, he said, "I won't laugh at you."

With a shrug, she said, "I have a kind of internal radar, if you will." She smiled a little, glad to straighten up and work the kinks out of her shoulders. "I call it my 'all-terrain radar.' I get a sense about a person or a situation—and I'm rarely wrong. It has saved my life a couple of times in the past with transporting brig prisoners—or tracking them when they've escaped."

Fear bolted through Joe as he stared across the horse at her solemn expression. "What do you mean?" he croaked, his fingers tightening around the horse's leather halter.

"Over the past five years, I've been flown in whenever brig prisoners escape. Various bases have used my skills to find the escapees. I've tracked through swamps, forests and about any kind of rough terrain you want to mention. I use these—" she pointed to her head and then her heart "—like radar. I can't really explain it except to say that I can literally sense if danger is near. Then I'm really careful and make sure my backup is in position."

"Intuition?" Joe could only guess at what she was talking about.

"I guess...." Annie smiled at him and held his blue gaze, which was now openly curious. But she noticed something else in the depths of his eyes that surprised her: fear. What kind? She wanted to ask, but knew she didn't dare. Joe would open up, if at all, on his time and terms, not hers. "Anyway, the few times I haven't paid attention to that internal red-flag warning, I've nearly bought the farm."

"Died?"

She gave him a wry look. "Listen, being a brig chaser automatically puts you in the line of fire, don't you think?"

Frowning, Joe muttered, "If you follow regulations and always work with a partner, it's safer." But not foolproof, as he knew all too well.

"I always had a partner." Annie laughed. "My partner is the other set of ears and eyes that can stop a bullet from nailing me."

A chill worked its way through Joe. "Tracking prisoners isn't some kind of lark," he snapped irritably.

Taken aback, Annie blinked. Joe's face was thunder-cloud dark with accusation. "Hey, wait a minute. I didn't say it was a lark."

"You act like it is. You laugh at nearly getting killed. That's stupid."

Working to hold on to her mounting anger, Annie said tightly, "I think we had better get back to our original topic: Garwood."

"What about him?"

Reeling from his suddenly cold attitude, Annie snapped back, "He's dangerous!"

Joe snorted. "Oh, sure."

"You asked what I felt, and I'm telling you!"

Joe's anger surged upward. Annie's blazing eyes triggered all of the tamped-down fury and frustration that had simmered for the past two days since her arrival. "I don't care how famous you are, Yellow Horse. To me, you're just a brig chaser—like the rest of us. This crap about sensing stuff is for the birds. Saying Garwood's dangerous is ridiculous. You can't prove it."

"Why..." Taking a deep breath, Annie stopped herself from saying anything else. Donnally was her superior. Her boss. Instantly, she clamped down on her anger. But what had stung him to make him attack her again? It seemed totally unjustified. Compressing her lips, but holding his furious gaze, she said tightly, "Let's get back to work."

"Yeah," Joe rasped, struggling to calm his overflowing fears and anger. Why was his heart beating this way? As soon as Annie had mentioned being in danger, a hard, unrelenting pounding had started in his chest. Dammit! It seemed as if he had no control over this automatic, protective urge toward her. Annie was a marine. A brig chaser on top of that. If anyone knew how to protect herself, she did. *But so had Jenny,* something deep within him warned. And look what had happened to her.

Chapter Four

Annie could barely contain the thrill that raced through her as she discovered the horse whose hoof fit the plaster mold. It was a big, rangy bay gelding, and she grinned triumphantly as Joe came around to examine the match.

"I'll be damned," he muttered as he straightened, his respect for her surging in spite of himself. She looked so completely at home here in the paddock, he thought, with the smell of sweet hay drifting from a nearby barn and the hot sun bearing down on them.

Annie patted the horse's neck. "Now we have to find out who this horse belongs to."

"Probably the stables, with our luck," Joe said unhappily. "Let's go talk to Garwood."

The stables manager had just returned from a ride and was once again standing on the porch as they approached. Annie didn't like the smug look on Garwood's heavily lined face. She decided to hang back a few feet and assess his response to what Joe would tell him.

"Our cast matches one of your horses in Paddock A," Joe said as he came up next to Garwood.

"Really?" Garwood raised his eyebrows in surprise.

Annie felt tension around the manager—and saw it in a slight narrowing of his eyes upon Joe.

"A big bay gelding with four white socks," Joe went on, holding the cast toward Garwood. "Who does he belong to?"

Garwood grinned a little. "The United States Marine Corps, Sergeant."

Joe grimaced. "I was afraid of that."

Annie spoke up. "May we look at the roster of people who rode the day Ms. Tyler was shot at?"

Garwood snapped a look in her direction, his eyebrows lowering. "What?"

"The horses are signed out when they're ridden, aren't they?"

"Yes, I suppose they are," Garwood agreed irritably.

"We'd like to look at the logbook, then," Joe said, giving Annie a glance that said, "Well done." He hadn't thought of that possibility. But then, he was unfamiliar with this business of horses and stables.

"You probably won't find anything," Garwood warned. "We don't have people on trail rides sign the roster or be assigned to a specific horse. Only A- and B-grade riders have to sign out and choose which horse to ride."

Annie followed Garwood into the office. "Is the bay an A or B horse?"

"No, just a trail horse."

Disheartened by Garwood's answer and puzzled by his vaguely amused attitude, Annie went over to the logbooks on Garwood's secretary's desk.

"You won't find anything," Garwood said again. "If you'll excuse me, I've got work to do."

Annie opened the logbook to the day of the shooting incident. She felt Joe moving nearer, and her heartbeat sped up. He had an incredible aura of power around him, she thought, like nothing she'd ever felt before. It wasn't a violent presence, though; rather, it was a beckoning strength that tugged at all her senses, making her vibrantly aware that she was a woman. Confused by the signals she was receiving—her heart and body responding even as her wary mind warned her that Joe didn't like her—Annie fought to ignore her rampant feelings.

Joe looked across her shoulder, more than just aware of Annie's nearness. He couldn't help but gaze at her parted lips as she leaned down to study the logbook. Softness. There was such inherent softness about her. And she was gentle. Like a lamb. Now, where had that notion come from? Joe chastised himself for letting his mind wander into forbidden territory.

"Find anything?" he asked roughly.

"No," she admitted, disappointed. When Joe stepped back, Annie felt as if a cloud had suddenly blocked the sun. How could that be? As she turned and looked up into his blue eyes, she almost gasped aloud. For the first time, Joe's eyes looked warm and inviting—and his intense gaze was pinned directly upon her. His pupils were large and black, encircled by only a thin crescent of blue. Annie's pulse bounded, and she felt breathless beneath his heated inspection.

Joe fought himself. The wild, unbidden urge to reach out and run his fingers through Annie's mussed black hair was nearly his undoing. Her eyes had turned golden, and the seconds strung between them melted like hot honey. Her face was upturned, its oval shape confirming her softness. She was all gentle curves—from the shape of her face to her high cheekbones, full lips and large, intelligent eyes. Annie's was a primal beauty, born of a heritage of living close to the land. Joe felt a gnawing need to explore her—on all levels. She had refused to protect herself with the hard exterior that many women in the military adopted in order to survive the harsh male environment.

With a slight shake of his head, Joe took a step back—knowing that if he didn't, he would reach out and touch that shining ebony hair. Shocked by the strength of his desire to know her, Joe stalked out of the office, the plaster cast in hand. As he walked toward where the HumVee was parked, he wondered if a medicine woman was the same thing as a witch. Had Annie cast a spell of some kind on him? Joe snorted to himself. Not that he believed in such things.

When they'd both clambered into the HumVee, Joe handed Annie their plaster clue. "Let's go tell the captain what we found," he said gruffly, refusing to look at her.

Annie murmured her assent, her heart still beating hard in her chest. For that one golden moment out of time, she had seen the intense hunger Joe held for her. It was as surprising as it was thrilling—and confusing. Grateful that Joe didn't want to talk, she held the cast on her lap and said nothing on the way back to brig headquarters.

"Well done," Captain Ramsey praised as Joe and Annie stood in an at-ease stance in front of his desk.

"It didn't get us anywhere," Joe noted.

"Perhaps not," Ramsey murmured, setting the plaster cast aside, "but put this in as possible evidence. Have you taken the bullet casings to the lab?"

"Yes, sir, they're over there right now," Joe said. "My guess is they came from an M-16, but that's all we'll get."

"Still, the evidence is mounting," Ramsey noted. He smiled briefly. "Good job, both of you. Dismissed."

Annie followed Joe into the passageway and shut the door behind her. It was well past noon and she hadn't eaten, she realized as her stomach growled ominously.

"I'm going to grab a bite to eat at the chow hall," she told Joe.

"I'll take you over there. I'm hungry, too."

Surprised, Annie said nothing. If anything, Joe seemed less tense toward her. Was it because she'd been able to match the plaster cast to a horse's hoof? Unsure, she followed him back to the parking lot.

"We'll take my Chevy Blazer," he said, pointing to a polished black vehicle.

The car fitted Joe's personality, Annie decided as she climbed into its spacious interior. Despite its off-road and recreational abilities, the vehicle was scrupulously clean, with no dust visible on the dashboard, no marks on the carpets. As she adjusted the safety belt, Joe turned the key, and the Blazer emitted a throaty roar. Indeed, the vehicle did emulate Joe, Annie thought with a secret smile. Because Joe seemed to be in a better mood and more relaxed than usual, she decided she might broach those defensive walls of his.

"You said you lived in National City. How close is it to San Diego?"

Joe guided the large vehicle out of the parking lot and onto the main road that would lead them to the chow hall.

"It's about ten miles south of San Diego," he responded noncommittally.

"You were born there?"

"Yes."

"A city slicker?" she teased, hoping he wouldn't take her comment the wrong way.

"Compared to you, yes."

"Did you like living in the city?" she asked, peering at him.

With a twisted grimace, Joe said, "As a kid growing up, I didn't mind it. After I joined the corps and began to realize that everything wasn't made of glass, concrete and steel, I felt differently."

"Oh?"

"I kind of like the outdoors."

Annie ran her hand along the door. "This Blazer suggests someone who might camp, hike or fish a lot."

"Fish," Joe admitted, again struck by Annie's unsettling ability to see beneath his surface. Just how much did she know about him?

"What kind of fishing?" Annie persisted.

"Fly-fishing for trout."

She smiled. "Ohh . . ."

He briefly glanced at her, taken by the warmth dancing in her cinnamon eyes.

Absorbing his interest, she smiled and murmured, "I might have known you would go for the toughest fishing in the world. Fly-fishing takes a lot of delicacy and timing."

"And I don't look like I have either one?"

Feeling heat flooding up her neck into her face, Annie avoided his amused look. "I didn't say that."

"A city slicker who can fly-fish. Pretty unique, isn't it?"

"Yes."

"Do you fish?"

"Not many fish on the desert where I grew up," she returned wryly, meeting and matching his first smile. When Joe's compressed mouth lifted at the corners, his entire demeanor changed—if but for a brief, heart-pounding moment. All the tension he usually carried in his face seemed to melt away, leaving a miraculously vulnerable man before her. The discovery dissolved Annie's fears. Joe Donnally wasn't an unfeeling man after all.

Joe realized Annie was blushing. The shyness in her was evident as she quickly looked away to stare out the window. Suddenly, he ached to know more about her.

"You said you grew up in New Mexico?"

"Yes. My parents live the old-fashioned way, in a hogan made of logs and mud, with no electricity."

"Sounds like my worst camping nightmare."

Laughing, Annie thrilled to the change in Joe. Perhaps he was adjusting to her, finding out that she wasn't like the tough legend that generally preceded her from base to base—and she was, after all, just a human being like everyone else. "I'm glad I had that kind of upbringing. It helps me feel comfortable when I'm out tracking where there are no modern amenities. My partners are often unhappy, but I can pretty easily adjust to the demands of the terrain."

Joe felt some of his happiness evaporate. "Captain Ramsey says you're like a bloodhound. Once you're on a trail, you won't ever let up."

"So far," Annie said, relaxing against the seat. "It's kind of precarious to try to maintain a perfect record of recapturing prisoners."

"Why?"

She shrugged and said, "I'm not perfect. Not by a long shot."

"Could have fooled me," Joe said dryly. He saw the hurt come into her eyes and instantly was sorry. "It's the captain," he added. "He thinks you walk on water. He was really excited about getting you to Reed."

"Captain Ramsey worries me," Annie said quietly. "I don't want to disappoint him, and I'm afraid I'm bound to someday."

"He's not going to mark you down on your personnel record the one time you can't find a prisoner," Joe soothed. "He's not that kind of officer." He pulled into the parking lot of the chow hall. Because it was 1300, no lines of marines trailed from the huge, two-story building. A green lawn, manicured shrubs and even a few palm trees graced the area, giving it the out-of-place look of an oasis in the yellow desert that surrounded it. He parked and shut off the engine.

"Reed has got some of the best navy chow you'll ever eat. Come on, I'll show you the ropes."

This time, Annie noticed as they walked side by side toward the chow hall, Joe shortened his stride for her sake. Had he done it consciously? Uncertain, she took in the bright yellow marigolds interspersed with red geraniums that lined the sidewalk, displaying the Marine Corps colors of crimson and gold. It was gung-ho landscaping and Annie smiled. Of course, just seeing flowers in bloom on the desert was a gift.

By the time they got through the line and sat down at a table opposite each other, Annie was starving. She marveled at how much Joe was eating, but then, marines in general led a highly active physical life.

Joe tried to concentrate on his food, but he couldn't help looking up once in a while. Annie ate delicately and without the hurry he did. Trying not to stare at her lips, or the graceful way she used the flatware, he forced himself to mind his own business. He noticed that she ate much less than he did. She had selected a huge salad with dressing, one pork chop and a baked potato, while he had loaded up with three pork chops and a huge mountain of mashed potatoes and gravy—and no salad.

For dessert Annie settled for a cup of steaming black coffee. The military tended to make its coffee strong, and she liked it that way. As Joe dug into a slice of cherry pie, she decided to try again to penetrate his defenses.

"Do you live on or off the base?" she inquired, taking a sip of coffee.

"Off," he answered between bites of pie, then surprised her by asking, "How about you? Are you staying at the barracks or are you going to rent off base?"

"Off, like you. I've rented a small apartment south of Oceanside. It's near the marsh and I can see a lot of ducks and great blue herons."

With a shrug, Joe said, "My apartment's almost in the middle of town."

"Once a city slicker always a city slicker," she teased.

Joe smiled a little and watched as she wrapped her long, expressive fingers around the heavy white mug of coffee. "In some ways, I guess I always will be," he admitted.

"But you go fishing to relax?" she ventured.

Her insight was unfailing. "Right again."

"Where?"

"Up in the Sierras northeast of here. I like to go on weekends when things are quiet. The past two years have been a special kind of hell because Jacobs wouldn't replace the people we lost through transfers or retirement, so we were all standing a lot more duty. I needed to get away to those mountains and lakes, but it didn't happen much.''

"It sounds like it has been a nightmare around here for you," Annie said, meaning it.

"I had to stand between my people and Jacobs a lot. I didn't like it. I didn't like him. He was a lousy officer and a poor manager."

"But Captain Ramsey is doing something about it."

"Yes." Joe wiped his mouth with his paper napkin and put his tray aside. Then he sipped at a large Coke to finish off his meal. "I hope in a month or so, I can take my Blazer, myself and my fishing pole up to the mountains. It will be the first time I've been able to get away in six months."

Annie's heart went out to him. He was obviously overworked, laden with too many responsibilities that shouldn't have been his to shoulder in the first place.

Uncomfortable at having exposed his personal life, Joe growled, "Let's saddle up. I've got a ton of work to plow through back at the office. And I want you to go over to the crime lab and see what they've dug up on those bullet casings."

Surprised at his sudden change of tone, Annie nodded as they rose and left the table. Joe was an enigma—one moment open, the next unreachable. Still, at least now he wasn't growly *all* the time. Maybe, as the days came and went, he'd get used to her being in his section and become less irritated with her. Maybe.

Annie was sitting at her desk a week later when she heard Joe scrape back his chair and get up. It was almost noon, and she was hurrying to finish processing some paperwork for a brig prisoner to be transported to Treasure Island the next morning.

"Here," Joe said, handing her a thick file. "This bastard is all yours."

Looking up, Annie took the heavy file and placed it beside her other paperwork. "By your expression, I'd guess this prisoner isn't very nice."

"That's an understatement," he agreed with a sigh. He sat down on the edge of her desk. The past week had convinced him that Annie wasn't the enemy he'd originally thought. If anything, she'd been a workhorse, helping him to see daylight for the first time in six months. The paperwork was getting done—on time—for once, and they'd avoided those last-minute scrambles. Today she was in her light green uniform skirt and blouse, and all day Joe had made an effort not to stare at her long, slender legs. But, as with avoiding Annie, it was a losing battle.

Pointing to the file, he said, "Ever hear of Corporal Dutch Gorman?"

Annie felt the hair on the back of her neck prickle, but said merely, "Him."

"You have, I see."

"I was at Camp Lejeune when I heard about Gorman killing his wife and two kids at their base house. It was horrible."

"I was on duty when it happened," Joe said with a frown. "Gorman's one of the most dangerous prisoners I've ever seen."

"He's being transferred?"

"Yes, you can start the paperwork for his transfer to Fort Leavenworth, Kansas."

Annie nodded. "I'll get to it right after chow." Leavenworth was the military equivalent of a federal penitentiary, where only the most dangerous of military criminals were taken. It was a hard-rock prison known for its harsh treatment of prisoners, although the Marine Corps wasn't kind to any prisoner, as Annie had found out early on. Brig prisoners were treated worse than "boots" in boot camp, which meant strict discipline. If a prisoner committed an infraction, he could be ordered to do a hundred push-ups or some other physically demanding work. She'd never liked brig duty and was glad, because of her tracking abilities, that she hadn't put in much time guarding prisoners. The brig itself was a depressing place, Annie admitted.

"I'm going over to the chow hall. You want to ride along?"

For the past week Joe had been scrupulously avoiding her. Startled, Annie looked up. "Well—sure. Thanks...."

"Let's saddle up," he said, easing off the corner of the desk. Joe frowned to himself as he went back to his desk, directly behind Annie's, and pulled open the drawer to locate his cover. Placing it on his head, he enjoyed watching her get up and retrieve her cap and black shoulder purse. He would never tire of watching Annie's graceful movements, more like those of a lithe cat than a woman, he often thought.

Joe tried not to think about the fact that he was breaking his own rule. He'd decided that complete abstinence from Annie was his only chance. Because she was officially his partner, he'd tried to put plenty of paperwork between them. Luckily, Captain Ramsey hadn't needed them again for the ongoing Libby Tyler investigation. But now, as he walked with Annie down the passageway toward the parking lot, his heart lifted. They stepped out into the bright sunshine to find the sky a pale blue accented with high, white cirrus clouds. People were streaming from the building, heading for the chow hall or one of the restaurants just outside the gate. On a whim,

Joe suggested, "Let's go offbase. There's a great little restaurant called Aunt Madge's. Best pancakes in town."

Annie couldn't hide her surprise as he opened the door to the Blazer for her. "Sounds exciting."

"That's all brig chasers need is more excitement. Right?" Against his better judgment, Joe let himself look into Annie's velvety, cinnamon eyes, now dancing with joy. In the past week, he'd come to realize that she wore every emotion on her very readable face. And how many times had he dreamed of Annie last week? Too many. He shut the door and walked around the Blazer.

Annie didn't quite know what to do or say. As Joe guided the vehicle onto the highway toward the main gate that would lead them into Oceanside, she bit down on her lower lip. All week, he had pointedly ignored her, only speaking to her when he absolutely had to. Every morning she'd come to work to find her desk stacked with transfer files to process and Joe already hard at work himself, having arrived early. He'd merely look up, nod and go back to work. Stymied by this new turn of events, Annie didn't know how to take his unexpected lunch invitation.

Joe glanced over at Annie. She was quiet, but that was nothing new. She wasn't a big talker. If Rose came over, they would chat, or if one of the other brig chasers needed something from her, she'd talk to them—but that was all.

"I'm having a tough time deciding whether you're happy here with us or not," Joe ventured. He slowed the vehicle as they neared the main gate. A marine on duty, resplendent in a summer tan uniform encircled by a white web belt with a shiny brass buckle waved them through.

"I'm very happy here."

"Yeah?"

Annie gave him a long, studied look. "I didn't realize my happiness or lack of it mattered to you."

Joe smarted under her honesty. His conscience was eating him alive for having so pointedly ignored her all week. He knew that Annie saw him interact with his section, and he was friendly, open and communicative—with everyone but her. Sometimes Joe would look over and see the hurt mirrored in her face. She knew she was being left out of the natural camaraderie—almost completely. Maybe that was why he hadn't been sleeping very well. But what could he do? And how long could he be an ostrich, sticking his head in the sand to avoid being a real partner to Annie?

Quirking his lips, Joe said, "All my people are important to me."

"I see...."

Frustration thrummed through him at the obvious doubt in her voice. Sooner or later, they'd have to work together in the field again, and his automatic overprotectiveness would begin working full-time. A brig chaser couldn't afford not to have a close, bonding relationship with his partner—not in their sometimes dangerous line of work. They were the cops of the military, and their job was just as demanding and dangerous as that of their civilian counterparts.

Scrambling to reassure Annie, because he knew Captain Ramsey, too, wanted her to be happy, he said, "You're doing good work. We're finally getting that backlog of paperwork cut down to size."

"Thanks."

"I imagine you'd rather be out tracking than doing desk work."

"I don't mind."

"The captain talked to me yesterday about you and me setting up a tracking school. When we get past this paper logjam, I want you to draw up a proposal."

Surprised, Annie lifted her chin and glanced at him. The freeway leading into Oceanside was typical, but the beautiful silver-barked eucalyptuses that lined it gave it a more rural, natural feel. "I thought you were going to handle it."

"Why should I? A good NCO delegates. You're the tracking expert, so why shouldn't I ask you to become involved?"

Annie sat in silence for a long moment. Joe hadn't allowed her to become involved in anything regarding their so-called partnership thus far. "I . . . just didn't think you wanted anything to do with me." There, the truth was out.

Needled, Joe took an off ramp and slowed the Blazer. The softness of Annie's voice pierced his guilt like a knife. As he slowed for the stop sign, he glanced at her. Her head was bowed, her profile silhouetted. Such sadness showed in the line of her lips that he winced. Making a right turn, he pulled into the restaurant's crowded parking lot. Struggling to identify and control his burgeoning feelings, Joe felt like a heel for hurting Annie. As a half Hispanic, half white kid growing up in a barrio, he'd learned the hard way what the hurt of nonacceptance could feel like.

Opening the door, he said, "Come on, I'll treat you to lunch."

Annie tried to hold herself at bay against Joe's sudden kindness as they walked into the restaurant. He obviously was trying to atone for his recent treatment of her. It had hurt her to think that she was so unwanted. Even the other people in Joe's section had stayed away from her, picking up on the way Joe was shunning her. Normally, Annie was good at making friends, but this time it was an uphill battle. Only Rose, bless her heart, was openly friendly with her. Otherwise, Annie felt like a trapped coyote that was beaten regularly, then handed scraps of food by the same person who did the beating.

Joe worked his way between the crowded tables, decorated with red-and-white-checked cloths and vases of carnations. Country music filtered through the background noise. His luck was holding today, he thought as he spotted a red-vinyl corner booth just being vacated. Annie was hanging back, her eyes wary, and he felt even worse, if that was possible. Somehow he had to convince her the problem wasn't her—it was him. But no way did he *ever* want to tell another living soul what he'd told Captain Ramsey. The pain of the memories was just too great. And for a brig chaser to lose his partner that way was shaming in his eyes. He'd done the unforgivable: he'd allowed his partner to die before his eyes, and he was damned if Annie would ever be placed in that situation. Not with him.

Before they got settled in the big, roomy booth, the waitress came over with menus. Annie stole a look at Joe, who seemed tense. Too, he was being overly solicitous, and it grated on her nerves. When the waitress left with their drink order, Annie said, "If you don't mind, I'll pay for my own meal."

Glancing sharply at her over the menu, Joe saw her determination in the firm line of her beautiful mouth. If only she wasn't so damned appealing. "Look, you've worked like a dog all week. I'm grateful for your help. It's my way of saying thank you," he said tightly.

Her hands clenched the menu and she lowered it to the table. "I'm doing work expected of me, and I'll buy my own lunch."

"Okay," Joe conceded in a strangled tone, "we'll go dutch."

Lowering her gaze to the menu, Annie felt any appetite she might have had dissolve. She'd seen the anger flare briefly in Joe's eyes, but she didn't care—not any longer. What had looked hopeful was rapidly turning out to be a miserable hour spent with a man who couldn't stand her— but was trying somehow to make amends. She closed her eyes for a moment, feeling the hotness of tears behind her lids. Never in her six years in the corps had she felt more alienated than she did right now.

Chapter Five

Joe sat at his desk, furious with himself. He was botching his relationship with Annie on every level. Lunch had been a stilted mess at best. He was angry, too, at Captain Ramsey, who'd refused to allow Annie to be transferred to another section. Joe rested his head in his hands and sighed. It wasn't Annie's fault. Somehow he had to apologize, to set things right between them. But how?

Twirling a pen absently between his fingers, Joe stared at her back. She had a long spine and a strong body despite her willowy looks. She worked out at a local gym every other day to enhance her upper-body strength, he'd learned. Although Annie was working diligently at her desk, Joe could swear her emotions were palpable—wounded by his less-than-glorious attempt at making up for ignoring her all week.

Private Shaw came into the office, and Joe sighed internally. The young marine was a screwup in the best sense of the word, but luckily, Captain Ramsey had realized he was illiterate. The kid's face was flushed and he looked excited as he wound his way toward Joe's desk.

"Sergeant Donnally?"

"What is it, Shaw?"

"Sir, we need some help transferring Gorman from his cell to solitary. Can I get somebody from the office here for just a second?"

"Gorman's fouling up again?" Joe demanded.

"Yes, sir, he is. He just got into a fight with his cell mate. We've called the ambulance."

"Damn it," Joe snarled, dropping the pen onto the desk. He saw Annie turn around. Obviously she'd overheard Shaw. "He's nothing but trouble. I'll be glad when he's out of here."

"I just got the paperwork done on him, if it makes you feel any better," she offered.

Joe shot her a glance. "Will you go with Shaw and help transfer Gorman?" Secretly, he wanted someone with brains involved in the transfer. Shaw didn't possess a whole lot of experience in brig matters and Joe didn't want their worst prisoner breaking out. Not on his watch, especially.

"Sure." Annie rose and smiled up at Shaw, who was a gangly six foot five, all arms and legs. "Let's go, Shaw."

"Yes, ma'am! Thanks, Sergeant."

"Just be careful," Joe warned them heavily before returning to the hated paperwork.

Annie led the way down to the brig area. Shaw followed, chattering all the way.

"You sure have a reputation, Corporal Yellow Horse. We're mighty glad you're here with us."

"Thanks, Shaw."

"Why, the guys and me were just saying that if anyone broke out, you'd nail them before they got off Reed."

The passageway leading to the brig consisted of a series of checkpoints and desks manned by brig chasers on duty. At each station they had to sign in. In addition to the metal badges above their left breast pockets, identifying them as brig personnel, they carried plastic ID cards with color photos. Annie didn't like the brig area, not at all. It was stifling, made of heavy concrete blocks, with no windows—just a dark rectangle lit with fluorescent lights. Unhappy prisoners stared at them as they walked by. Because she was so sensitive, Annie could feel their rage at being confined, their hatred, their grief.

Her nose twitched at the special odor always associated with brigs. Even though prisoners were ordered to shower once a day in a special area, the stale scent of sweat and cigarettes remained. As the brig guard opened the main gate to the cell block, Annie longed for fresh air. She picked up a wooden baton, the three-foot stick that was their main weapon in these crowded quarters. They'd been trained to break bones with the baton to stop an escape, if necessary. Although Annie wore a pistol at her side like every other brig chaser, the baton was the first line of defense.

Shaw nervously moved his own baton into position as they halted at Gorman's cell. Annie felt the hair on the back of her neck stand on end as she got her first good look at the dangerous prisoner. Gorman was built like a bull. Heavily muscled, with no neck, he stood at least six foot two. He must weigh about two hundred and fifty pounds, she estimated—none of it fat. As she met the prisoner's black, angry gaze, Annie's gut automatically clenched and her hand tightened around the baton tucked beneath her right arm. A third guard began to unlock the cell door.

"Hit the deck, Gorman," Annie ordered. Gorman glared at her and didn't move. "Now!"

Gorman looked at Shaw, then back at her. His fleshy lips pursed and rolled into a smirk. Sullenly, he obeyed.

It was normal procedure to have a dangerous prisoner lie on his belly, hands behind his back. That way, cuffs could be placed on him with relative safety. Still, Annie didn't trust the thirty-year-old prisoner convicted of such brutal crimes. She was in charge of the transfer because she was the only corporal present. She was responsible for enforcing correct procedure for moving a prisoner from one cell to another. Tensing, Annie watched as the third marine opened the cell.

Her gaze never left Gorman, who lay on the deck, his hands behind his back. "Shaw, put the cuffs on him," she ordered grimly.

"Yes, ma'am." Like a gangly pup, somewhat uncoordinated and tense, Shaw moved gingerly into the cell, the cuffs dangling from his right hand.

Annie watched Gorman closely, but her body was giving her all kinds of warning signals. Her skin crawled. Her heart began to pound. Just as Shaw approached Gorman and leaned down, she saw the prisoner's arm shoot out. Shaw tottered momentarily and let out a yelp, the cuffs sailing through the air and hitting the cell's bulkhead. The private's feet were jerked out from beneath him, Gorman's superior weight and strength sending Shaw flying backward. The marine slammed into the bulkhead, let out a gasp and sank semiconscious to the deck, his eyes glazed with shock.

Instantly, Annie yelled to the guard at the desk, "Lock the outer door!" Her eyes narrowed, and she felt a cold wash of terror slam through her. Quickly she moved to the door of the cell to stop Gorman from escaping, her baton in position to defend herself.

With a snarl, Gorman got to his knees. His mouth twisted into a lethal line as he sized her up in the millisecond before he sprang to his feet. Annie was the only one between him and escape. She stood at the cell door, the baton in position.

"Freeze, Gorman," she snapped, hunching slightly for the attack she knew was coming.

"Get outta my way," he roared, and launched himself at her.

Annie thrust the baton forward with all her strength, her body behind the forceful jab. The end buried itself deeply in Gorman's belly. The prisoner let out a gasp. His eyes bulged in disbelief, and then shrank to slits of murderous rage. He flailed forward, trying to grab her, and his fingers sank desperately into her shoulder. Pain flared in her neck as he threw her off balance. Blindly, acting out of years of training and inborn survival instinct, Annie shoved the baton upward as hard as she could toward Gorman's granitelike jaw. The *thunk* of the stick connecting solidly with bone echoed eerily through the cell.

Gorman groaned. He staggered backward, his hand still like a claw in her shoulder. Annie heard the shouts of other marines who had been alerted to the escape attempt echoing through the brig. The alarm went off. Good! Even if Gorman got past her, she knew all cell doors would be locked to prevent his further escape.

Breathing hard, Annie wrenched backward to break Gorman's death grip on her shoulder. At the same time, she kicked out with her right leg, sending him flying off his feet. Her head snapped back hard. Gorman still hadn't released her shoulder, and he was dragging her down with him. As he landed heavily on the deck, Annie felt herself falling. She tried to prepare, but she hit the deck on her shoulder and hip, the baton clenched in her fists. If she lost the baton, Gorman would kill her. She saw the glitter of absolute hatred in his black eyes, heard the ugly rasp of his bull-like breathing, and knew beyond doubt that she was locked in a battle of life and death.

With all her strength, Annie rolled half a turn and forced herself to her feet. Gorman was dazed, blood on the side of his jaw, but his eyes never left hers. She had to disable him. Disregarding her puny size and weight in comparison to his, she straddled him with her legs and jammed the baton down across his throat. Gorman's eyes widened. He croaked. His hands started to flail, his breathing nearly cut off. Annie shifted all her weight forward into the baton, her fists locked on the wood. Spittle erupted from Gorman's lips as he tried to buck her off.

Another brig marine finally raced into the cell and grabbed one of Gorman's hands, cuffing it. Before he could get the other one secured, Gorman growled and doubled his fist. Annie had to get off of him in order for him to be cuffed. Gasping for air, her weight still on the baton to keep him subdued, she didn't see his fist arching upward.

The side of her head seemed to explode with stars and light. Pain followed, and Annie felt herself flying through the air. She landed with a thud against the bunk, the baton dropping nervelessly from her hands. For a moment, everything went black, although she could hear the shouts of the brig chasers and Gorman's nonstop cursing. Through the combined din of the shrieking alarm, the brig chasers subduing Gorman and his evil curses, Annie fought to clear her head. She knew she was on the verge of losing consciousness. But she couldn't. She just couldn't.

She lay sprawled on the deck, gasping for breath, her hand against her temple where she'd received the blow. Gradually, the blackness changed to gray, then back to full clarity. A brig marine, his face etched with terror, came and helped her into a sitting position. It was Shaw.

"Ma'am, you okay? Are you? Oh, geez, you're bleeding." His hands moved jerkily from her hair to her shoulder to her arms. He didn't know what to do.

"I'm okay," Annie rasped, sitting up. Breathing raggedly, she watched through wary eyes as Gorman was jerked to his feet by two brig marines and dragged away toward solitary. He hadn't escaped. That was what was important.

"I've got to get you help. Hold on," Shaw rattled, completely shaken.

"No!" Annie reached up and gripped the private's arm. "Just settle down, Shaw. Give me a minute, will you?" She hung her head, her left ear ringing badly where Gorman had hit her. She closed her eyes momentarily, trying to get a grip on herself. This was no time to faint. Gorman could still try something.

His voice wobbled as he said, "But you're bleeding bad on the side of your head."

So she was. Annie looked at her hand. "Don't go," she rasped, feeling a little woozy. This was only the second time in her career that she'd foiled an escape attempt by a prisoner. Nausea stalked her. If she hadn't been as aggressive as she had been in attacking Gorman, she knew he'd have snapped her back like a pretzel and killed her. Just the thought made her feel like vomiting.

Just then, she heard several more footsteps running down the passageway toward the cell block. She lifted her head. "Open the door for them, Shaw."

"Y-yes, ma'am," he responded hesitantly, leaving her side. Halting at the cell doorway, he looked back at her worriedly, then hurried toward the outer door.

Annie heard Joe Donnally's authoritative voice above the din of marines and the wailing of the brig siren. What would he think? She'd nearly allowed Gorman to escape, and it would have been on Joe's watch—not something any section leader ever wanted to happen. Internally, she tried to brace herself for Donnally's wrath, but it was impossible. The feelings roiling through her now were ugly, scared and nauseous.

Still, Donnally's arrival meant she could finally relax. Shaw was too shaken to take command, and she was too incapacitated to assume it. Relief, sharp and powerful, moved through Annie. Joe would take over. She rolled over to try to at least sit up on the bunk.

Shaw opened the door and leapt back as Joe came running in, his face taut and utterly unreadable. His blue eyes were slits, his mouth tight, his body filled with tension. His gaze swept the area, then riveted on her. Shame filled Annie as she saw his eyes go wide with shock. Probably shock that she'd allowed Gorman to nearly escape.

Joe turned in one motion toward Annie, who sat pale and bleeding on the cell's bunk. Her eyes looked dazed and his heartbeat seemed to triple in time as he took huge strides toward her. What the hell had happened? Annie was hurt, that much was clear. She tried to sit up and straighten her back as he approached, her lips parting as if to give him an explanation. The entire left side of her face was swelling, blood dripping down the line of her jaw. She looked devastated, Joe thought. A flashback of

Jenny, lying on the ground, dying, slammed into him. He hesitated fractionally as memories of the past became a haunting overlay to the present.

What had he done? He shouldn't have ordered Annie to the brig. She was too new to Reed, too new to the system. As he raised his hands to reach out for her, guilt flooded through him. He should have sent someone else—anyone but her.

Annie saw the glitter in Joe's eyes as he halted in front of her. When he reached out, she stiffened, waiting to be yelled at for screwing up. Instead, hands, strong and gentle, cupped her shoulders.

"Annie?" His voice was terribly off-key.

It was Joe's voice. His hands. He wasn't angry. At least, not yet. But he seemed as shaken as she was. She managed to quirk one side of her mouth as he crouched in front of her. "I'm okay. Just give me a few minutes and I'll be okay...."

Worriedly, Joe quickly assessed her condition. What had happened, anyway? He wanted to ask, but those details were secondary to Annie's injury. His heart was pounding so hard with fear that he could barely think. Annie was his partner. He'd allowed her to get hurt. He hadn't been here to back her up. He saw the blood flowing from a cut along her hairline.

"What the hell happened?" he demanded as he took his white handkerchief from his back pocket. Annie was beginning to slowly collapse on him. She was still groggy. Unwinding from his crouched position, he moved to her side and sat down, allowing her to sag against him. She was pale and her eyes were dark and dazed looking. As he pressed the cloth against the cut, she sat stoically without reacting to his touch.

"Gorman tried to escape," Annie murmured. "They got him cuffed and they're taking him to solitary right now. It's okay, Joe. Everything's okay...."

"Yeah," Joe breathed angrily, "everything except you."

Shaw came racing back into the cell, a glass of water in hand. "Here, Corporal Yellow Horse. Drink this. You'll feel better. I called the ambulance."

"Thanks, Shaw." Annie held the glass with both hands, knowing if she didn't, she would drop it. She sipped the water, realizing the young marine was terribly agitated. "It's okay. I'm okay."

"I—I'm sorry, Corporal Yellow Horse. I really am. I didn't know Gorman was going to grab my leg."

Joe glared up at Shaw, who stood nervously before them, his face totally devoid of color, his eyes shadowed with fear. "What the hell happened, Shaw?"

Annie reached out and touched Joe's arm. "It wasn't his fault." It hurt to talk, but she didn't want him chewing out Shaw.

Shaw stammered, "Corporal Yellow Horse ordered Gorman down on the deck, hands behind his back. I went in to cuff him so we could transfer him. The next thing I knew, Gorman grabbed my leg and threw me clear over him and against the bulkhead. My head hit first and I dropped to the deck." Shaw gave Annie a look of awe. "Sergeant, she jumped into the open cell door, her baton in position, and stopped Gorman. I couldn't believe it. He charged her and she delivered a blow to his belly. That stopped most of his forward motion, but then he grabbed Corporal Yellow Horse by the shoulder and yanked her down to the deck next to him. Gorman started to hit her, but she gave him an uppercut to the jaw that felled him like an ox. And then she leapt up on him with her baton against his throat so they could cuff him. At the last moment, Gorman hit her. Right after that, me and Perkins subdued him enough to cuff him.'' Shaw shook his head. ''Man alive, I was on the deck, half-conscious after I hit the bulkhead, when I saw Corporal Yellow Horse move to the door. I thought he was gonna kill her for sure. She's so little in comparison. I just couldn't believe my eyes. It was like David taking on Goliath!''

Annie gave the private a dark look, embarrassed by his dramatic embellishment of the facts. She had been the one in charge, and she was responsible for what had happened. She deserved at least a chewing out—from Donnally, and probably from Captain Ramsey. ''Shaw, just tell the sergeant what happened, okay? Don't overdramatize.''

Laughing a little nervously, Shaw raised his hands. ''I couldn't help myself, Corporal. I mean, you're a woman, and Gorman's a bona fide murderer. You put yourself in harm's way without a second thought.''

Annie muttered, ''That's our job, Shaw. If we don't do it, innocent people could get killed. We are the last stop. You got that?'' The adrenaline that had helped her overcome Gorman when it counted was beginning to ebb from her bloodstream, and Annie was feeling very shaky. But Joe's steadying presence next to her helped. He kept his handkerchief against her temple, and no matter how much she tried, she couldn't keep herself from sagging more and more heavily against him. She was feeling very weak all of a sudden.

Joe flashed an irritated look at Shaw. ''Go out and meet the ambulance. Bring them back here with a stretcher.'' Desperately, Joe tried to stuff his escaping terror and guilt deep inside himself again. Right now Annie needed his help, his care.

"Yes, sir!" Shaw hightailed it out of the cell, having the guard open the first door leading out to the main brig area.

"That kid is too hyper to work here," Joe grated as he slowly stood up. "Come on, lie down on the bunk, Annie. You're more hurt than you let on."

Annie smiled brokenly and did as he ordered. She closed her eyes. "I'll be okay, Sergeant," she whispered. "This isn't the first time I've tangled with a brig prisoner who wanted to run over me to freedom." Internally, she was trying to prepare herself for Joe's anger, which she knew was coming. He might be shaken up right now, but later, after he'd reviewed the report on the escape, he'd hunt her down for a good chewing out. But that was the last thing Annie wanted to think about right now. She felt stripped and horribly vulnerable emotionally. It was one thing to work with prisoners day in and day out, but quite another to have one attack you with the intent to kill.

Joe stood, feeling helpless. Annie was exhausted, her eyes closed, her lips a line of unspoken pain. At that moment, he wanted to pulverize Gorman into dust. The bastard was a killer, and Joe knew that Annie's heroic stand against him at the cell door was remarkable—enough to make even a marine of a similar weight and height to Gorman's cringe with fear. Gorman was a sociopath; he lived by no rules but his own, and human life meant absolutely nothing to him. Annie easily could have been killed if she hadn't fought back as viciously as she had. Rubbing his jaw, Joe knew he had never felt more guilty than right now. Annie was his partner, whether he wanted her to be or not. He'd had no right to send her down to the brig alone—he should have gone with her, shadowed her movements and been here when Gorman turned on them. What the hell was the matter with him?

Trying to get a hold on his unraveling emotions, Joe crouched down and touched the handkerchief to Annie's wound again. It was swelling even more and looked very bruised, but at least the bleeding had stopped. For a moment, they were alone. Without thinking, he pushed several strands of dark hair away from her tense brow.

"It's going to be okay," he whispered unsteadily. "You're going to be okay...."

Just the tender touch of Joe's fingers moving shakily across her brow, however briefly, brought Annie's lashes up. His fingertips were roughened; he loved the outdoors as much as she did, even if he had been born in a city, she realized. As her gaze drifted upward, she felt the touch of his hand again, this time cradling the side of her face to give her solace. Annie's lips parted as she met and held Joe's turbulent gaze, fraught with fear. Fear? Why? For her? More likely over the possibility of an escape on his watch, she tried to tell herself. Still, she closed her eyes, capitulating to his gentle touch. As she lay with Joe crouched at her side, Annie felt a wealth of warm, good feelings flowing to the surface to dissipate the fear of combating Gorman. Joe cared. He could have left her here alone or with Shaw to await the ambulance, but he hadn't. He was here, at her side. Tears welled up beneath her eyelids.

Joe saw the beaded tears gathering on Annie's thick, dark lashes. Unthinkingly, he reached down and smoothed them away with his thumbs.

"You're going to be okay," he said softly. *Where the hell was the ambulance?* Worriedly, Joe lifted his head and looked toward the passageway, but heard nothing.

Annie gulped back the rest of her tears. She knew it wasn't right to cry; marines had to be tough. Joe probably thought she was a wimp for crying.

"I didn't mean to cry," she whispered as she looked up into his set face. He appeared haggard and far more shaken than he should be. Why?

"Tackling Gorman would be enough to make any marine cry, believe me," Joe rasped.

Annie managed a twisted smile through her pain. "I wasn't crying over Gorman's attack."

"What then?"

She sighed and held his ravaged stare. "I—I thought you hated me, didn't want me as a partner. And now..." She sniffed, her eyes filling with tears again. "You're taking care of me, like a partner would. I didn't think you cared enough to stay with me after I got hurt...."

Joe hung his head, his heart exploding with such shame that he gripped her shoulder gently with his hand. Forcing himself to look her in the eyes, he muttered, "It's a long story, Annie." His mouth curved downward with pain—her pain. "I'm sorry. I've been a real bastard to you ever since you came. It's not your fault, it's mine."

She studied his suffering features, the anguish clearly written in his eyes, and felt an avalanche of such despondency that it took away her voice for a good minute. Finally clearing her throat, she whispered, "Something happened, didn't it? You lost a partner. I've seen that look before...."

Joe heard the ambulance people arriving, and he heard Shaw's off-key voice giving instructions as they ran toward the cell block. He forced a tight, broken smile and gently squeezed her shoulder. "I owe you an explanation, Annie. But let's get you over to emergency. We'll talk later, I promise...."

Joe refused to leave Annie as she made her way up the concrete ramp toward the emergency room of Reed's navy hospital. And he kept his hand cupped around her left elbow without asking permission. She'd given him a strange look when he'd helped her out of the ambulance, but had said nothing. She was barely able to walk a straight line by herself, and that was enough of an excuse to keep a hand on her.

Inside the emergency room, a nurse directed them to the first cubicle on the right. A small, pert woman doctor came over immediately.

"I'm Dr. Karen David. You must be Corporal Yellow Horse?" she queried.

Annie whispered, "Yes, ma'am," barely noticing Joe helping her sit up on the gurney. The overhead lights were bright and made her headache worse. Annie was amazed that Joe remained standing next to her, tenacious as a bulldog, refusing to move when Dr. David came forward.

"Excuse me, Sergeant," Dr. David said, quirking an eyebrow at him.

"Oh...sure." He quickly moved to the other side of the gurney, never letting his eyes leave Annie. Her voice had grown very faint and he figured it hurt her to talk.

Dr. David gave her a slight smile as she gently began to examine her injury. "You can't tell me you slipped and fell," she murmured, removing strands of hair from the wound.

Annie said, "No. I got in a fight."

"Hope you punched the sucker out, Corporal."

Annie grinned a little, liking the spunky doctor. "Not exactly."

Karen smiled more broadly and began to clean the wound quickly and efficiently. "Well, it doesn't matter. I think you're going to need about six or seven stitches to close this."

Annie groaned.

"Now, just let Dr. David handle this, Annie," Joe said sternly. He glanced over at the doctor. "All she wants to do is go home."

"Really?" Karen put the gauze aside and inspected her work. "I don't think so, Corporal. First, I'm going to have them wheel you down to X-ray to make sure you don't have a concussion. When you get back here, I'll sew you up."

Annie was wildly aware of Joe's overwhelming presence. She could hear the concern in his deep voice and felt him come around the end of the gurney to stand on her right, opposite the doctor. Giving Dr. David a pleading look, Annie said, "But then I can go home, right?"

Karen rubbed her nose and thought for a moment. "I don't know yet...." She checked Annie's eyes with a light. "I want to see X-rays first." Looking around the patient, she said to Joe, "Are you her partner?"

"Yes, ma'am."

"Okay, then you can go with her down to X-ray." Karen gestured for a navy corpsman to come over and gave him instructions to wheel Annie down to the lab.

Muffling a groan, Annie lay down on the gurney and the corpsman began pushing it out of the cubicle.

"Take it nice and slow," Joe admonished. "This isn't a road race."

Smiling to herself, Annie closed her eyes. Joe was like an overprotective mother hen with a newly hatched chick. His care was surprising, and part of her still waited for him to realize that she wasn't as badly hurt as he thought, and to chew her out for messing up with Gorman. Still, she was glad he was here. Hospitals were far from her favorite places in the world, and it was nice to have her partner with her.

After X-ray, Annie was brought back to the cubicle. Joe continued to wait patiently next to the gurney, his arms crossed over his broad chest. The look on his face was dark and stormy.

"Will you relax? I'm not going to die."

Joe cast a furious look in her direction. "You look like death warmed over," he muttered.

"Would you be hovering over me this way if I was a man?" she challenged.

"Yes, so just lie there and take it."

Her mouth pulled into a slight grimace.

Joe fought the need to reach out and touch Annie's shoulder. He was worried about how pale she looked. When her lips moved into a grimace, he wondered for the first time if she really didn't want him around. If not, could he blame her? He'd behaved very badly toward her. Still, his fingers ached to reach out and stroke her shiny black hair to give her solace.

"When you were a little girl, did your mother hold you when you stubbed your toe?" he asked.

Annie barely opened her eyes. Just lying down felt heavenly right now—exactly what she needed. Joe stood facing her, his brows drawn into a frown, his eyes unreadable. "Well...sure. Why?"

"Good." He reached out and gently smoothed several strands of her hair away from the area of the swollen injury.

Shocked again by his care, Annie stared up at him in disbelief.

Joe saw the look on her face and felt heat surging up his neck into his face. Was he blushing? He hadn't done that since he was a kid! Clearing his throat, he frowned. "Don't look so shocked. I may be a bastard, but I still have a heart, Annie."

Her eyes softening, she whispered, "I know. Thanks ... I'm glad you're here...."

"You are?" Joe couldn't stop himself from blurting out the words. Somehow, he felt terribly shy and self-conscious around Annie, in a way he'd never experienced before.

"Why wouldn't I be?"

He could think of plenty of reasons, but with a shrug, he muttered, "I don't know."

"Partners are supposed to take care of each other," Annie said, her voice growing thin and tired. She closed her eyes, the thought of having to get up and move anywhere right now becoming increasingly unappealing.

Joe's throat constricted as he stared down at Annie. She looked serene despite today's violent events. *Partners.* Yes, they were, and he'd already screwed up badly in that department. He opened his mouth to apologize to her, to tell her how sorry he was for not being there for her, but just then Dr. David appeared with X-rays in hand.

"Well, Corporal Yellow Horse," she said airily as she halted at the edge of the gurney, "you're clear of any serious head injury."

Joe felt a mountain of tension dissolve from his shoulders. "Good," he growled.

Annie barely nodded. "You'll sew me up so I can go home?"

"I'll sew you up," Dr. David said briskly, "but I'm holding you overnight, Corporal."

Annie's eyes widened. "But—"

"Now, don't argue," Jo warned.

"I hate hospitals!" Annie told the doctor, her voice rough with emotion.

Dr. David nodded. "Any sane person would." She laughed at her own joke, then got serious. "You're staying, Corporal."

Resigned, Annie murmured, "Yes, ma'am."

Joe inched around until he had Dr. David's attention as she prepared to stitch up Annie's wound. "Doc, er, you're sure Annie's okay? Nothing else wrong with her?"

David shot him a look. "I'm positive, Sergeant. Why?"

"Uh, no reason. It's just that—" he gestured helplessly at Annie "—she looks terrible."

Annie steeled herself for the impending stitches. "You'd look terrible, too, if Gorman had just nailed you," she whispered through clenched teeth.

The doctor chuckled. "Sergeant, go back to work, okay? Your partner is going to be fine, believe me. All she needs is some quiet, uninterrupted time to rest and get plenty of sleep. I'll release her tomorrow afternoon. Is that okay with you?"

Joe met the doctor's demanding look. "That's fine with me, Doc." He stuffed his hands in his pockets. "When are visiting hours?"

"Nineteen hundred hours to 2100."

Annie closed her eyes. Joe was behaving like the ideal partner. But was it real? Or just a show he was putting on? She wasn't sure.

"Great." Joe reached out and barely touched her shoulder. "I'll see you tonight, Annie."

Opening her eyes, she drowned in his concerned blue ones. How could she think he was not sincere? The burning anxiety in his eyes, the emotion bleeding through his gruff voice told her all she wanted to know. "Okay...."

He patted her shoulder awkwardly. "Yeah, tonight...." Joe took a step backward, still reluctant to leave. He knew stitches smarted like hell. What he really wanted to do was hold Annie's hand in his and comfort her through that pain. But he, of all people, didn't deserve that honor. Attempting an encouraging smile, he turned away.

"Sergeant?" Dr. David called.

He turned back. "Yes, ma'am?"

"Make sure you don't tire out Corporal Yellow Horse tonight, please. She really does need a lot of rest."

"Of course." And again, reluctantly, he turned away.

Many hours later, Annie sat unhappily in her hospital bed, looking slowly around the room at the other two empty beds. She sighed. At least she was the only one in the room and closest to the window. From where she sat she could see the evening sky, watch the bats flitting around catching bugs, enjoy the sunset. Still, she hated hospitals. She hated the smells and the awful feelings that came with them. Feeling trapped, she stared down at the plastic wristband printed with her name.

A knock at the door made her start. Her heart pounding, her hand against her breast, she said, "Come in."

Captain Ramsey entered and smiled a greeting. He was dressed in his summer uniform of tan slacks and short-sleeved shirt. He took off his garrison cap as he approached her bed.

"How are you doing, Annie?"

She managed a wan smile. "Fine, sir."

Ramsey walked over to where she lay propped up on several pillows. "You're a heroine. I hope you know that. There isn't a brig chaser on Reed who isn't talking about the way you placed yourself in the cell doorway to prevent Gorman's escape. That was something, Annie. I don't know that I'd have had the guts to do the same thing. Gorman's a killer." He scowled. "If you hadn't gotten the drop on him, you could have died."

Annie lowered her lashes beneath her superior's praise. "I was just doing my job, Captain."

Chuckling, Ramsey said, "Shaw's telling everyone on base about it."

With a groan, she said, "He's just an excitable kid, that's all."

"Well," Ramsey said, smiling down at her, "I'm glad you were there. You kept your head."

"I just followed procedure, sir." Annie felt a little uncomfortable at the captain's praise—especially when she'd expected a chewing out! Swallowing her surprise, she said, "There's really nothing to make a fuss about, sir."

"Well," he said lightly, "I'm writing up a commendation for your bravery and it will go in your personnel jacket."

Annie felt heat nettle her cheeks and knew she was blushing. A commendation from one's superior never hurt one's chances for promotion later on. They were rare gifts handed out by officers to their enlisted subordinates, and Annie was grateful. "You didn't have to do that, Captain, but thank you."

"It was Sergeant Donnally's idea. After he told me what you did, I agreed with him. Good work, Annie."

Warmth flooded her as she met the captain's serious gaze. "Thank you, sir."

"Is there anything I can do for you? Anything you need while you're staying here?"

Touched, Annie shook her head. Ramsey was going way beyond duty, and his kindness left a lump in her throat. "No, sir, but thank you...."

He settled the garrison cap back on his head. "Get a good night's sleep, Annie. I've ordered Donnally to let you have the next three days off to recuperate."

"But, sir, we're shorthanded!"

"That's my problem, Yellow Horse, not yours. Now get a good night's sleep."

Glumly, Annie whispered, "Yes, sir." She watched as Ramsey left and then closed her eyes, feeling suddenly exhausted—and more than a little weepy. Sinking back against the pillows, she fell into a light, restless sleep. At the sound of the door to her room opening and closing, she woke with a start.

"Dinner," a young, blond navy corpsman said with a smile as he brought her tray into the room.

Annie wasn't really hungry. She managed to sit up as the corpsman placed the tray on the mobile table, which he wheeled to her bed and swung across her lap. "Thanks," she said.

"Enjoy!" With a lift of his hand and a smile, he left.

Annie toyed with the food, in the end eating only the tasteless Jell-O and drinking the coffee, leaving the rest untouched. Finally, she gave up and pushed the table away from her bed. A knock sounded at the door. She lifted her head, wondering who else would be visiting her. Joe's promise to see her still tugged at the back of her mind— although she knew it was probably silly.

"Come in."

Joe opened the door to Annie's room to find her lying propped up on a lot of pillows on the bed closest to the window. Her attempt to smile didn't succeed, and he could see her eyes had widened in obvious surprise at his appearance. Didn't she remember he'd promised to come visit her? Or maybe she hadn't wanted to remember. A bitter taste filled Joe's mouth. "May I come in?" He saw her look of surprise change to wariness, and his stomach clenched in knots.

"Sure," Annie said, her voice raspy. Her heart had started an erratic pounding. Well, Joe Donnally had been good for his word; he'd come back to visit her. But she wasn't sure of his motives. Had he come because he had to, because she was his partner, or had he come because he wanted to be here to see how she was? Annie wished she didn't hope so much that it was the latter. Joe was dressed in civilian clothes instead of his usual marine utilities, looking dynamic and completely masculine in tan chinos, a smartly pressed, light blue, short-sleeved shirt with a button-down collar and a pair of tennis shoes. And if she wasn't seeing things, it looked as if he had shaved— again. Usually, by 1700, she knew, he had a shadow of beard growth that lent a dangerous edge to his appearance. But tonight his skin was scraped free of that telltale shadow, and Annie wondered why he'd gone to such pains on her account.

Joe, she was realizing, was a complex man of great depth and many secrets. As he slipped into the room, she saw a dozen yellow roses clasped in his left hand. Her mouth lifted in disbelief. Were they for her? No, they couldn't be. "Gosh, roses," she blurted.

"They're for you," Joe offered shyly, wondering if Annie would accept his apology by taking them.

Annie's eyes grew round. "They are?"

Joe was taken aback by her shocked look. Wasn't she used to getting flowers? Granted, brig partners didn't normally give each other bouquets, but this was a different situation, for many reasons. "Well...sure, they're for you...." His stomach tightened again and he wondered if she was going to tell him to take a walk, roses and all.

Not that he wouldn't have deserved it. Still, deep in his heart, Joe hoped she would accept his peace offering.

Shaking her head, Annie murmured, "No one has ever given me roses," and she held out her hands as he extended the bouquet to her.

Joe smiled for the first time, relief combining with a heated pleasure in finally having done something right. Annie's face glowed with sudden joy as she took the lush bouquet, and she promptly buried her face in the dark yellow blooms and inhaled deeply. A wild, euphoric feeling flooded Joe, and he nervously shifted his weight from one foot to the other. Annie did like the roses; it showed in her eyes, which had lost some of their initial wariness. When her mouth curved upward, heat streaked through him like lighting on a hot, muggy night.

"This is heaven," Annie murmured, surrounded by the heady fragrance. She laid the roses gently across her lap and looked up into Joe's dark and worried-looking blue eyes. "Thank you, Sergeant Donnally. You didn't have to do this, you know."

With a one-shouldered shrug, Joe stood restively beside her bed. Absently, he ran his fingers across the light blue bedspread. "Call me Joe, will you?" He motioned to the roses, which she delicately stroked with her long, graceful fingers. "Partners are supposed to protect each other," he muttered apologetically. "It's my way of saying I'm sorry I wasn't there when things got out of hand with Gorman. If I'd been thinking, I'd have gone down there with you. I know Gorman. You don't."

Annie lifted her chin and melted beneath his gaze. Warmth emanated from him, and she felt wave after wave of his care deluging her, healing her. Trying to hide her shock at his change of attitude toward her, she said, "You had no way of knowing Gorman was going to try something. Besides, there will be plenty of times when we aren't working together."

With a sigh, Joe nodded. "That's partly why I dropped over tonight. I promised I'd talk about the way I've been acting toward you, Annie. The other reason, though, was to see how you're getting along. Are you feeling any better?" She looked better, but he knew that individuals in this line of work were notorious for hiding how miserable they might feel. Showing weakness to anyone—even a partner—just wasn't the marine way.

When he spoke her name, a small shiver rippled through her—a delicious sensation. "I'm feeling okay...." Annie whispered. Again, she had to hide her surprise at his solicitous gesture. Sensing his sincerity, she realized this might signal a change between them. "What's on your mind?" She tried to prepare herself emotionally for whatever he might have to say. The fact that he'd called her his partner made her hope that whatever obstacle had cluttered their way thus far would finally be removed—or at least explained.

Joe nodded and brought over a chair. Turning it around backward, he threw his leg across it and rested his arms across the top. "First of all, I owe you a big apology," he murmured, his voice low with feeling. Opening his hands, he said, "I didn't expect to be saddled with a new brig partner so soon after Captain Ramsey arrived at Reed. I guess I just expected things to go on the way they had. We were shorthanded and everyone was short-tempered and morale had gone to hell in a hand-basket. Ramsey sized up the situation fast and ordered four more brig chasers transferred to Reed. You were one of them. I guess because I was the glue holding the section together by myself for so long while Jacobs was running the place, I didn't expect to get a partner."

"You were like a lone wolf," Annie murmured, "used to running without a mate...I mean, a partner." Embarrassed by the slip, she hoped he wouldn't catch the inference.

Joe lowered his eyes for a moment. *Mate.* He withdrew inwardly at how easily she saw through him. His last partner *had* been his mate. Swallowing hard, working not to reveal his true feelings, he met and held Annie's gaze. Her glorious, gold-flecked, cinnamon eyes were so unguarded, he nearly got out of the chair to go over and hold her. That's what she really needed, he realized belatedly. He'd let himself forget that she was a woman who lived in the very harsh, dangerous world of brig chasers. She'd put herself on the front line, never giving a thought to the fact that she was a one-hundred-forty-pound woman up against a brute of a man almost twice her weight. Joe found himself respecting Annie more than any woman he'd ever met. When he'd written out the report on Gorman's escape attempt with Shaw, he'd begun to grasp the magnitude of Annie's courage.

He realized he'd stopped speaking and gave her a slight smile. "You amaze me, Annie. You really do."

She looked at him, nonplussed. "I don't understand."

"Gorman was twice your size. From what Shaw said, you fearlessly placed yourself in his path." With a shake of his head, he added, "Shaw said you weren't even scared. Hell, I'd have been shaking in my boots."

"There wasn't time to be afraid," Annie told him quietly. "Why can't I make anyone understand that I was just following procedure? I'm sure any marine would have done the same thing. You're making too much of this, Joe. You shouldn't have asked Captain Ramsey to give me a commendation. I feel I'm getting it because I'm a woman. If I'd been a man doing the same job, would I have gotten one?''

Joe cocked his head and held her gaze. "What you don't understand is that Gorman is one of our worst military criminals. I'd have written up Shaw if he'd placed himself in front of that bastard. Okay?''

Pretending to examine the roses, Annie murmured, "Okay...."

"Brig chasers are heroic," Joe pointed out, "just like the police and fire fighters. Our work often goes unnoticed, but even while Jacobs was here, I wrote up personnel commendations for my people—although he refused to sign them. Captain Ramsey has promised to review my commendations, though. What we do is damned dangerous, Annie. You know that more than most, because you're out there hanging ten over the edge, tracking the worst of those bastards.''

Annie nodded and looked up to meet and drown in his compassionate blue eyes. She could see respect in them now—and a touch of awe. With a tiny smile, she said, "You aren't going to buy into that silly legend that follows me around like a bad shadow, are you?''

"Maybe a little.''

"Keep it at a minimum, will you?''

"I guess if we're going to be partners we need to see each other realistically, warts and all.''

Her smile widened. "Something like that. Yes.''

"Well, speaking of warts," Joe said in a quiet tone, "I'm going to share my past with you. It's to go no further than you and me. Captain Ramsey knows about it, but I don't want anyone else knowing. Fair enough?''

"I won't say a word to anyone," Annie solemnly promised. She placed her hands on the bouquet, sensing a terrible wall of grief surrounding Joe. "I know something has been standing in our way. I just didn't know what it was."

"In some ways, you scare me to death, Annie," Joe admitted, shaking his head.

"Why?"

"Because I feel like you can look right through me to the depths of my soul."

Gently, she reached out until her hand rested on top of his. "Joe, I would never use my intuition, my sights, to hurt anyone. I only use them to protect."

Her touch was butterfly light, warmly stirring the coals of a need Joe had thought had died with Jenny so long ago. When Annie pulled her hand back, he felt bereft. Such genuine compassion and care burned in her eyes, which looked old with wisdom. It must have something to do with her Navajo forebears, he thought, his heart expanding with such incredible longing that he had to take a deep, steadying breath.

"A brig chaser who does no harm," he said wryly. "I believe you, Annie."

Shocked by her unthinking physical contact with Joe, she murmured, "I guess this battle with Gorman has me more shaken than I first thought."

"Don't say you're sorry," Joe rasped, "because I'm not." If anything, he wanted more of Annie—more of her touch, more of that radiance that seemed to envelop her like an invisible rainbow, lighting his darkened soul and helping him hope again. Hope was something he'd believed had died with Jenny.

Her eyes widening at his statement, Annie remained silent. In her heart she knew Joe needed to be touched, to be comforted over the grief he carried clutched around him like a heavy coat. Their relationship had to be professional, not personal, she chided herself. Yet how could she help herself? Joe was excruciatingly vulnerable right now, and her own protective mechanisms were working overtime, wanting to save him from the terrible, dark secret he evidently carried.

Gathering all of his strewn emotions, Joe swallowed hard. He was barely able to hold Annie's compassionate golden gaze as the silence became almost palpable. "I was stationed at Treasure Island, a navy base up in San Francisco, three years ago." Joe felt his voice go wobbly. He gulped convulsively and went on. "Lance Corporal Jenny Long was my partner. She'd been with me two years." Joe looked away, then down at the bedspread. "We had to transport a prisoner from TI to Fort Leavenworth in Kansas. The prisoner grabbed Jenny from behind and took the pistol she carried. I was standing with my gun drawn...." Joe forced himself to look up into Annie's devastated eyes. "I had a bead on him...." He felt his armpits become damp at the memory of that terrible moment. "I—I didn't know what to do. I knew what the manual said, but Jenny's life was on the line. The prisoner had his arm around her throat, and she couldn't do anything. He yelled at me to drop the pistol or he'd shoot her in the head."

"Oh, no...." Annie whispered, automatically reaching out to grip Joe's hand again.

He felt the warmth, the soft strength of her touch, and it gave him the courage he needed to go on. "We were under directives never to drop our pistol or rifle in such a situation. Jenny knew that. The prisoner we were transporting was a murderer. I could tell by the look in his eyes that if I dropped my weapon, he'd kill us." Joe wiped his upper lip with the back of his hand, a whole range of emotions including grief and guilt eating at him.

Annie felt tears come to her eyes. The pain in Joe's gaze was tortured. "What happened?" she asked brokenly.

Swallowing hard, he rasped, "Jenny knew what I was thinking. We had this mental telepathy between us, in a way. I mean, she was my partner for two years. We knew each other so well.... Jenny smashed her boot back into the prisoner's leg. He let out a howl and released her. I fired and missed." Joe's voice died. "I missed. I'm an expert marksman...."

Annie tightened her grip on his hand. "Joe, it's not unusual in that kind of a situation."

With a shake of his head, he looked up at her with misery-laden eyes. "I'll never forgive myself for what happened next. It was my fault. I'd missed an easy shot. Twenty feet away. My God."

Annie shook her head, feeling his grief as if it were her own. "What happened next?"

Painfully, Joe forced out the words that had grown like a lump in his throat. "Before I could get off a second shot, the prisoner fired on Jenny and—and killed her. I fired and killed him." Bleakly, Joe looked at her. "But Jenny died because I missed that first shot."

Her hands had flown to her mouth at Joe's tragic confession, and now Annie stared mutely at his ravaged face. She felt tears coming to her eyes and rapidly gulped them back. The bleakness in Joe's blue eyes tore at her heart.

"There's more," he said in a choked voice. "You need to know I loved Jenny." He closed his eyes, the tears smarting behind them, his voice rough. "We were going to get married. The date was set...."

At that moment, Annie simply wanted to throw her arms around Joe's sagging shoulders, draw him against her and hold him. But she knew that she couldn't, no matter how much she wanted to. She remained very still, watching the play of powerful emotions across his unforgiving face. How badly life had hurt him. Finally finding her voice, she whispered, "Stop blaming yourself for her death, Joe. You were shaken up. She was in danger. We've all missed shots at close range. We will in the future. That's part of being human." Against her better judgment, she reached out and laid her hand on his tense shoulder. "I'm sorry, Joe. So sorry—for both of you."

Her hand was steadying, and Joe felt some of the raw emotions begin to dissolve beneath her gentle touch. Opening his eyes, he blinked away tears and held her sad gaze. "Now you know," he whispered brokenly. "That's why I didn't want another woman partner. God knows, I've tried to put Jenny's death behind me—and I have, to a degree. It happened a little over two years ago. Shortly after her death, I was transferred here to Reed and started tangling daily with Jacobs. I went from one hell to another, but at least being here forced me to focus on other things...."

"I understand, Joe," Annie whispered, lowering her hand to cover his once more.

Joe felt himself drowning in Annie's velvety brown eyes. Her unerring vulnerability amazed him. For some reason, she had no need to protect herself from this large, hurtful world they lived in, and he marveled at her obvious inner strength. His heart ached from retelling the story, but Annie's warm, strong hand on his seemed to dull some of the pain. She had a healing touch, he realized somewhere in his spinning senses. And her response was more than he'd ever dared expect. Generous. Annie was a very giving person, Joe admitted. Over the past week he'd seen her pitch in and help the entire office staff, giving of her time, never selfish or stingy despite his own cold treatment of her. Shaw doted on Annie, but after all, the young marine needed good role models—and Joe couldn't think of anyone better.

"No wonder you were angry when I showed up," she said pensively as she hesitantly removed her hand. She could see the glimmer of tears in Joe's eyes, but she'd also seen the way he'd pushed them back deep within himself. Had he ever grieved for Jenny? Ever cried for her loss? Her intuition told her no.

"I took my anger out on you and that wasn't right," Joe agreed. "When Captain Ramsey ordered me to take you as a partner, I was hot." He looked up at the window. "I even asked him to transfer you to another section, to another brig chaser."

Annie sat very still. Joe was looking at her, his face heavily lined and weary. She couldn't be angry with him; she understood his predicament. Her heart told her that he possessed a special kind of magnetism that made people gravitate to him. He was a natural-born leader, and she could understand how Jenny might have fallen in love with him.

As she sat, head bowed, eyes on her clasped hands in her lap, Annie warned herself that no matter what, she would have to maintain her relationship with Joe on a professional—not a personal—level. She couldn't afford to give her heart to another marine. Her own loss had been too great.

"I guess," Annie said, her voice cracking, "we both need to come clean." She held Joe's cheerless gaze. "Two years ago I was engaged to Sergeant Jeff Green. We met and fell in love on base in North Carolina. Then Desert Storm came along, and we were shipped to Saudi Arabia together. He was a recon marine." Opening her hands, Annie said, "He was stationed at my base, and he was wounded three days into the war. He was brought back to us because of the hospital on base." She looked down and struggled to keep her voice from shaking. "I watched him die that next day."

Joe grimaced. "Loving a marine isn't very safe, is it?"

She shook her head. "No, and that's the greatest lesson I've learned from all of this, Joe." Looking up to hold his gaze, she said, "I'm never going to fall in love with a marine again. I'm like Libby Tyler: never again."

"That makes three of us," Joe said, clearing his throat. "It's just too risky."

"Especially as brig chasers," Annie added. "Even with peacetime making other marine occupations safer, ours don't change."

"Not ever," Joe agreed glumly. Slowly easing out of the chair and pushing it back against the wall, he again approached Annie. "Partners?" he asked, extending his hand.

Annie looked at his large, callused hand and recalled the roughness of his fingertips as he'd caressed her cheek. Joe had tried to soothe her, and she would never forget his touch. As much pain as he'd been in, something in his heart had allowed him to reach out and unselfishly help her. Searching his eyes, Annie realized just how special he really was—even if he never realized it himself. She could still see guilt in his eyes, and sadness.

"Partners," she whispered brokenly, sliding her smaller hand into his. As his fingers curled around hers, Annie felt the latent strength in Joe, his backbone of steel. Despite the way he had initially treated her, he'd had the courage to admit he was wrong. "This is a good way to start over," she offered.

Not wanting to release her but knowing he must, Joe did so. He stuck his hands into the pockets of his chinos and stared down at his shoes. "Seeing you lying there on the deck with blood on your head scared the living hell out of me," he told her quietly. "I saw flashbacks of Jenny lying there instead. He shot her in the head...."

Swallowing hard, Annie forced herself not to cry, not to give in to the urge. She wanted to open her arms so that Joe could come and sit on the edge of her bed and she could hold him while he cried. The glitter was back in his eyes, and Annie felt he was close to weeping. She didn't know what to do. She didn't want to embarrass him, and the newly intimate connection between them was fragile.

"I was never so glad as when I heard your voice coming down the passageway," she admitted softly. "And when you helped me off the deck, I felt safe for the first time."

Safe. Inwardly, Joe winced. Jenny had always said he made her feel safe, too. "Well," he grumbled, "my feet are made of clay. You've already seen that, Annie, so don't get any ideas. The only way to stay safe is to rely on yourself first."

"I understand." And she did, more than Joe could ever realize. Rallying, she said, "We're professionals, Joe. We both know our jobs and we're the best at what we do. I'm not Jenny and you're not Jeff. I think we can handle our partnership despite our pasts, don't you?"

Joe wasn't sure at all, but he couldn't tell Annie that. "Yeah," he said as he headed to the door, "we'll handle it."

Chapter Six

Annie tried to hide her pleasure when Joe showed up the next afternoon while she was being released from the hospital. She hadn't expected him, despite last night's admissions. It was obvious that he was still hurting from Jenny's death, and she knew he wouldn't want to get anywhere near as close to her as he had been with the woman he'd loved and lost. She was standing at the nurse's station signing out when she felt a warmth flow across her. Accustomed to the sensations provided by her ultrasensitive awareness to her surroundings, Annie looked up, pen poised over the papers. Her heart skipped a beat. Joe was coming down the passageway, his face arranged in a typically stoic marine expression. But it was his eyes that sent her pulse fluttering wildly. They were aqua and intense—and gently held her captive.

The heat in his appraisal as he approached was unmistakable, and Annie froze momentarily beneath his hooded look. Forcing herself to snap out of it, she looked down and jerkily signed the forms. Joe was one of the few people she'd met in her life that she could feel coming without a need to see where he was. His larger-than-life presence seemed to send clear signals to her inner radar, creating a feeling she could only describe as a warm cloak surrounding her, providing a sense of protection as well as of desire on the most intimate of terms.

What a silly thought, Annie chided herself as she smiled and handed the Corpswave the forms. She turned and looked up at Joe. His eyes were alive with welcome, with care—and with some intangible emotion that made Annie hotly aware she was a woman.

"Are you the welcoming committee?" she asked playfully.

"I'm it." Joe smiled slightly, absorbing Annie's upturned face and flushed cheeks. "Your eyes look clearer. You must be feeling better." Her eyes had taken on a reddish earth tone, luminous and flecked with the gold of the sun in their large depths. How beautiful and how simple Annie was, he thought with a thrill of further discovery. Her Native American heritage had allowed her to stay close to the soil, close to things he'd never entertained— or maybe had laughed at because they weren't part of his cultural upbringing.

Annie picked up her purse and slipped it over her left shoulder. "I didn't expect an escort," she told him as she walked down the passageway to the exit doors at the other end.

Joe fell into companionable step with her. Annie was dressed in the same clothes as yesterday, and he castigated himself for not thinking to ask last night if she needed a fresh uniform. It showed just how much he'd shut himself off from being sensitive to a partner's needs, and that was disturbing. What if they had to transport a prisoner? That situation was one where an almost intangible sense of teamwork had to be cultivated because it could save a life—or both their lives. Frowning, he opened the door for her.

"How are you feeling?"

With a shrug, Annie moved out into the bright, hot sunlight. She stood, absorbing the energy of the rays, and smiled. "I'm better now...."

Joe saw her lift her face skyward, her lips slightly parted, like a flower starved for sunlight.

"I guess having been raised outdoors all your life, a hospital room is the pits," he murmured.

A soft smile crossed Annie's mouth. She lifted her lashes slightly and saw a naked, heated hunger in Joe's eyes—for her. Or was it? Could she be imagining things? "Thank you for understanding."

Scratching his jaw, he muttered, "If I was so understanding, I'd have gotten you a fresh uniform from your apartment last night."

Annie's smile grew tender as she held his frowning gaze. "You've been without a partner for two years, Joe. That's a long time. A lot of old habits you might have had are a little rusty, that's all."

She was right, and he appreciated her insight, as well as her way of forgiving him. "Well, I'm trying to make amends. Do you feel like driving home, or would you like me to drive? You could leave your car at the brig. I'll pick you up when you're ready to work again and bring you back to the base."

The offer was tempting on many levels. Annie knew Joe was trying to be a good partner. Although she probably felt well enough to drive, she said, "If you could take me home, I'd appreciate it."

Joe felt as if a ton of weight had flowed off his shoulders. He pointed to his Chevy Blazer in the visitor's parking lot. "Come on, I'll get you home so you can rest."

On the way off the base, Annie asked, "How's Gorman doing?"

"He's in solitary where he belongs," Joe muttered, cold fury in his voice.

"And Shaw? How is he?"

"Still pretty shaken up." Joe grimaced. "I don't know if Shaw should stay in a brig occupation. He hasn't got the mentality or savvy of most brig chasers."

"Have you been able to shadow him and teach him?" Annie queried.

Joe drove out the main gate of Reed and headed for the freeway. "No, you're right, I haven't been able to put the kid into the kind of training he needs. I was too busy fighting brushfires from Captain Jacobs."

"I feel if you give Shaw a fighting chance, he'll turn out to be good material to work with. He didn't have to get back into the fray with Gorman after I was knocked down. He could have faked it and stayed in the corner."

"You're a pretty savvy lady yourself, you know that?" Joe liked her smile, liked the banked warmth he saw in her eyes.

"I think of it as common sense," Annie stated. "Shaw is energetic, enthusiastic and he wants to please. Those qualities spell the kind of potential that could be developed through some intensive training."

"You're right," Joe said grimly. "And that lack of training damn near cost a couple of lives yesterday. I've talked to Captain Ramsey about instituting a training program for the newer brig people. He approved the idea yesterday." Glancing over at her, he said, "I'd like you to teach our section. Will you?"

Pride that Joe would choose her to do the teaching flooded Annie. "But we have to work on getting that tracking school set up, too," she reminded him.

"The in-house training will require only two hours a week."

"Oh..."

"Will you teach it? I'll help you develop the program. I'm just worried that if Gorman tries another escape, we might not be so lucky. That bastard wants his freedom so bad he can taste it."

"I know. Sure, I'll spend the next couple of days setting up a syllabus," she agreed.

"The captain said you'd helped him set up a tracking school at Camp Lejeune. I don't see any reason why we can't use the same curriculum here. That way, there's not so much stress on you to come up with new programs while carrying out your normal brig duties."

"I was hoping he'd let me do that. The lesson plans and classroom material are all in place. All we have to do is set up an outdoor tracking course here at Reed."

Joe nodded, savoring Annie's animated features. She almost looked good as new, except for the white dressing that stood out starkly against her coppery skin and raven hair. How close he'd come to losing her already. How close... Sleep hadn't come easily to Joe last night. He'd turned and tossed, with blips of Jenny's death haunting him, overlaid like a transparency with scenes of Annie lying on the deck, the side of her head bloodied. Adrenaline still pumped through him today, making him more irritable than usual at the office.

Annie guided him south of Oceanside to an off ramp where a group of apartments were located on the edge of the extensive local marshlands. Her apartment was on the first floor, and Joe drove into the parking space reserved for her car. Curious to know more about her, he said, "I'll walk you to your door."

Pleased, Annie nodded and got out of the Blazer. It was nearly 1700, and she was hungry for some real food after suffering through hospital fare. As Joe came around the vehicle, she asked, "Would you like to stay for dinner? I'm starving after not eating most of those hospital meals."

Joe was torn. He badly wanted to mend the fabric of their relationship after his poor start with Annie. And his heart wanted him to stay. But his head warned him it was a stupid idea. Somehow, though, the pleading look in Annie's eyes melted away his mind's logical advice. "Yeah, I'd like that. Thanks."

Opening the door, Annie stepped inside. "I live fairly sparsely," she said almost in apology. "Make yourself at home. I'm going to change clothes, then I'll get dinner started."

Joe nodded and shut the door behind him. Annie's apartment had shining wood floors, waxed and glowing in soft tones of yellow and red. Probably cedar, he surmised as he put his hands in his pockets and moved from the foyer into the living room. Annie did live sparsely, he realized. A black-and-gray Navajo rug was laid out before a huge picture window, which looked directly onto the marshlands where so many birds made their homes.

As he glanced around the apartment, Joe was more curious than he liked to admit to himself. Her furniture, he saw, was Shaker style, made of wood, the lines clean and without embellishment. An ivory-colored couch was covered with a Navajo blanket woven in rich tones of brown, yellow, red and black. The only lamp in the room was of stained glass, in colors to match the blanket. Two end tables displayed small, round pottery and an array of tiny cacti, some of which was in bloom. What he liked the most about the room, Joe thought, was the incredible sense of serenity that reached out to embrace him. Maybe it was the beauty of the marshlands, with thousands of spindly green cattails waving in a slight breeze. He saw several flocks of ducks bobbing here and there in the patches of blue water, and a great blue heron was hunting frogs at the edge.

Turning, Joe noticed several dark brown feathers sprinkled with white spots near their tips hanging on the wall. Sprigs of dried greenery were with them, all tied together with a thin strip of soft black leather, fringed and feminine in appearance.

"It's a medicine fan given to me by my mother," said Annie, coming into the room and following the direction of Joe's gaze.

His eyes widened as Annie's soft voice drifted across his heightened senses. He turned, perplexed. "I didn't even hear you coming."

She smiled a little and pointed to her bare feet. "As a kid I went barefoot everywhere. I had calluses an inch deep on my soles. I still don't wear shoes except when I have to."

Joe couldn't tear his gaze from Annie. She'd put on a simple white, short-sleeved blouse and dark blue slacks that complemented her tall, willowy form to perfection. Out of uniform, she looked like a young woman who might own her own company or who was in the fast track of some corporation. There was a cleanness to Annie, and that haunting simplicity began to wrap tendrils around his heart. Tearing his gaze from her, he focused again on the feathers on the wall.

"Can you tell me more about them?" he asked, pointing.

"As I've mentioned, my mother is a medicine woman," Annie explained, reaching over and touching the feathers. "She used this fan for many years in healing ceremonies. They're eagle feathers tied with sage, a sacred herb we use to cleanse ourselves with before a ceremony."

Joe took off his garrison cap and placed it on one of the end tables. "When I saw it, I felt the power around it."

"I'm not surprised. My mother is a very powerful healer. She's known throughout the reservation. Many come to her who haven't been helped by other medicine people."

Joe looked at her. "Your world is so different from mine."

"Yes, it is." She smiled a little. "Come, I'll show you my quiet room."

Mystified by the term, Joe followed Annie down the hall. On a door hung another handful of dried sage wrapped carefully in a red ribbon. When she opened it, a subtle fragrance struck his nostrils and he inhaled deeply. The room was small, decorated with another Navajo rug, a much smaller one, in the middle. No furniture or pictures filled the space, but on the rug sat a piece of pottery with more dried sage lying across it. Annie moved aside and gestured for him to come in.

Joe stood just inside the door, feeling as if he were trespassing on a very private part of Annie's Navajo way of living. He looked at her, and she smiled with her eyes.

"I can never be far away from Mother Earth," she told him quietly as she knelt upon the rug. She lifted a small bowl of pottery filled with reddish-colored soil. "This is from my home, the earth I was birthed upon." She handed it to Joe and he held it cupped between his hands as if it were something fragile. "Every night for about an hour, I come in here and sit. I hold that bowl of earth, I sing the songs my mother taught me and I remember my past and how it has brought me to my present."

Joe's hands tingled strongly as he held the small bowl of earth. Annie's voice had taken on a husky, emotional quality, and as he gazed down at her, he saw tears in her eyes.

"I guess," he said awkwardly, carefully handing the bowl back to her, "the word you used, *sacred,* fits all of this."

She placed the bowl gently on the rug and got to her feet. "All things are sacred, not just what I believe or what I was taught."

Joe looked around and felt the intense serenity in the room. It was amazing to him. He'd never felt so relaxed or safe. Looking at her strangely, he said, "There's a sensation in here—all through your apartment."

"Oh?" Annie led him out of the room and closed the door.

"Yeah, I can't figure it out. It's just a feeling."

"The Navajo call it the Beauty Way. It's another word for harmony," Annie said as she led him into a spacious kitchen fitted with all the modern appliances she could ever want. "Have a seat," she invited, gesturing to the table and chairs.

Joe sat down at the wooden table, obviously lovingly handcrafted. In the center of it sat a bright vase of wildflowers, the yellow-and-white daisies as naturally beautiful as Annie herself. An invisible blanket of peace cloaked Joe, and he felt the tension he usually carried in his shoulders dissolving like fog beneath hot sunlight.

"Tell me about this harmony," Joe said, realizing how important the concept was to Annie. He tried to tell himself he wanted to know because she was his partner, and a good partner should know damn near everything about the other person.

Annie worked efficiently at the kitchen counter. She had purchased some lamb chops the day before and wanted to broil them. Glancing over her shoulder, she said, "Harmony is another word for balance. We know that if we're in harmony within ourselves, that state translates outwardly to the world around us, and no one can throw us off balance."

Joe frowned. "Is it like *chi*—the Chinese way of explaining energy and harmony? The yin and the yang?"

"Very much so. The Navajo way of living parallels some of the Far Eastern mystic ways."

"I understand *chi* because I have a black belt in aikido," Joe explained.

"Ah...then you know." Annie put the lamb chops into the oven and began to make a salad.

"If you are in your center, nothing can throw you off stride." Joe paused, watching her graceful movements. "That's why you could stand in front of Gorman to stop him," he murmured, half to himself. "You had your center, your *chi,* in balance within you."

With a laugh, Annie said, "It wasn't easy to leap in front of that cell door and try to stop Gorman, believe me. But yes, I work hard always to maintain my inner balance, my harmony."

"So you meditate nightly to bring yourself back to your center?" Joe guessed.

"Kind of...." Annie sliced tomatoes and cucumbers, then added some alfalfa sprouts to the lettuce. "When I go in my room, I don't really meditate, as you call it. I sing songs that bring me close to my heart and back to the land that birthed me. It's hard to explain."

"No," Joe murmured, "I know what you're getting at. When I practice my aikido every morning before I go to work, I go through the *katas*, or routines. I feel a oneness in myself as I do them, and I sure couldn't explain that feeling to anyone else."

"It's nice to know you understand." Setting the bowls of salad on the table, she said, "Coffee?"

"Sure. Thanks."

Curiosity was eating away at Joe. "You have any brothers or sisters?"

"Yes, plenty of them! Mother had eight of us."

"Eight?"

"Big number nowadays, isn't it?" She took down plates and place mats and arranged them on the table. The place mats depicted Navajo symbols. "Look at it this way, Joe—on a reservation in the middle of nowhere, with a herd of nearly five hundred sheep to care for, and having to survive off the land, you need a big family to help with all the chores. My brothers gathered firewood, herded the sheep and hunted. My sisters helped with the cooking, wove rugs that could be sold for money and assisted my mother with her medicine work. We also helped raise the young ones growing up after us."

Amazed, Joe smiled. The enticing scent of fresh coffee wafted through the room. "So were you the firstborn?"

"No, I was number three. Mother had the four girls first, then came all my brothers."

"So you really became a little mother at an early age."

"You could say that." Annie saw the pensive look on Joe's face, and her heart sang with such joy that she felt breathless. His presence, whether he realized it or not, was like having the sun in her apartment. Was he aware of his personal power? Annie wondered. That unseen energy that swirled around all living things?

"I remember you said you wanted to be a sheep herder, not a weaver."

With a wry smile, Annie continued setting the table. "I loved the animals. I couldn't sit still for hours the way Mother and my sisters could. I was sort of a mixture of boy and girl. Not that I was looked down on for it, because we believe in honoring who and what we are. My mother is a very wise woman. When she saw I'd rather be outdoors in all kinds of weather, she told me to try my hand at becoming a herder."

Joe savored the look in Annie's eyes and felt what she meant. Never had he met a woman who spoke so eloquently with her eyes. "Maybe you have a little of your mother's medicine-woman ways?" he ventured.

"What made you say that?" Annie went to the refrigerator and drew out fresh broccoli, which she rinsed carefully.

With a shrug, Joe said, "I don't know. There's something around you... I can't put my finger on it. It's as if you know more than you let on."

"Don't worry, you're safe," she teased, cutting up the broccoli and placing it in a steamer.

"Is that why you're so good at tracking? You have this other ability?"

"I don't know. I never felt or thought about it that way. My mother is a very gifted clairvoyant. All the women in the family have that talent to some degree."

"But you got a lot of it?" Joe guessed.

Annie went to the counter and poured the fresh coffee into two white mugs decorated with spring flowers. She placed two potatoes in the microwave to be baked. "My mother wanted me to train to be a medicine woman," she admitted as she sat down opposite him at the table. "But I was too restless. I wanted to see the world. I'd always loved any challenges that were thrown at me. Several times I faced cougars stalking our herd with just my staff."

Joe looked up from sipping the hot coffee. "You what?"

With a laugh, Annie brought her leg up and tucked it under her on the chair. "You have to put what I said in the context of being a Navajo, Joe. We believe that we have invisible spirits who are our teachers, who guide us, protect us and try to help us throughout our lives. When I was ten, my brother Tom got sick and had to go back to the hogan, eight miles away. Our collie dogs and I had to keep the herd safe until my father could send someone else out to help me. That night I built a fire and didn't sleep much, because I could feel a cougar stalking the herd. The dogs were restless and sensed him, too. Near dawn, the cougar got bold. I felt where the cat was hiding and went to the rock outcrop to scare him away. We couldn't afford to lose any of our sheep. They were not only our food source, but a source of wool to weave the rugs.

"We don't believe in killing anything, not even a cougar, but I was taught to use the staff to defend myself. It's about eight feet long and made of stout cottonwood. As I approached the rocks, I saw the cougar sitting in a crouched position. Our eyes met, and for a moment out of time, I felt as if he had pulled me out of my body into his. It was such a startling, unusual feeling that I knew something sacred was happening. I remembered my mother telling us that the way we receive our medicine from our spirit guide is through a transfer of one to the other. At the time, I hadn't understood what she meant, but when the cougar stole my spirit, I suddenly knew.

"I also knew I had to get out of the cougar or he'd kill me. I used all the internal strength—my *chi*, if you will—to come back into my body. When I did, I felt as if someone had snapped me back into it like a rubber band. The instant I escaped the cougar, he bounded out of his hiding place and left." Annie shook her head and took a sip of her coffee. "The next day I went home and told my mother what had happened. She gave me a sad look and told me that I was not meant to be a medicine woman, but a warrior for Mother Earth. She really wanted me to follow in her footsteps, but she honored what had happened."

Joe ran his fingers lightly across the warm mug. "There are many ways to protect the earth," he ventured. "Working with prisoners and keeping them behind bars to protect the public is one way."

She smiled at him. "You understand."

"I'm trying to," he said. "I don't understand about this transfer thing between you and the cougar, but it doesn't matter. I see the symbolism."

"Exactly," Annie said approvingly. "My spirit guide is a cougar, and I have to learn to emulate him. In that way, I will learn."

"No wonder you went into the Marine Corps," Joe chuckled. "We need brig chasers with cougar medicine."

Laughing, Annie stood up. The garlic-laced lamb chops were filling the kitchen with their delicious scent. She crossed to the stove and checked on them. Satisfied it would be another five minutes, she turned and rested against the counter. "Two of my brothers are marines, and of course, my grandfather was one during World War II, so it was kind of a natural transition for me. I knew what to expect of the corps, and I wasn't scared by the challenge it presented. I saw opportunities."

Joe nodded, absorbing her story. The Annie standing relaxed before him now was not the woman he'd encountered at the base. She looked so fresh and appealing in her slacks and bare feet, and he smiled. "I've got a lot to learn about you, about the way you live and see your life."

"I think I've told you enough for now," she said wryly.

"You probably don't let too many people into your life like this, do you?"

Annie eyed him. "You're a little intuitive yourself," she challenged softly.

"It's saved my miserable neck from time to time."

Going to the stove, she put on the oven mitts and opened it. "You're right," she said over her shoulder, "I let very few people into my personal world. It's so different from most people's. I love the ancient traditions of my people. I don't ever want to give them up. I want not only to live them, but to become them." Annie set the broiled lamb chops on top of the stove. Taking the potatoes from the microwave, she scooped butter and sour cream onto them.

Joe got up to help. "That's the way it is in aikido. You become the *chi* and live in a balanced state."

As she handed him the platter of meat, Annie's hand touched his. In that moment, she thought she had never felt happier. Though the brief touch of his fingers was gone, her skin still tingled. Turning, she placed the steamed broccoli in a clay bowl and set it on the table. Then, joining Joe at the table, she said, "Let's eat."

After dinner, Joe sat back, totally relaxed. Annie had cleared the dishes and served up two large portions of blackberry pie with vanilla ice cream. Over a second cup of coffee, he said, "I can't remember ever feeling this good—or this full." He grinned.

Annie nodded. "I was starving."

"Hungry like a cougar?" he asked, baiting her.

Her smile was instantaneous. "Exactly."

"Gorman didn't stand a chance with you."

Laughing outright, Annie leaned back in her chair, the mug of coffee in her hands. "Cougars don't always capture their quarry," she warned him more seriously as she drank the sweetened brew.

His smile was dangerous. "I'm beginning to understand where you're coming from. You said you learned the skills of the spirit—in this case, the cougar. They survive on their ability to track down their quarry."

"Not only that, but their ears are their most important sense."

"So, you sense with your ears?"

"I've been accused of having 'dog hearing' because I pick up sounds long before most other people hear them. If you've studied wild animals, you know there's something else going on besides just a good set of ears and a good nose. They *sense* their surroundings; the least little perturbation or vibrational change, they pick up. How could animals know of an impending earthquake? Yet, they know days in advance. They sense it with their heart, their intuition. I do the same thing. It's an internal kind of knowing. I can't be more defined than that about it. I can sense the presence of an escaped prisoner. I can follow this inner knowing, and pick up even a bad trail. In fact, even if I lose a trail, I follow this inner guidance." She pointed to her stomach region. "Eventually, I'll find the trail again."

"That's the 'all-terrain radar' you were telling me about when we first met."

"Yes."

"I have it to a degree," Joe admitted. "I've never known what to call it, except maybe a sixth sense. I honed mine through years of being a brig chaser. You either do that, or you're in big trouble."

"Exactly. It is something that can be developed," Annie murmured.

"Well," he said, putting the coffee mug aside, "I think I'd better go. I'd keep you up all night talking about your background."

Annie nodded. "I am kind of tired."

"Letdown from getting out of the hospital," Joe said, rising. He didn't want to leave. It was the last thing he wanted to do. But he could see the fatigue in Annie's eyes, and she'd lost some of her usual radiance.

"Hospitals are terrible places," Annie said, getting to her feet. "They take more out of you than give back. That's not balance, in my opinion." She went to the living room and retrieved Joe's cover. He nodded his thanks when she handed it to him.

"You and Libby Tyler. She hates hospitals."

"With good reason, from what I hear," Annie said as she walked Joe to the front door. "Her husband died in a terrible helicopter crash here on base three years ago. Being in the same hospital must have brought a lot of bad memories back to her. I think it was nice of Captain Ramsey to take care of her over at his apartment."

Joe grinned. "I think that our captain is head over heels for Libby Tyler."

Annie opened the door and smiled. "I feel you're right. He likes her, but because of her past, she's afraid to open herself up to him."

"Because he's a marine," Joe said, "and marines live dangerous lives. Makes sense, doesn't it?"

She tilted her head. "My mother always said that the heart makes more sense that our heads, and to listen closely to it."

Joe opened the door and hesitated. "And do you always listen to your heart, Annie?"

She felt his appraisal. In the shadows, Joe Donnally's face looked dangerously alluring. His eyes had lost their frosty edge entirely. Now they were warm with life, glittering with interest, and she felt as if their mutual energies—his *chi* and her harmony—had met, integrated and become one. It was an exhilarating sensation that made her feel light and joyous.

"I—I try...." She found her voice stumbling in response to his intensity. "But sometimes, it's too scary for me to follow what I feel."

"Yeah," Joe said wryly, looking out the door toward the parked cars, "I know what you mean. Living life is for people who have *real* guts."

With a laugh, she watched him move out onto the porch. "I won't disagree with you."

Joe shoved his hands into his pockets, noting the play of light and shadow against Annie's soft eyes and mouth. An ache built within him, hot and immediate. "I've decided one thing, though," he added, reluctant to step away.

She stood in the doorway. "What?"

"That you're an enigma, a mystery."

Chortling, Annie pointed her finger at him. "Me? What about you?"

With a grin, he said, "Just take care of yourself, Yellow Horse. I want to see you in three days looking good as new."

"Yes, sir." And she allowed his crooked smile and tentative, shy look to fill her, just as the luminescence of a full moon filled the ocean with a special kind of light.

Chapter Seven

"Annie, the captain wants us to meet him down at Motor Pool in fifteen minutes," Joe said as she entered the office her first morning back at work.

Taken aback, she hesitated. Joe looked worried. Dressed in her utilities, she placed the soft cap in her hand back on her head. "Okay, let's go." After being away for three days, Annie had planned on arriving a few minutes early, wanting the time to adjust to the tension the office always contained. She laid her briefcase on her desk and slipped her purse into a drawer. Turning, she followed Joe out of the office. As she walked with him down the passageway, she felt concern radiating from him. "How have things been since I left?"

"Getting real interesting," Joe said. "I'll let the captain fill you in." He slanted a glance in her direction. "You look good as new." In fact, she looked more beautiful than ever, in his eyes. The simple unisex uniforms didn't detract from Annie's femininity in the slightest. She never wore makeup or lipstick, but she didn't need to.

"I'm fine." Annie hooked a thumb back toward the office. "I got the tracking-school proposal in order for training the new brig chasers."

Joe nodded. Obviously, industrious Annie had made the most of her sick-leave time at home. "Good. We'll go over it as soon as we get a chance."

Flushing, Annie felt him smile, but she didn't look up. How she'd missed Joe, even in these few short days. Although her time at home had been productive, she'd been lonely—for him.

At Motor Pool Annie met Captain Ramsey and Libby Tyler. After saluting, the captain ordered everyone into the HumVee. Joe drove and Annie rode with Libby in the rear of the green-and-brown-camouflage vehicle, which looked more like an ugly bug than anything. The array of antennae that sprouted out of the HumVee added to its gangly, awkward look, although it had proven to be a reliable replacement for the jeeps they'd used in the old days.

Annie listened intently as Captain Ramsey filled them in on what Libby had discovered the day before—that the fence surrounding Camp Reed had been cut many times along the freeway. Annie saw Joe's face become expressionless, and she felt the worry around Captain Ramsey. Libby didn't seem to realize the implications of her find, but Annie hadn't expected her to. The fact that she'd noticed that the fence had been cut was a fine piece of investigative work.

When they arrived at the fence from within Reed's property, the captain ordered the HumVee to a halt. Annie disembarked with the other two marines while Ramsey ordered Libby to stay in the HumVee for safety

▼ SILHOUETTE ™

AN IMPORTANT MESSAGE FROM THE EDITORS OF SILHOUETTE®

Dear Reader,

Because you've chosen to read one of our fine romance novels, we'd like to say "thank you"! And, as a **special** way to thank you, we've selected <u>four more</u> of the <u>books</u> you love so well, **and** an Austrian Crystal Pendant to send you absolutely _FREE!_

Please enjoy them with our compliments...

Nora Gavin Senior Editor, Silhouette Special Edition

P.S. And <u>because</u> we value our customers, we've attached something extra inside ...

EDITOR'S
FREE GIFT SEAL
THANK YOU

PEEL OFF SEAL AND PLACE INSIDE

HOW TO VALIDATE
YOUR
EDITOR'S FREE GIFT
"THANK YOU"

1. Peel off gift seal from front cover. Place it in space provided at right. This automatically entitles you to receive four free books and a lovely Austrian Crystal Pendant.

2. Send back this card and you'll get brand-new Silhouette Special Edition® novels. These books have a cover price of $3.50 each, but they are yours to keep absolutely free.

3. There's no catch. You're under no obligation to buy anything. We charge nothing—ZERO—for your first shipment. And you don't have to make any minimum number of purchases—not even one!

4. The fact is thousands of readers enjoy receiving books by mail from the Silhouette Reader Service™ months before they're available in stores. They like the convenience of home delivery and they love our discount prices!

5. We hope that after receiving your free books you'll want to remain a subscriber. But the choice is yours—to continue or cancel, anytime at all! So why not take us up on our invitation, with no risk of any kind. You'll be glad you did!

6. Don't forget to detach your FREE BOOKMARK. And remember...just for validating your Editor's Free Gift Offer, we'll send you FIVE MORE gifts, *ABSOLUTELY FREE!*

NOT ACTUAL SIZE

YOURS FREE!
*You'll look like a million dollars when you wear this lovely necklace! Its cobra-link chain is a generous 18" long, and the multi-faceted Austrian crystal sparkles like a diamond! It's yours **absolutely free** — when you accept our no-risk offer!*

reasons. Because it was a potentially dangerous situation, Annie tuned in all her senses. The area consisted of small sand dunes, rounded and topped with sparse strands of thick salt grass, something like a lot of almost-bald men with a few sprouts of long, untamed hair on top, Annie thought. She smiled to herself at the analogy and followed on the heels of the two men. Farther inland the terrain eventually smoothed out and turned rocky and more desertlike, with plenty of prickly pear cactus around to jab anyone who wasn't paying strict attention.

They split up, looking for tracks to indicate unusual activity. Joe went to the fence to check it out, the captain in another direction and Annie stood assimilating for a moment before she decided which way to go.

"Annie!" Captain Ramsey called.

She looked toward her superior and saw him gesture for her to come over. Immediately, she jogged toward him.

"What do you make of this, Corporal?" He pointed to a set of prints.

The sand was torn up with a great deal of horse-hoof activity. Crouching down, Annie quickly looked the area over. With her fingers, she lightly touched the surrounding sand. The tracks had been protected by a small sand dune from the wind that blew almost constantly from the ocean. If the sand was still loose, it would mean the tracks were fresh, but if it had hardened slightly, becoming more firm from regular nightly dew, it would indicate they were older. Testing the sand very carefully so she wouldn't disturb the nearly perfect hoofprint, Annie felt the firmness of the soil. "These are old, Captain."

"How old?"

She hesitated. "Hard to tell. Sand's different than soil."

"Your best guess?"

Annie didn't want to be wrong, but there was no way to accurately tell about these prints. "Maybe three weeks?" She twisted to look up at Ramsey's set features. He nodded and placed his hands on his hips, frowning heavily.

"That would have been the last new moon."

"Sir?"

"Good work, Corporal. Can you tell me how many animals were here?"

This was the work Annie loved. She began to track, her senses fully engaged and operating. The hoofprints were many. The first thing she had to do was sort the different sizes and shapes; each horse would be a slightly different size. Some horses had large, splayed hooves, while others had smaller, more rounded ones. She felt Captain Ramsey shadowing her movements as she knelt, barely touching the prints, then rose and moved on to another set. The tracks all led from the fence inland toward the heart of Camp Reed, there was no doubt of that.

Annie straightened and took her cap off to wipe the sweat forming on her brow. The captain stood next to her, patiently waiting for her assessment. Placing the cap back on her head, Annie studied the tracks one last time.

"There are five horses' prints here, Captain."

He grinned a little. "Bingo."

She studied his tense features, the bill of his soft cover shadowing his face. "Maybe the same five horses Ms. Tyler reported being ridden illegally?"

"Maybe," Ramsey murmured. "Come on, let's see what Joe has found."

Later, as the three of them gathered after taking photos, Annie stood next to Joe. His face was unreadable, but she saw worry in his eyes.

"I don't like this, Captain," Joe said, gesturing to the fence. "Something's going on here on a regular basis.

That fence has been cut at least five or six times, then carefully repaired to look as if it hadn't been cut at all."

"And the horses are carrying a lot of weight," Annie surmised, "more than just the weight of an adult rider. It doesn't make sense."

"No." Ramsey sighed. "Well, let's get back to the office. We've all got a heavy schedule ahead of us today. Joe, will you write up an investigation report on our findings and place it in Ms. Tyler's file?"

"Of course, sir."

Back at the office, Joe invited Annie to lunch with him off base. He was thrilled when she accepted. They drove over to Aunt Madge's Restaurant, then lingered over the tasty bacon and pancakes.

"What do you make of this latest development on the Tyler case?" Joe asked as they sipped coffee after the meal.

"Strange."

"What's your sense about it?" he pressed.

Annie rolled her eyes. "A lot of danger. I don't know...."

"I think Libby Tyler has run into something a lot bigger than she realizes."

"Or perhaps than *we* realize," Annie said wryly. She smiled a little and took another sip of the strong black coffee. "It felt good to be tracking again," she admitted.

"I looked up a couple of times and saw you were really enjoying yourself," Joe said with a nod. It took every ounce of his control not to reach out and touch Annie's flushed cheek. Her hair was pleasantly mussed, and he ached to thread his fingers through it and smooth it back into place.

"I do love it. I'll take outdoor work any time."

"I know you don't like brig work."

She shrugged. "I may not enjoy it, but I do it because someone has too."

"You remind me so much of Maria."

Annie heard pain in Joe's voice, and he refused to look up at her. Instead, he was studying his coffee darkly. Tentatively, Annie asked, "Who is Maria?"

With a sigh, Joe set the cup down and sat back in the red-vinyl booth. The restaurant was filled with a noontime crush of people, but the corner booth afforded Joe and Annie a great deal of privacy. Joe felt as if his heart was twisting in his chest, and he felt a sudden compulsion to tell Annie about Maria. "She was my sister. Two years older than me." He ran his hands slowly up and down the sides of the warm coffee cup. "Maria was . . . well, she was my best friend growing up. We lived in the barrio with our parents. My dad is Anglo and my mother is Hispanic. I don't know if you know anything about a barrio, but it's sort of like your reservation—different from the white world in a lot of aspects. My mother is Yaqui Indian and Mexican, so she mixes Catholicism with Indian ways."

Annie saw the troubled look in Joe's eyes, but she felt him reaching out to her in spite of his pain, which touched her deeply. "So you're part Native American, too?"

"Yeah." He chuckled in a strained tone. "I'm kind of a Heinz Variety, you might say. A little Indian, a little Mexican, a little Irish and German thrown in from my dad's side of the family."

"You have a good heart," Annie said softly, "that's all that counts. People's skin color means nothing, it's what they do on a daily basis for themselves and others that matters."

He raised his eyes and met her warm gaze. "I know you know about prejudice."

Her lips lifted wryly. "A little."

"I do, too...." His brow wrinkled and his hands stilled around the cup. "Maria was a lot like you. She wasn't conventional, and Mom had a tough time with that. She wanted Maria to be tame and submissive, but she inherited my dad's temper and my mom's stubbornness. I was always getting Maria out of trouble. She joined a gang of girls when she was twelve years old." Joe shrugged and shook his head. "That's how I got involved in gangs. Mom was worried sick over Maria because of the gangs."

Annie felt such a volume of pain surrounding Joe at that moment that she reached out, her hand touching his arm. "You said 'was.'"

Joe felt Annie's warm, long fingers settle on his arm. Even though they were in uniform and such fraternization was discouraged in public, he didn't care at that moment. His chest ached with grief, and Annie's touch was soothing. Joe desperately needed the care she automatically gave to him. Casting her a somber glance, he said, "Maria died at sixteen of a cocaine overdose. She was dealing drugs in her gang, making the money she wanted for buying new clothes and jewelry. My parents were torn apart when the police came to our door and told us Maria was dead." His hands tightened around the mug. "I don't think any of us ever got over the shock of the news."

Her grasp tightening on his arm, Annie whispered, "I don't think you ever do. They're a terrible thing, drugs."

"Yeah." Joe's voice grated. "I hate them. I hate the pushers. Maria wanted her freedom, but she didn't go about it right. She hated the barrio, what it stood for, and she wanted out. But she couldn't see a way to get out, so she turned to drugs as a way to escape, even for a little while...."

Annie realized they were in a public place with prying eyes. Not wanting to risk starting gossip, she forced herself to reclaim her hand. There was such hurt mirrored in Joe's eyes that she began to understand on a far deeper level about the women in his life and how they had profoundly and irrevocably changed him.

"You said you were in a gang, too?"

With a snort, Joe lifted his head and held her compassionate gaze. "Not after Maria died. It scared me straight. I wasn't doing drugs, but I had been getting into fights and running guns. When I saw how devastated my parents were by Maria's death, I swore I wouldn't end up like her. They were afraid of losing me, too, so I quit. It was hard, though, because the guys in my gang were the only friends I'd ever known."

"I can't imagine the pressures on you," Annie said gently.

Shrugging, Joe took a sip of the cooled coffee. "I did it because I wanted to. I didn't want to make my parents cry the way they had at Maria's funeral."

"You wanted them to be proud of you."

"Yeah, I guess so. So I went the opposite direction. I went into law enforcement with a personal vendetta against drugs."

"Captain Ramsey has one, too."

"I know..."

Annie gazed at Joe's misery-laden features. "Women have brought you a lot of grief," she ventured.

Joe nodded. "I never looked at it that way, but I guess it's true. First Maria, then Jenny." He rubbed his face and refused to look at her.

"And now you're thinking, 'I've got Annie Yellow Horse. Will I lose her, too?'" she posed quietly.

His heart reacted violently to her question, and his hands tightened around the coffee mug. "Are you reading my mind?" he asked hoarsely.

"No, just your heart." Annie ached for Joe, for the tears she saw glittering in his eyes. Somehow, she knew he'd never really cried for the loss of Maria *or* Jenny. She wanted to cry for him—cry with him.

Clearing his throat, Joe rasped, "After you shared with me about your life, your growing-up years, I got thinking about my own. Your childhood was different. The fabric of it, your way of life, was stronger than ours."

"I've found," Annie said, "that if I move away from my beliefs, a lot of things get out of balance in my life."

"You're right." With a quirk of his mouth, he looked beyond her and out the window at the busy lunchtime traffic at the stoplight in front of the restaurant. "I've been trying to get back to that center in myself since we lost Maria. I haven't done it yet, but I'm trying."

"Just talking about your loss is important to the healing process, Joe."

He smiled a little. "Maybe you're more medicine woman than you realize."

"Why do you say that?"

"Because I feel better now." He moved his shoulders as if to rid himself of an invisible load. "It's you, you know."

Flushing, Annie avoided his warm, dark gaze. "I feel when people open their hearts to one another and speak their personal truths, healing always comes. Don't you?"

Reaching out, Joe picked up her hand. Her skin was warm, her fingers long and graceful looking against his. He was surprised at his own gesture, but in his heart it seemed the most natural thing on earth for him to do in that precious moment. Joe didn't care if he was in uniform, or if people were watching. Annie's eyes shone with wisdom beyond her years, as if all the wise, good spirits of her family were contained within her. "Whatever is happening between us," he told her in a low, unsteady tone, "is good, Annie. Although it scares me to death inside." His hand tightened around hers. "I felt it from the moment we met, and I tried like hell to fight it. I blamed you for my fear, when really, it was me all along."

Joe's hand was strong around hers, absorbing Annie's shock at his gesture. She found herself getting lost in the stormy honesty that burned in his eyes, and her voice was unsteady when she spoke. "That's because you've lost two of the most important women in your life, Joe. Don't you see that?"

"I do now." He squeezed her hand once more and released it, knowing if he didn't, he would surely make a fool of himself. What he wanted to do was get up and sweep Annie into his arms. There was something so healing about being with her that Joe felt less empty inside for the first time in his life.

Her heart beating erratically, Annie avoided his smoldering look. Yes, she felt it, too, she allowed to herself, but she didn't have the courage Joe did to admit it. Swallowing against a lump of tears she knew she didn't dare shed, Annie whispered, "I think you needed to talk about this in order to heal your past, Joe."

"Thanks to you," he said as he picked up the check and dug in his rear pocket for his billfold. Rising, he watched Annie closely. He could see fear in her eyes. He knew undeniably that he liked her. And there wasn't a damn thing he could do to stop it. Would his life repeat the same cycle again? Would Annie be torn from him? Killed like

Maria and Jenny? The serrating pain that zigzagged down through his chest at the thought frightened him. He must continue to fight his attraction to Annie, fight to keep their partnership professional. If he had any doubts about that, all he had to do was look into Annie's eyes and see that she was just as deathly afraid of a personal relationship with him.

With a tight smile, he said, "Let's saddle up. We've got work waiting for us back at the office."

Two mornings later Annie was sitting at her desk finishing off the final paperwork on Gorman's transfer. Captain Ramsey had ordered her and Joe to drive the dangerous prisoner from Camp Reed to USNAS Fallon, Nevada. From there, Gorman would be transferred to another Brig Chasing team to take him the rest of the way to Fort Leavenworth, Kansas just three days from now. Since that heartwrenching lunch with Joe, he'd been less accessible, but Annie knew why. She was fighting an attraction to him just as she knew he was to her. Somehow they would have to maintain a purely professional relationship. The emotional cost of anything more was simply too high—for both of them.

Annie was so absorbed in her paperwork that she didn't hear Joe approach until his voice cut into her concentration.

"I think we've hit pay dirt."

Annie looked up, startled to see Joe in front of her desk. "What?"

"Take a look at this lab report. Libby Tyler followed that trail from the freeway on horseback yesterday into Reed. The trail intersects with a little-used back road. She found a piece of torn cloth on a low branch, and Rose sent it to be analyzed." He handed Annie the report, a look of triumph in his eyes.

Rapidly, Annie scanned the proffered paper. Suddenly she gasped and jerked a look back up at Joe. "They found cocaine traces on it?"

"Yes, and the lab is saying the scrap of material is from one of those burlap bags you put horse feed in."

Annie's mouth fell open, then she snapped it shut. "The stables! They use those bags there."

"Exactly." Joe took the report back from her. Raising his eyebrows, he said in a low voice, "I'll bet my sergeant's stripes that we've got a drug ring operating on base. Captain Ramsey is due back this morning. Wait until he sees this report."

Frowning, Annie put the paperwork on Gorman aside. "What about Libby, though? Might she be in danger?"

"I don't think so. She didn't have any trouble out on the trail when she found this cloth. She got back to the stables without incident."

Rubbing her brow, Annie stood up. "I don't know, Joe. I've got a bad feeling on this one...." Before she could continue, she saw Captain Ramsey enter the office.

Joe said, "I'm going to let him see this right away. Don't go anywhere."

Originally, Annie had planned to take some samples over to the lab, but they could wait. Her heart was pounding and she tasted fear. But over what? And fear for who? She saw Ramsey beckon Joe into his office immediately, and the door was closed. No more than ten minutes had passed when Joe reemerged, looking worried. He headed directly to his desk, his gaze pinned on her.

"Get your cover, we're going over to the stables," he said tightly, opening a drawer to retrieve his weapon.

"Why?" Annie asked quickly, grabbing her hat.

"Libby Tyler didn't show up for work this morning," he said as he placed the pistol in the shiny black-leather holster on his web belt.

Annie's heart dropped and her stomach clenched. "She's in trouble."

Joe hurried toward the door, in step with her. "What kind?"

"I wish I knew...."

"Well," he said as he opened the door for her, "we're going over to the stables to check it out. Captain Ramsey is fit to be tied. He wants every lead followed up—fast."

As Annie hurried to the HumVee, she said, "Isn't it possible she's not missing? What if she's in Oceanside doing her weekly grocery shopping?"

"The captain is aware of that possibility." Joe jerked open the door and climbed into the driver's seat. Annie hurriedly followed and slammed the door shut on the passenger side. On their way to the stables, he told her, "The captain agrees with us about a drug ring operating on base. We think they're dropping the drugs from either the ocean or the freeway, then using those five horses to transport the stuff to the stables area under the dark of the moon each month."

"So," Annie quickly added, "if the horses bring it here, then it can be loaded into a car or cars. They could drive out the back gate, undetected."

"Yeah," Joe said grimly, his hands tightening on the wheel. He was immune to the early morning beauty of the silver-barked eucalyptuses lining the road to the stables.

"I wonder if Garwood is involved," Annie murmured, more to herself than to Joe. "I got a bad reading off him the first time I set eyes on him."

Joe nodded. "We'll do a thorough investigation. There's no telling how this thing is going to start unraveling, but it's starting—and in a hell of a hurry."

Annie nodded. She clenched her hands in her lap as the HumVee pulled into a parking space in front of the stables. Her intuition told her that by the time darkness came, they would have some answers.

The feeling of a stone in Joe's stomach continued unabated. They had thoroughly searched the stables and found no sign of Libby. Stuart Garwood was too busy to help—or so he said. Now Joe stood at ease in front of Captain Ramsey's desk, Annie at his side. The captain was obviously unhappy and worried.

"Annie, take that dirt and straw you found in the back of Garwood's Cherokee over to the lab and see what they find," he ordered.

"Yes, sir." Annie came to attention, made an about-face and left the office.

"Joe, I'm worried about Libby."

"Yes, sir...." Joe stood awkwardly, wanting to tell the officer everything would be all right. But he didn't know that. He knew how Ramsey felt, though. Libby might be in danger and Ramsey loved her. Those bare facts affected Joe more than he could ever express.

"If traces of cocaine show up in Garwood's Cherokee, what will you do?" he asked instead.

His eyes narrowed, Ramsey sat back in his chair, resting his chin on his fist. "I'll call in the local police and ask them to tail Garwood in an unmarked car. I want his activities constantly monitored."

"You think there might be a drop tonight?" Joe asked.

"A very good chance. It's a new moon." Ramsey's nostrils flared as he exhaled forcefully. "Damn, I wish I knew where Libby was. She can't just have disappeared off the face of the earth.''

"We searched every building in the stables facility," Joe said.

"I know, I know...."

Internally, Joe was worried, too. He knew without a doubt that a stakeout would be set up to try to capture the drug runners—whether or not they located Libby in the meantime. And that meant that Annie would be there. His stomach tightened painfully, and he wrestled with his own fear and anxiety.

"Dismissed," Ramsey muttered, and stood up.

Joe came to attention and left the office. It was nearly 1600, an hour before the brig office closed. What would the lab find from Annie's samples? Nothing, he hoped as he sat down at his desk to try to work. But his mind wouldn't stay focused on the papers staring back at him. If Ramsey ordered a stakeout, Annie would be involved. Oh, God, he couldn't risk her being in the line of fire. He just couldn't.

Annie saw Captain Ramsey's face become closed and still as he read the lab findings. She was elated, nearly walking on air at her find, but she maintained a stoic expression.

"Cocaine traces?" Ramsey muttered.

"Yes, sir."

Ramsey looked up. "Good work, Corporal."

"Thank you, sir."

"Ask Sergeant Donnally to come in here, will you?"

Annie turned and left. It was 1700 and the day people were leaving, although Section A personnel were still on duty until their relief arrived at 2100. Joe was at his desk,

a heavy scowl on his face, struggling over the neverend-
ing paperwork she knew he hated.

"Joe?"

Joe's head snapped to the left at the sound of Annie's
husky voice. "Yes?"

"The captain wants to see us."

Again, Joe's pulse skyrocketed—out of fear. He probed
Annie's calm, cinnamon-colored gaze as he quickly rose
from his chair. "What did the lab find?"

"Cocaine traces." She smiled a little. "Garwood is im-
plicated."

Joe's heart fell as he walked quickly out of the office
toward the captain's office. His mouth hardening, he realized a stakeout now was unavoidable.

"I wish you hadn't found anything," he said harshly.

Annie glanced at him. She saw the fear in his eyes.
Reaching out, she gripped his arm and brought him to a
halt before they reached the captain's door. "Joe, wait a
minute."

"What?" he demanded testily.

"I know why you're upset."

"I have a right to be, dammit!" He placed his hands on
his hips and stared down at her. Annie had such an open,
expressive face. Flashbacks of Jenny's face moments before she was killed slammed into him. "I don't want you
on the stakeout I know is coming down. I want you safe,
Annie."

"I know you do," she whispered, "but Joe, you have
to get over this fear. I'm very capable of taking care of
myself. What I worry about is that your mind will be on
me and not the stakeout. That could get *you* hurt." *Or
killed.* Annie didn't even want to think it, but the reality
was there. She saw the absolute frustration and blazing

anger in Joe's eyes, heard it in the vibration of his deep voice and felt his raw state with all her senses.

"Annie, you could have a wall of medals and commendations proving your ability as a brig chaser, but it wouldn't mean a thing to me right now." Some of the anger left him as her eyes turned dark and compassionate. Lifting his hands in a gesture of defeat, he rasped, "I don't know what to do. I know if I ask the captain to take you off the case, he'll refuse. I know you'd fight my request, too."

"I would," Annie agreed with a sad smile. She moved aside as several civilians, including Rose, left for the day. Smiling at Rose, Annie waited until they were out of earshot before she continued. Making sure no one else was in the passageway, she reached out and gripped Joe's arm momentarily. "All my life, Joe, I've lived by one rule, and that's to face my worst fears. In the Navajo way of walking, we learn to make friends with our fear. We let it stay at our side, but we don't feed it anything. We acknowledge its presence, but we don't give our power away to it." Releasing his arm, she took a step closer, her voice low with feeling. "Don't you think I'm afraid for you?"

Startled, Joe gave her a quizzical look. "What are you talking about?"

"Hasn't it hit you that I might be worried about you on this stakeout? You're my partner. I feel a sense of responsibility for your safety, too. It's a two-way street, you know...."

Joe stood for a long, silent moment, digesting Annie's admission. "I guess I never wondered how you might feel," he admitted.

"When you're caught up in the kind of fear you have, Joe, it's easy to forget other people's feelings or concerns."

He hung his head and stared down at his boots. "I guess you're right."

"Let's try to make the best of this stakeout," Annie urged. "I'm not going to take any stupid chances with my life, Joe. And I know you won't, either. We're both trained to follow safety procedures."

With a one-shouldered shrug, Joe raised his head and met her fervent gaze. "I'm just scared for you, that's all."

"Can we be scared together?" Annie had never lost a partner, and she didn't want to start with Joe. Besides, they had a special tie to each other, an invisible one, and she wanted what they had to grow and become strong between them.

His mouth thinning, Joe said, "We don't have a choice, do we?"

"No...."

Exhaling, Joe moved forward. "Let's go and get this over with."

Annie sat at her desk, her mug filled with cooling coffee and a sandwich in hand. The brig office had hummed with activity since Captain Ramsey had ordered a stakeout operation to begin at dark tonight, now an hour away. Someone had brought in sandwiches from the chow hall earlier, and Joe's section was eating on the run. The din of noise was high, with people constantly coming and going. Phones rang nonstop as plans were coordinated with state and local police. Further, Drug Enforcement Agency personnel were coming in to take part in what everyone hoped would be a major drug bust.

As she sat munching the meat-loaf sandwich, Annie's only job was to monitor the unmarked police car assigned to follow Stuart Garwood's Cherokee. Since he hadn't yet left the stables, she had little to do. Worriedly, she turned around in her chair. Joe was up at the front of the office working with Captain Ramsey over a terrain map of the area. They were making plans on how to set up the operation. A recon captain by the name of Harris was with them. Yes, it was going to be a large, coordinated effort, and Annie hoped that it would net them the bad guys.

Crinkling the sandwich wrapper and throwing it into the wastebasket next to her desk, Annie wondered about Libby Tyler. There was no doubt in any brig chaser's mind that she had either been kidnapped or was dead somewhere. Captain Ramsey was holding up well, Annie thought, under the circumstances. She didn't know Libby that well, but what she'd seen of the woman she liked. Her heart turned to Joe, who stood at the map, his finger tracing a route for the two officers.

Wiping her lips with a paper napkin, Annie dropped it, too, in the wastebasket. Whether she wanted to admit it or not, her heart was opening to Joe Donnally. But she couldn't let it. She'd loved a marine before and lost him to a bullet. It could happen again, and she knew she wasn't strong enough to take the loss of a second man she loved. Glancing at Joe's set, rugged profile, Annie felt the magic that seemed to simmer between them. She knew Joe felt it, too. He was more honest about his feelings toward her than she was with herself.

Somehow you're just going to have to hold him at arm's length, Annie told herself sternly. Somehow... Joe emanated the self-confidence bred with experience that always appealed to her. And he was honest—perhaps the trait she cherished most. Despite his tough marine veneer, Annie knew that Joe was a man whose heart was easily touched by everything—he just hid it better than most. He wasn't sexist, and he accepted her fully as someone who could do her job—even if he was overprotective. She tried without success to find something to dislike about him.

More than anything, Annie liked his love of his family. She was sorry he'd lost his sister, Maria. It was important to her that the man she someday would fall in love with should be family oriented. Not that she wanted children right away; that could wait until she had put in her twenty years in the corps. But after that, becoming a mother was something Annie looked forward to with great relish. She had joined the marines at eighteen, and by the time she was thirty-eight, she'd have her pension and retirement. Her late thirties was a perfect time to be a mother, she felt. By that time she'd have accrued the wisdom and experience to be, she hoped, a very good parent.

Her gaze moved back to Joe. Instinctively, she knew he'd make a wonderful father. He was a man who loved the outdoors, and she smiled, thinking about him teaching fly-fishing to his daughters and sons. Heat moved through her, and Annie tried to ignore the sensation. Joe would cherish his family, being just as protective and fiercely caring as he was with her, she realized with a start. Actually, being in charge of a section of thirty marines was a lot like being a parent, she surmised. Joe had a lot of experience with his Marine Corps family, and it was obvious the men and women in his section not only respected him, but liked him. Yes, he'd be a very good father.

When Joe turned toward her, Annie automatically tensed. His blue eyes looked turbulent as he slowly walked toward her. She pulled the chair closer to her desk and sat stiffly with her hands folded on top of it. He pulled a chair from another desk and sat down in front of her.

"Well," he grumbled, "the stakeout's set."

"Good."

He gave her a searching look. "I don't know how you manage to look so calm and cool when things are in high gear around here."

She smiled softly. "Remember? I've got six years under my belt. This isn't my first stakeout, Joe."

"I suppose not...." He rubbed his face with his hands. Pushing several dark strands off his forehead, he met her inquiring gaze. "We're going to be up on the front lines."

"I thought so. What about the recon squad?"

"They're our backup if we get blown away."

A cold shiver wound up her spine, but Annie kept her face carefully arranged, conscious that Joe was probing her for some kind of reaction. "We won't."

"Humph." He looked at her phone. "Garwood move yet?"

"No."

"If he doesn't, then this stakeout will probably be a bust."

"Maybe not. What if Garwood stays at the stable, waits for the five horsemen to come back to him, loads the drugs in his car and takes it out the back gate?"

Joe gave her an assessing look. "You've thought of that, too."

"Why are you surprised?"

"I don't know," he said wearily. "We're the only two who did. I'd be impressed if I wasn't so worried."

Annie nodded. The phone on her desk rang. She answered it and listened closely, pen in hand. When the caller hung up, she said, "Garwood's leaving the stables right now."

Rising, Joe said, "I'll let the captain know. Looks like this stakeout won't be the quiet one I hoped for."

"No," Annie said, feeling bad for Joe. The worry burning in his eyes ate at her. For the first time, she was getting a sense of just how much he was bothered. But short of refusing to go on the stakeout, there was little she could do, even if she wanted to. The only thing that might help Joe right now was for her to put her arms around him and just hold him for a moment—and that was certainly out of the question.

The activity in the office increased even more as periodic radio calls began to come in from the unmarked cruiser tailing Garwood. Night fell, and Annie felt the tension rise accordingly. Very soon they would be picking up their weapons, preparing for war on a small scale. She didn't fool herself; brig work was always dangerous. Annie had never killed anyone, and she hoped she'd never have to, either. Her conscience nettled her as she got up from the desk. What if she did kill someone? The burden would rest heavily on her, she knew.

As she made her way toward Joe, a cold fear shot through her. An even worse nightmare would be to have him injured—or killed. It was funny how they each worried only about each other. It seldom entered Annie's mind that *she* might become a target. Other brig chasers who had been wounded had told her that after being shot, a huge shift in reality took place—every one of them became far more conscious of their own delicate hold on life in the line of duty.

Well, tonight she wouldn't be concerned with her own safety. Annie knew her focus would be on memorizing her part of the assignment involved and keeping her partner, Joe, safe. As she walked up to him and met his shadowed gaze, she tried desperately to ignore the way her heart automatically blossomed around him. No personal feelings could interfere in their teamwork tonight. None.

* * *

Annie lay behind a rounded sand dune, her M-16 rifle in prone position, waiting. It was midnight, moonless, with low-hanging clouds blotting out what little starlight there was. To her left was I-5, the main interstate up the coast of California. Less than half a mile away the Pacific Ocean beat on the shore, the interstate running between them and the foaming surf. Annie's heart was thudding hard with anticipation. The unmarked car had reported that Garwood was northbound on the interstate—heading toward them. To her left lay Joe, his M-16 cradled in his arms, his profile hard, his silence palpable. To her right lay Captain Ramsey.

They had been in position for the past three hours, just waiting. Annie felt Joe's anguish as clearly as she felt her own. Everything had piled up like an avalanche toward this moment. Was Libby Tyler dead? Killed by the men who had discovered her getting too close to their drug operation? Annie died inside a little for Ramsey, who she could feel was strung tautly as a bow, ready to break.

Annie had tried to settle her own feelings down, but it was impossible. She knew Joe was agitated by the fact that she was at his side, but nothing could prevent that from occurring. Somehow, he was going to have to wrestle with that demon on his own.

Glancing down at the watch on her wrist, she saw by the luminous dial that it was half an hour past midnight. The night was cool and her body heat had been sapped from her during the hours of lying unmoving in the sand. It was possible no one would show up at the fence line at all. What they were doing was a gamble. A big one.

Joe looked to his right, where Annie lay prone, no more than three inches away. Everyone had painted their faces with greasepaint camouflage except her. Her copper skin blended perfectly with the surrounding darkness. As if knowing he was looking at her, she twisted to look in his direction. For the first time he was truly seeing Annie the professional, not the woman, he realized. He saw how her eyes were narrowed. Her lips were compressed in a tight line, conveying the tension they all shared. He managed a slight smile for her benefit, and in the passing headlights of cars on the interstate, he saw her own expression soften for just an instant. It was enough.

Despite his best attempts to stay cool, Joe lay drenched in a cold sweat of terror—for Annie. He kept telling himself that she knew what to do. She was trained to handle a myriad of weapons, and the fact that she'd handled Gorman earlier had proven she could take care of herself. But what if there was a firefight? Groaning softly, Joe pressed his head against his weapon momentarily. The excruciating awareness that any of them could be wounded or killed was very real. Suddenly, he wanted to know everything about Annie, to endlessly explore her serene world, to learn more about her growing-up years on the reservation. She spurred a hunger in him he'd never encountered, and a molten heat flowed through him, embracing his heart.

Joe's mind switched instantly to the interstate as a final call from the unmarked cruiser came in, telling them that Garwood was slowing down and would probably be pulling over to the side. His eyes squinting against the constant glare of headlights coming at them, Joe held his breath. There! He saw Garwood's black Cherokee moving onto the shoulder of the road. His hand tightened around the stock of the rifle and he quickly glanced toward the captain.

"They're coming," he said in a low tone.

"Roger," Ramsey said.

The small communication headsets they all wore in their left ears crackled to life, and Donnally tensed even more as he heard the captain alert the entire force. A recon squad was backing them up inside Reed property, three hundred feet along the horse trail. The brig chasers were the front line of defense, on the opposite side of the fence, hidden behind several small sand dunes that paralleled the road. Within a mile in either direction, state and local police waited to be called in once the trap had been sprung on Garwood and his men. Sweat trickled down Joe's temples, and he swallowed rapidly against his constricted throat. More than anything, he wanted Annie safe.

Annie controlled her breathing, lying very still, becoming a part of the sand dune. Without thinking, she flattened against the sand as the headlights of the Cherokee flashed momentarily in their direction. Her fingers tightened around the M-16 she shouldered. All her senses were screaming as the vehicle stopped and the lights were switched off. Her eyes narrowing to slits, Annie saw someone get out, walk quickly to the rear of the vehicle and open it. Four other men got out and looked toward the ocean on the other side of the eight-lane interstate.

"They must be waiting for that tuna boat the coast guard's been shadowing up the coast," Donnally whispered tensely.

"Lock and load," Ramsey ordered quietly.

Annie heard the heavy bolt action of ten M-16's, but the sound was easily drowned out by the constant traffic that prowled the most heavily traveled freeway in the state.

A gasp tore from her. "Wait!" She jabbed a finger in the direction of the Cherokee. "Look, Captain!" It was Libby Tyler. Two men were dragging her away from the

Cherokee, but they seemed to be having trouble holding her up. Something was wrong with her. Annie watched in silent terror as they brought her toward the other two men clustered in front of the vehicle.

"It's Libby," Captain Ramsey said in a cracked whisper.

"They've drugged her," Annie whispered tautly. "Drugged or injured her. She can hardly stand on her own."

"On my order, Tiger Three and Four lock and load," Ramsey whispered. "Now! Be apprised that Libby Tyler is their prisoner. She's the smallest person in the group. Be careful not to injure her. Out."

Her heart pounding hard, Annie felt every muscle in her body tense, but her eyes never left Libby. She heard Joe curse softly to her left and heard the raspy breathing of Ramsey on her right. Then, without warning, she saw Libby suddenly tear loose from her captors and run drunkenly into the line of traffic.

"Close in now!" Ramsey cried as he leapt to his feet.

Annie flattened and, in her sights, picked up one of the men starting after Libby. She pulled the trigger, missing the man, but a puff of dirt shot up warningly in front of him and he halted. Suddenly, all four men drew weapons and began to fire back at the marines.

Annie felt Joe get to one knee and shoulder his M-16. Bullets whined and danced around them. She fired again, and saw one man fly backward, struck by someone's bullet.

She heard the rest of the recons firing methodically, and the screeching brakes of several cars. Horns blared. Her attention tore to the left, to where Captain Ramsey was running across the freeway. Annie's eyes widened, and she rose to her knees. A huge eighteen-wheeler was bearing down on Libby in the fast lane, where she reeled drunkenly, seeming dazed or confused. Didn't she see the truck coming? It was going to hit her!

Without warning, Annie heard a groan to her left, and she saw Joe pitch forward, the rifle dropping from his hands. It took her precious seconds to realize he had been hit. No!

"Joe!" she cried, and lunged to the sandy earth, wriggling toward him.

"Sonofabitch!" Joe snarled, holding his left arm tightly, the stinging, burning pain racing up into his shoulder. A trickle of blood leaked through his fingers as he rolled behind another sand dune, safe from further bullets. Before he could do anything, Annie was there, covering for him, firing toward the men below.

"I'm okay!" he shouted above the din of rifle fire. With his right hand, he reached out and jerked Annie back against him in order to give her the full protection of the sand hill. Breathing hard, he patted her shoulder to signal that he was all right.

Seconds later, the firefight was over. Annie saw the other brig chasers moving forward to capture what was left of the perpetrators. She noted that Captain Ramsey had managed to rescue Libby before the truck hit her. Getting swiftly to her knees, Annie jerked her head toward the Cherokee. As she made sure that all the prisoners were on the ground, handcuffed and no longer able to fire a weapon, she saw Ramsey bending over Libby on the grassy median strip.

Turning, she put her rifle aside and devoted her attention to Joe. He was lying on his side, his back to her. With shaking hands, she turned him over so she could see his face. "Joe? Joe, you okay? Were you hit?"

Grunting, he sat up. "It's just a nick," he said, gripping her hand to reassure her. In the flash of headlights, he saw the naked terror in her eyes as she crouched over him. "We have to help Ramsey. Something's wrong with Libby," he went on. "Help me up."

Nodding, Annie hauled him to his feet. She picked up both rifles.

"You stay here and find that recon paramedic. We may need him," Joe ordered, then he turned and ran across the freeway.

Though she was still stunned by the fierceness of the firefight, Annie kept her head and located the paramedic. In no time, Joe had run back across the interstate to get him. She remained where she was, senses alert, watching the whole scene. There was nothing she could do. Two of the prisoners had been wounded in the firefight and the others had given up. All of them were loaded into a waiting ambulance provided by the state police. Traffic had been stopped now, and police cars' flashing lights stabbed through the blackness of the night. It was a surrealistic scene, Annie thought as she saw Captain Ramsey carry Libby Tyler across the highway to an ambulance.

Had anyone else been hurt? Annie rapidly took a head count. Luckily, there was no one—except Joe. How badly had he been hit? she wondered. She waited at the roadside impatiently as he walked across the highway yet again. He was in charge now, and she simply fell in at his side, his partner, ready to do whatever he asked.

Wearily, Joe ordered his people back into the Hum-Vees that had been hidden behind sand dunes on Camp

Reed property. There would be a mountain of paperwork to do. But now the local and state police would handle the snarling traffic problems and get the cars moving again. He watched as the van drove off with Garwood and his men. Turning, he realized belatedly that Annie was there, looking up at him, worry etched in her gaze.

"Come on," he said. "I need to get to the base hospital and have this arm looked at."

She slipped through the barbed-wire fence after him onto Reed property. "How bad is it?"

"It's a scratch." He motioned to the HumVee. "Will you drive?"

"Sure." She placed the two M-16's in the rear of the vehicle and climbed in. Worriedly, she glanced at Joe as he got in on the passenger side. The HumVees bearing the rest of the squad were already heading back to brig headquarters. Turning the vehicle onto the horse trail after the others, Annie found the dirt road that would eventually intersect the main highway on Reed.

"Hell of a firefight," Joe muttered as he tentatively pressed his hand along his injured arm.

"Yes," Annie whispered. She was beginning to feel an adrenaline letdown, and was becoming shaky. Her voice was trembling.

Reaching out his good arm, Joe rested his hand briefly on her shoulder. "I really am okay."

She glanced at him. "It's my turn to be worried, all right?"

Sitting back, he closed his eyes. The muscles in her shoulder were tense. "I'm sure it's just a nick. We'll know soon...."

* * *

Annie refused to leave Joe's side as he sat on a gurney in the emergency room. Despite the fact that his injury was minor, as he'd promised, Joe saw how agitated she had become over the past hour. Her eyes were dark, her lips thinned. Still, he marveled at her coolness under fire.

"You know," he said as the nurse dressed his wound, "you've got the night vision of an owl. I didn't realize it was Libby Tyler they were hauling out of the back of that Cherokee."

"My gut told me she had to be with them," Annie whispered tiredly. "Either that or she was already dead."

"Still, you did a nice job, Annie. I'm proud of you. Proud that you're my partner...."

The words, so sincerely spoken, brought tears to her eyes, and Annie turned away, not wanting the nurse or Joe to see them. "Excuse me for a moment, will you? I've got to get a drink of water...." She turned blindly on her heel and walked quickly out the sliding doors. Moving to the women's rest room, she was relieved to find it empty.

Almost by accident, Annie glanced up as she washed her hands and splashed cold, reviving water across her face. Her brown eyes were dark with anguish, driving home the depth of her feelings. She could no longer ignore the emotions for Joe that had been brought out during the firefight. She cared about him so much—personally as well as professionally. Standing there, Annie gripped the sides of the washbasin, suddenly dizzy with fatigue and adrenaline letdown. Even her knees felt shaky. Bowing her head, water dripping off her nose and chin, she was overwhelmed by a flood of feelings—all focused on Joe. Her heart ached with the thought that if he'd moved just a few inches, the bullet would have killed him rather than merely scratching him.

Trying to get a hold on her unraveling emotions, Annie scrubbed her face and hands with soap and cold water. When she finally left the rest room, she saw Joe standing at the nurse's desk, signing forms. Evidently they were going to release him right away.

He looked up as she drew near. "Take me home? I'm feeling a little groggy right now."

"Sure."

Once in Annie's car, a sensible Japanese compact, Joe closed his eyes and relaxed. It was 0300 and all he wanted to do was get a hot shower and go to sleep. Reaching out, he placed his hand over Annie's. He didn't feel the tension in her any longer.

"How are you holding up?"

Annie clasped his hand. Joe's gesture had melted her heart and touched her soul. He cared for her. "Going downhill fast," she admitted. "I'm shaky and exhausted, just like you."

He sighed, turning his head to study her clean, soft profile in the streetlights as they drove off Camp Reed. "You hold up well."

"Practice," she said wryly, trading a slight smile with him. "It's all show, believe me. I feel like mush inside right now."

Joe nodded. "That's right, there are no heroes in our business, just scared people trying to do their duty." His own fear was dissolving along with the last of the adrenaline rush as Annie continued to allow him to hold her hand. Right now, he needed that physical contact, and so, he sensed, did she.

"I'm just glad that Libby is going to be okay," she said fervently.

"Yeah. I don't know what the captain would have done if she hadn't pulled out of that drug overdose."

Annie glanced over at him. She saw the ravagement in Joe's slack features and her heart went out to him. "Seeing Libby like that probably brought back memories of Jenny."

Joe closed his eyes again, keeping his focus on Annie's warm, soft hand captured in his. "It did, but having you beside me in the firefight was worse. It was hell."

Chapter Eight

Annie walked with Joe to his apartment door. It was nearly 0400, and just the briefest hint of dawn lay along the eastern horizon of the night sky. At the door, he fished around in his pocket for the key and finally found it. His hands were shaking, but Annie understood. Hers weren't very steady, either. Such a large part of her wanted to walk through that open door, to go inside with Joe. She could feel his churning emotions and saw the burning darkness in his eyes as he turned to her.

Her heart began to pound slowly as he lifted his hand and settled it gently on her shoulder. More than anything, she wanted to step into the circle of Joe's arms and be held. She saw the silent question in his eyes as his fingers tightened slightly on her shoulder. Her lips parting, she rested her hand against his chest.

"No..." A terrible sadness wrenched her. If she allowed Joe to hold her, it would signal a different kind of relationship between them, one of intimacy. Annie knew what her professional response should be, but she was equally caught up in a human response, having passed through this life-and-death crisis together. It had shown her just how much she cared about Joe Donnally as a human being, as a man.

She wanted to kiss him. The smoldering look in his eyes tore at her reeling senses, and she whispered, "Joe, we can't ... we don't dare...."

She saw understanding come to his darkened eyes, combined with sadness and raw desire—all there for her. Annie felt Joe's fingers loosen on her shoulder. Feeling bereft as he lifted his hand away, she tried to find the right words.

"I'm sorry, I don't mean to hurt you, Joe. I—I want it as much as you do, but it's the past. The past..."

"I understand," he rasped. "I'm sorry, too, Annie. I shouldn't have placed you in this position. It's my fault." Joe felt a terrible strain wash through him. Annie's eyes were huge with need. He sensed how much she wanted to be held—if only for a moment. But he also remembered somewhere in his spinning senses that Annie had loved a marine and lost him. Tonight, they could have lost each other. If she had willingly stepped into his arms, it would have meant she had come to grips with the fact that loving a marine was worth more than possibly losing him.

"It's okay," he whispered unsteadily, one corner of his mouth trying to lift in a reassuring smile. "Go home, Annie. Take a hot shower and hit the sack. Come in at 1300 tomorrow. Okay?"

Tears stung Annie's eyes as she stood in the doorway. Joe looked so alone, so in need of her, of what they might have if she only was brave enough to step beyond the bounds of her past. She reached out, barely touching his cheek, feeling the stubble beneath her fingertips.

"Y-yes, I'll be there at 1300. Good night, Joe...." She turned away.

"Good night, Annie...." He watched her become swallowed up by the night as she walked back to the parking lot. Never had he felt more alone, and the pain ate at his heart. He'd wanted to kiss Annie, to feel the heat of her full mouth blossom and open beneath his. There was something fragile about her, he realized as he woodenly turned and walked into his apartment. Closing the door, he headed straight for the bathroom, unbuttoning his utility shirt as he went.

Despite his own exhaustion and shock at being grazed by a bullet, Joe wanted to focus on Annie. Tonight, she'd acted coolly under fire. He had no doubt she could be trusted in a tense, dangerous situation. Professionally, she was very good. Dropping his shirt in the hall, he entered the bathroom and turned on the light. He winced at the brightness as he crossed to the tub and turned on the water. The doctor had said no showers for the next week, so as to keep his wound and dressing dry.

Glancing in the mirror as he straightened, Joe saw how bloodshot his eyes appeared, how dark they looked, with shock lingering in their depths. His mouth was still twisted in a thin line. Shedding the rest of his clothes and leaving them in a heap on the floor, he climbed into the tub with a groan. Taking the washcloth, he sluiced the hot water over his face, causing rivulets to race down his darkly haired chest. The heat felt good, loosening his tense muscles, and he lay back, allowing himself the luxury of the experience.

After shutting off the tap, Joe rested in the tub, drifting somewhere in the twilight zone of sleep. Annie's face appeared before his closed eyes, and he felt his heart stir in response. He'd nearly kissed her tonight. What had he been thinking when he'd reached out and gripped her shoulder to pull her against him? At least Annie'd had enough presence of mind to say no. Disliking himself for his own weakness, Joe opened his eyes and glared up at the white ceiling. What the hell was wrong with him? Tasting bitterness in his mouth, he sat up and began to scrub himself free of this night of fear.

Annie's face had mirrored hurt when he'd removed his hand. And sadness. Joe knew he shouldn't have reached out, but he hadn't been able to help himself. He'd needed her so much in that moment. Just the act of holding her hand on the way to his apartment had soothed his raw, screaming nerves. Her very presence was healing, he thought, not for the first time, as he climbed out of the tub and began drying himself with a large, soft, yellow towel. It was that calm center she had within her that he'd needed so desperately—that and the warmth of her mouth against his.

Groaning, Joe wrapped the towel around his waist and headed for the bedroom, his damp feet leaving prints on the wooden expanse. Opening the door to see his still-unmade bed, he realized what a great difference there was between Annie's home and his own. His apartment mirrored him: it was cluttered. Releasing the towel, Joe dropped it on a chair. Maybe that was his problem—he had too many messes that he needed to clean up before he got some proper perspective and order in his life.

As he lay down, a long, ragged sigh escaped. Placing his hands behind his head, he closed his eyes. The only thing missing was Annie next to him. He knew she'd be warm and sensuous, reflecting the sun's rays from within her like the moist earth itself. And she'd be so damned loving.

Sensing all of this about Annie, he felt starved for her, for what she could bring to him. But what could he bring to her? A jaded past featuring the loss of two of the most important women in his life? Emotions cluttered to the point where he didn't respect Annie enough to allow her the room to remain on a strictly professional level with him? Joe agonized even more over his mistake tonight as he began to drift off into a deep, badly needed sleep. Tomorrow he would try and let Annie know how sorry he really was. Somehow...

Annie's nerves were frayed and she still felt jumpy as she arrived at work at 1300 the next day. Her heart leapt in powerful response when she saw Joe already sitting at his desk, working. All her senses, whether she wanted them to or not, veered to him, intuitively checking him out. Joe had recently shaved, but his skin looked pasty, his black hair washed and shining against his head. His uniform was flawlessly pressed, his boots highly polished. But it was his mouth that made her want to reach out and touch his shoulder as she approached. His mouth was pulled tight in obvious suffering, the corners holding back pain of some sort. And his brow was wrinkled, as if he were laboring mightily with the paperwork before him.

Sensing her presence, Joe looked up. The moment his shadowed blue gaze met and held hers, Annie halted. She felt such a delicious sense of warmth tunneling through her, melting the icy pit lodged in her stomach and making her feel almost human again, that she stood frozen beneath his intense inspection. Without a word, he set his pen aside, shoved back his chair and stood. Stunned, Annie saw his eyes lighten and grow warm as he approached.

"We have to talk somewhere private," Joe said in a low voice. He placed his hand briefly at her elbow, silently asking her to turn and walk with him toward the door. Stunned, Annie followed his lead, falling into step with him. They walked down a long passageway that hummed with activity and out into the small courtyard shaded by eucalyptuses.

"Let's sit down," Joe invited, gesturing to one of the redwood tables.

Annie felt all the emotions she thought she'd captured last night and this morning begin to unravel. The second time Joe touched her elbow, she wanted to cry. Confused, she sat down on the opposite side of the picnic table, facing him. Struggling to appear calm, she clasped her hands in front of her and placed them on the table. "What is it, Joe?" He looked terrible, his face taut, his eyes bleak.

"It's us," Joe began heavily, his voice low. He, too, clasped his hands in front of him. At the moment, the courtyard afforded absolute privacy, but he didn't want someone to stumble upon their intimate conversation by accident. In no way did he want to embarrass Annie. "Last night," he began, "I was way out of line—"

"No!" Annie surprised herself by her vehemence, and lowered her voice. "No, you weren't, Joe. I felt my way through it later, and what you did, what we both wanted, was normal."

"No, it wasn't." He gave her a dark look. "If you were a male partner, I'd never have done that. I was taking advantage of the situation, even if I didn't know it here." He pointed to his head. "My feelings—hell, my heart—was ruling me at that moment, Annie. You were right to say no. I just wanted to let you know that you were the one who acted professionally." His mouth flattened. "I didn't, and I put you in a compromised position. I want you to know it won't ever happen again."

Annie felt even more raw after Joe's statement, if that was possible, and she had no idea why. Joe's words seemed to cut into her, making her bleed, and she felt tears stinging her eyes. As she forced them back, her voice became low and off-key. "Last night, one or both of us could have been killed, Joe." She opened her hands in supplication, begging him to understand what she was trying to say. "It pushed buttons in both of us. We like each other. We're more of a team than we want to admit, even if our partnership is less than a month old."

Joe nodded grimly. "You're right—we are a damn good team. We think and act like one person."

"And we did last night out there along the interstate when Garwood's group opened fire on us." She touched her brow and said softly, "Joe, I knew how much the bullet hitting you shook you up. I saw it in your eyes. I felt your shock, your devastation that you could have been killed out there. I've seen other brig chasers who were wounded have the same reaction. It's as if you realize you're no longer invincible." She smiled sadly and tapped her head. "There isn't a brig chaser alive who doesn't think that somehow, he or she is impervious to bullets, that they'll never be wounded in action. And when you do get wounded, it shatters that concept."

Annie ached to reach out and hold Joe's hand, but it was impossible. They were in uniform and at work—and worse, it would signal to him that she was willing to become more than just a partner to him, to continue the intimacy they'd shared last night.

"Don't you see?" Annie asked hoarsely. "When you reached out for me last night, it was out of a very human need to be held." Bowing her head, unable to hold his gaze, she added, "I was afraid, Joe. Not of you. Of myself."

He rubbed his mouth. "What do you mean, Annie? Afraid of what?"

Lifting her head, she said, "I discovered last night, as I lay in bed unable to sleep, that I like you very much. Too much, under the circumstances."

Joe was stunned.

"I can't be less than honest with you," Annie went on. "I wanted to come into your arms, Joe. I wanted to hold you." *And kiss you.* But she couldn't say that. "When I realized you'd been hit, my world exploded on me. I got in touch with feelings about you that I'd been fighting all along. I was afraid you were hurt a lot worse than we first realized, and so many scenarios ran through my head." She looked away, her voice low and unsteady. "I thought of my past, of my love for Jeff, and him dying in that base hospital in Saudi Arabia. I thought much of my heart had died with him, but I was wrong...."

She made herself look at Joe. "Last night I was forced to look at emotions that I hadn't known were there. I've been so busy trying to hold you at a distance, but somehow, you always touched me here." She pressed her hand to her heart. "I didn't know what to do. I was so scared, Joe. I was scared of even admitting I liked you, because that meant risking the past all over again." She shook her head. "I can't love a marine again. My heart can't stand it. Not again...."

Joe sat for a long time assimilating Annie's admission. He saw the tears in her eyes and wanted to reach out and console her, but he couldn't. His own feelings were too alive, clamoring to be noticed, making him emotionally unsteady. Finally, he sighed and said, "I think it best that I talk to Captain Ramsey about this. You should be transferred to one of the other sections, Annie. It's not fair to you, because I can't promise I'll keep my distance. Something happened last night during that firefight. I can't explain it. Whatever the fear was that I had after Jenny died is gone. I woke up this morning dreaming about you and how I feel toward you."

Annie sat very still. Her heart had nearly broken when Joe suggested that she get another partner, yet her head saw his reasoning and agreed. But she didn't know if she could stand being separated from him. He leaned back on the bench, searching for words, and she wanted to reach out and reassure him that everything would be all right. But it wouldn't.

"When I woke up this morning, I realized a lot of things I hadn't last night," Joe admitted. "The fear I had about a woman brig chaser being unable to defend herself in a crisis blew apart. I saw you under fire, and this morning, I realized that you aren't Jenny." His mouth quirked and he gave Annie an apologetic look. "I guess my heart knew that way ahead of my mind. That's why I reached out for you last night at my apartment. I wanted you. I needed you. But it wasn't a partner thing, it was strictly a man wanting his woman. Somehow, you sensed that, and said no. I saw the terror in your eyes, Annie. I felt the grief around you when I wanted you in my arms. Afterward—" he gave a deep sigh and leaned down to pick a blade of grass "—I understood why."

His woman. Joe's words, the powerful feelings behind them, rocked Annie inwardly. Never had she wanted to be anyone's woman more than his. Tears started to dribble down her cheeks and she quickly wiped them away. Joe looked utterly defeated. He absently played with the blade of grass between his fingers, unable to make eye contact with her. "It's me," she said in a wobbly voice. "It's my fear of the past. I haven't been able to put it to rest, Joe. You have, and I honor you for your courage to do that."

"I know." Joe gave her a tender smile. "And it's okay, Annie. I'm glad I understand now. But you need to be assigned someone else. You know that."

Bitterly, she nodded her head, a lump in her throat. The need to cry nearly overwhelmed her, and she couldn't speak.

Joe gave an apologetic shrug. "I'm afraid we're going to have to take Gorman to Fallon, Nevada, though. I talked to Captain Ramsey this morning. He's still over at the hospital with Libby, pretty shaken up over this, and I didn't want to mention transferring you to another brig section."

"I understand," Annie whispered, raising her head. The tender look in Joe's eyes made more tears come. "I— I shouldn't be crying. What if someone sees me?" She made a gesture of apology before swiftly wiping the tears from her eyes.

Joe handed her his handkerchief. "Here, take this...."

Just the brief touch of their fingers made her heart break open and bleed with such intense feeling that she could no longer talk as she daubed at her eyes.

"To tell you the truth," he went on quietly, "I don't want anyone but us driving Gorman to Nevada, anyway. He's lethal, and we're the best in our section because of our years of training. After we get back, I'll talk to Captain Ramsey about getting you a new partner. In the meantime, I promise to keep my hands off you, Annie. I won't put you in that kind of situation again. You don't deserve it."

Handing him back the handkerchief, Annie said brokenly, "I agree that we should transport Gorman. And it's okay with me if you talk to Captain Ramsey after we get back to Reed.''

Nodding, Joe self-consciously stuffed the handkerchief into his back pocket, more than a little aware that Annie's tears were on it. ''I don't know what happened. Somehow, visiting your home tore down a lot of barriers of fear I had in me.'' He gave her a crooked smile touched with shyness. ''There's just something about you that draws me. You have this quiet center, and when I'm around you, I feel more at peace with myself than I ever have in all my life. I can't explain it. I can't even apologize for it.''

Her heart breaking, Annie didn't even want to think about being transferred out of Joe's section. The only time she might see him then was when one section came on duty as the other was going off—just the briefest of contact. But wasn't that what she wanted? What she'd asked for because her fear of trying to live again, of possibly allowing herself intimacy with another marine, stood in her way?

Joe could feel Annie's terrible dilemma. She cared for him. The admission was as sweet as it was bitter. The only viable answer was to get her another partner. That way, they would rarely see each other. Choking down a lump that wanted to form, he rose slowly and said, ''Come on back to the office when you feel like it.''

Annie sat and watched him walk deliberately toward the door. Joe showed such pride in the way he threw back his broad shoulders as he walked. He was proud to be a marine, and he had the confidence to back up that esprit de corps. More than anything, she applauded his honesty with her, as much as it hurt both of them—and she knew it had. Scrubbing her eyes one last time, she got to her feet. First, she'd go to the women's rest room and wash her face with cold water. No one could know that she'd been crying.

In the bathroom, the cold water felt good on the heat of her skin and her burning eyes. Annie took paper towels and blotted her face, then looked at herself in the mirror. Her eyes reflected tragedy; the gold that normally showed in them was missing. Like a building thunderstorm, the clouds of her grief had blotted out the sunlight within her. She dropped the used paper towels in the wastebasket. The shape of her mouth spoke eloquently of her vulnerability, the corners pulled in to deal with the pain—her own and Joe's. Such an incredible umbilical cord of feeling stretched between them, she thought, an invisible trading of emotions.

As she walked slowly down the passageway to the office, Annie frowned. More than anything, during this two-day drive to Nevada with Gorman, they would have to focus on their dangerous task and not allow their personal feelings to get involved. No, Gorman was going to require every nuance of their attention, experience and alertness, because, Annie knew, he would kill them if given half a chance.

"Ready?" Joe asked Annie as he approached the gray station wagon at Motor Pool. Two days had passed—two of the most miserable days of his life, as far as he was concerned. Annie looked better, but he saw the distress in her eyes and it made him wince internally. The sun hadn't even risen yet, and the horizon was washed with pale pink to the east.

"Ready as I can be," Annie said. "I just went down the safety checklist with Motor Pool. The car is ready."

Joe looked at the long, heavy station wagon, specially built for transporting prisoners. The rear seat allowed the prisoner plenty of room to move around in, but a heavy metal grate divided it from the far rear, where two M-16's and other needed equipment were stored. A thick partition made of a special kind of glass that couldn't be broken by a determined fist or heavy implement separated the prisoner's area from their front seat. Further, the doors in the prisoner's section were permanently locked and couldn't be opened except by a switch located under the dashboard.

"How about the radios?" Joe asked, ducking into the driver's side and inspecting them.

"I checked them myself," Annie said, getting in the other door. She strapped on the seat belt. "I called the state police, the sheriff's department and our special line to the FBI office in Sacramento. The radios are up and running." If the car they were driving was in an accident or had a flat tire, they could use one of the radios to contact the nearest source of help. Further, their route had been given to all the police agencies along the way. If the prisoner did escape, they would be aware of the potential areas to search.

Nothing was left to chance when transporting a prisoner, and Annie felt glad of the security measures—especially when taking someone as dangerous as Gorman from one facility to another. Joe got in and shut the door. They would drive from Camp Reed to Sacramento for the night, a sixteen-hour journey. There, Gorman would be placed in the sheriff's custody overnight, and the next morning they would pick him up again and drive across the Sierras to Naval Air Station Fallon, Nevada, where Gorman would stay in the brig overnight. The third morning they'd transfer him to another set of brig chasers who would deliver Gorman to Leavenworth officials.

As Joe drove toward the brig, he glanced over at Annie. "I feel like we're transporting a slippery rattlesnake," he commented.

Grimly, she said, "Gorman's dangerous. Worse than a rattler."

Dawn was brightening the horizon, the morning cool but not cold. Joe looked up and saw clouds approaching from the west. "What's the latest word on the weather?"

She took the meteorological report that she'd picked up earlier out of the glove box. "There's a major storm coming in over the Pacific Northwest. We'll have cloudiness and a few sprinkles going up to Sacramento." She scowled. "It's tomorrow I'm worried about."

"Why?"

"We've got to go over Donner Pass in the high Sierras tomorrow, and the weather people are calling for heavy rain, possibly turning to snow showers. We'll be at eight thousand feet, and that's definitely snow altitude."

"Hmm," Joe murmured, "we'll have to watch for black ice on the road over the pass, then."

"Yes. I'm uneasy about it," Annie admitted.

"We'll be careful," he reassured her. The past two days had been a special kind of hell on Joe. He hadn't slept very well either night, because of his rampant feelings for Annie. Once he'd admitted that he was beyond the fear of possibly losing her, it had seemed as if the floodgates of his heart opened to allow an avalanche of never-ending feeling. He was confused by it, because it had never happened before. They were good emotions, though—solid, heartfelt vibrations that went far beyond the merely sexual, although those desires were an intricate part of them, too.

Right now Joe was vividly aware of Annie sitting less than two feet away from him, looking even more beautiful than usual, if that was possible. Since their talk, she had withdrawn a great deal from him. Much of their normal chatter, their sociability, was gone. Joe understood why. He didn't take Annie's retreat personally, because he knew she was afraid and that she was grappling with the past. Hadn't he, for years, gone through the same kind of hell? He could do no less than give her the room to heal in her own way—although it was the last thing he wanted to do.

Still, he was beginning to realize, even appreciate, that grief in a person's life had to be honored and left alone to be worked out on its own time schedule. For the next four days, he was going to enjoy Annie's presence, the wonderful nuances of her being, and he was going to absorb her into his heart. He wouldn't try to push her in any way, but he was going to appreciate her and let her know in little ways how much he cared for her.

Suddenly, Joe was looking forward to the trip as never before. He might be a man bound for a personal hell, but this four-day reprieve was going to be like getting a taste of heaven—or as close as he was likely to come. Annie was his sunlight, the woman who had given him the courage to shed his past. In some small way, Joe hoped he could help her in turn. Just the fact that he knew she liked him made him hum softly to himself. Optimism sprang up within him, and he savored it as never before.

Chapter Nine

The transfer of Gorman to the car had been tense, but had gone without a hitch. Annie lifted her hand to Private Shaw, who looked terribly worried as Joe eased the vehicle away from the brig. To be honest, her heart was still pounding, from a little fear mixed with a lot of adrenaline. Gorman had glared at her but said nothing as he hobbled toward the station wagon. His ankle and wrist manacles were bound to a chain around his waist, not to be removed until he was placed in the jail in Sacramento sometime after dark today.

Tension showed in Joe's face, but his expression was hard and merciless looking. Annie was coming to realize that he was far more open and accessible to her than to the world at large, and she tried to put those feelings and discoveries gently aside. Right now, as they made their way to the interstate that would take them north to Sacramento, she had to be completely focused on her job.

Once on the freeway, because she was riding "shotgun" in the copilot position, it was Annie's responsibility to call all police authorities involved and let them know they were on their way. Once an hour she would call in their position to the state police, and they would be tracked. If something should happen, the police would have a fairly good idea where they were and would be able to send out search parties if the prisoner escaped.

Joe kept his eyes on the traffic around and ahead of them. He could feel Gorman's black gaze drilling into his back and knew that the prisoner would like to kill him. Keeping both hands firmly on the steering wheel, he obliquely listened to Annie calling the authorities and stating their location.

It was standard procedure to drive in the middle lane of traffic, because in case of an accident, they'd have more room to maneuver. Joe kept to the maximum speed of sixty-five miles an hour, his gaze roving across the dials and gauges in front of him, then shifting back to the road. All his senses were on high alert. A fine tension thrummed through him whenever he transported a brig prisoner, but this time was different because their passenger was so dangerous. Although Gorman had been strip-searched before leaving the brig this morning, Joe didn't trust the murderer in the least.

Special sets of mirrors were located on the dash so that in one glance, Joe could see Gorman no matter where he sat. He was looking around now, his mouth hard and set. An alarm went off in Joe when Gorman pinned his angry gaze on Annie as she spoke on the radio. He saw the man's eyes grow slitted, and he longed to slap that look off his face. It was a look of lust at best, and it repulsed Joe, making him feel nauseated.

His hands tightening on the wheel, he glanced over at Annie, who sat with the log sheet across her lap, noting the times of the radio calls. Although Gorman couldn't hear them through the thick glass, they could hear anything he might say through a two-way speaker system hooked up to his small prison.

"This is one transport I'll be glad to get over sooner rather than later," Joe admitted.

Annie glanced at him and nodded. "You're lucky you can't feel the vibrations around him." She shivered and compressed her lips.

"I can feel a little bit," Joe said grimly. "Enough, believe me."

"Yes...."

He wanted to add, *I'm looking forward to tonight, at the motel.* And he was. But saying it would place another unfair pressure on Annie, and they had enough to do just getting safely to Sacramento with Gorman.

It was nearly 2100 when Annie met Joe outside their respective rooms. She'd changed into civilian clothes, and they were going to eat at a restaurant located near the motel. Joe smiled tentatively at her as he came down the sidewalk, his hands in his pockets. He wore dark brown slacks and a short-sleeved, light blue shirt, open at the neck. To Annie's surprise, he'd shaved again, and it made her feel special.

"Ready?" he asked.

"More than ready. I'm starving!"

Joe fell into step with her, marveling at her transformation from brig chaser to feminine woman. She wore a pair of light tan slacks, a pale pink blouse with ruffles around the collar and tan sandals. The sky was dark above them, the clouds threatening.

"Well, Gorman's safely in the county jail for the night," he murmured.

"Everything went like clockwork," Annie agreed.

"Thank God," Joe said, meaning it. So many variables could throw a monkey wrench into transport plans. Auto accidents or near accidents weren't common but were always a threat. Civilians on the freeway around them didn't know they were transporting a dangerous criminal. During her stint, Annie had driven with the same intense focus he had, and Joe had been able to relax. She was just as good a driver as he was, perhaps better in some ways.

The rain started again, this time coming down in a sudden shower. They both ran for the door of the restaurant, their hair damp as they entered. Joe slid his hand beneath Annie's elbow and pointed to a corner booth in the large, clean restaurant, fairly empty of customers at this time of night.

Annie smiled up at him and nodded, absorbing his steadying touch. She longed for more of it, and tried to tell herself no.

Reluctantly, he released her elbow and allowed her to lead them down the dark green carpeting toward the booth. A waitress was already coming toward them with glasses of water and menus in hand. The booth was black vinyl, comfortable and just what his back needed after their long drive.

Waiting until after they'd given their food orders to talk, Annie took a sip of steaming black coffee. "I wanted a chance to tell you how much I enjoyed working with you today. You really are good, you know," she said softly.

Joe flushed, sipping his own coffee. He set the mug down between his hands. "I was thinking the same of you," he said.

It was Annie's turn to blush. "Great minds think alike, I guess."

He laughed a little. "I don't know. Maybe great hearts."

Annie mutely agreed. She was amazed how easily they fell into a comfortable work routine with each other. Twice she'd seen a look of longing in Joe's eyes, but as soon as he'd realized she was aware of it, he'd quickly hidden it. Annie knew he was trying desperately to keep his real feelings toward her at bay, and it made her feel bad. If only she could get over her fear. If only...

"Tomorrow is going to be the toughest," Joe said, breaking the pleasurable silence. "Did you see that weather report at the sheriff's office?"

With a grimace, Annie said, "Yes. Rain mixed with sleet all the way up through Donner. You'd think in the middle of summer those sleet conditions wouldn't occur. I don't like it."

"It's the altitude," Joe groused.

"We'll do it, though. Whatever it takes," Annie added more firmly. Joe looked exceedingly tired, shadows plainly visible beneath his blue eyes. Hadn't he been sleeping well? Probably not. After all, she hadn't, either. "I feel so awkward," she blurted out. "I know how much of a stress this is to you, Joe. You've got enough to worry about with Gorman without—"

"Annie, it's okay. I'm a big boy. I've got a pretty broad set of shoulders, and I'm used to carrying loads." He smiled a little, trying to relieve the guilt that shadowed her luminous eyes. How pretty she looked, with her black hair softly brushed into place, her eyes giving away her real feelings, her mouth full and beckoning. He wondered if Annie realized how beautiful she was. Joe wanted to be the man in her life to tell her those things, to share with her those wonderful discoveries. Frowning, he said, "Can you tell me about Jeff? If it's none of my business, say so."

With a shrug, Annie said, "Jeff was a recon marine— a good one. He was a sergeant and had been in the corps for six years before I met him." Running her finger slowly up and down her coffee mug, she whispered, "He was very outgoing and gung ho. We fell in love over a year's time. It wasn't anything fast, and it didn't hit me over the head."

"That's the way it happened between Jenny and me."

For a moment, Annie was silent. Then she looked up and met Joe's tender gaze. "Jeff's parents were pretty shocked when they met me, after he'd announced our engagement."

"Why?"

"Because I'm an Indian." She held up her arm with a wry smile. "Dark skinned."

"I see people out on the beaches burning themselves to a crisp trying to get that shade," Joe muttered.

"Jeff came from a very well-to-do-family, and I think his parents had hopes that he'd get the Marine Corps out of his system, go back to college, get a degree and meet a woman with better bloodlines than mine."

"But he loved you despite what his parents felt?"

"Yes."

"Good for him."

She smiled tentatively and held his gaze. "You'd have liked Jeff. He was the opposite of you in some ways. You're quiet, and he was always the life of the party. But both of you fought fiercely for the people under your command. Jeff was called 'Mother' by his recon team, but it was an affectionate term. He cared deeply for his men, and they would have and did die for him...." Her voice trailed off and she swallowed hard. "In Desert Storm, Jeff's team was dropped behind Iraqi lines. Four out of the five men on that team didn't make it. Jeff told me before he died that two of his men had given their lives to rescue him. He'd been shot out in the open, and they got killed getting him to safety and medical help."

Joe nodded, his lips pursed. "I'm sorry, Annie."

She moved her shoulders, as if the invisible load she carried was getting heavier. "Jeff taught me about not being afraid to show how I felt. Remember, I'm Navajo, and we're a pretty shy, introspective people. He taught me so much. So much . . ."

Stopping himself from reaching across the table to grip her hand, Joe rasped, "I'm sure you gave him a lot in return, Annie."

With a small, pained laugh, Annie said, "I don't know. Jeff was like sunlight, if you know what I mean. Everyone liked him. He didn't have an enemy. He was that kind of human being."

"You were his moonlight, then," Joe whispered, his voice husky with feeling. When he saw the startled look in Annie's eyes, he added, "Believe me, any man worth his salt would see what you bring to a relationship. Jeff was the lucky one in this deal. No doubt in my mind." Or his heart. It hurt just then, because Joe wanted so badly to speak of his feelings for Annie—how she had affected his life, his scarred heart, in the most positive of ways.

She touched her hot, tingling cheek. She was blushing heavily and she avoided Joe's glittering, hooded look, sensing his emotions clearly. She found herself grieving for what she was denying both of them, yet she knew she couldn't just sweep away the fear that still stood between them. Trying to extricate herself from the ebb and flow of turbulent emotions, she tried to think ahead—to tomorrow. The danger of ice on the highway would keep them fully involved through the first half of the day, and that was good. Annie wasn't sure how long she could continue to shield herself from Joe's care and need for her—despite her fear.

It was very quiet in the station wagon as, near 0900, they encountered heavy sleet conditions on the approach to Donner Pass. Annie was riding shotgun again, her hands tightly knotted in her lap, and Joe was at the wheel. His face was set, his eyes glued on the twisting, curving, two-lane highway ahead. On their left a jagged cliff rose a thousand feet into the air. To their right, past the guardrail, the cliff continued downward a good three hundred feet before it stretched into thousands of acres of dark green forest.

The sleet thickened until visibility was limited to about six feet. Pinging ice pellets barraged the vehicle, the noise high and sharp, rubbing Annie's nerves raw. Dangerous "black ice" covered the asphalt. It had rained throughout the night, and with the front passing, the temperature was plummeting, leaving the invisible coating of ice on the pavement. Would drivers of oncoming vehicles realize the dangerous, slippery conditions? Annie strained to see through the sleet. Traffic was light, but still she was tense. Not everyone knew how to drive in snow and ice. She felt their station wagon slip every once in a while even though Joe was driving with maximum care.

Picking up the clipboard from its spot on the dashboard, Annie placed it in her lap, her hands tightening around it. "I hate this kind of weather," she admitted.

"Yeah," Joe rasped. "I'm not so worried about *our* driving—it's the other people out there I'm on edge about."

"I was just thinking that a lot of folks from the Nevada side live in the desert and aren't used to these kinds of weather conditions."

"Bingo," Joe said, his hands tight on the wheel as he tried to peer through the thickening veil. The ice pellets were larger and were falling faster now, making the highway very slippery. He handled the wheel delicately. One wrong move and he knew they would go spinning out of control—and there was no place to go except over the edge of that damn cliff.

Out of the wall of rain, just as they crept around the corner of a narrow curve, a pickup truck careened toward them, out of control.

"Joe!" Annie screamed, throwing up her hands to protect her face. Horror shot through her as the truck slid sideways toward them. There was no place to go, no room to maneuver. Joe could either hit the guardrail or wrench the car to the left and smash into the cliff. Everything slowed down to individual frames of movement for Annie. She heard Joe suck in a sharp breath. The truck loomed in their vision. They were going to be hit!

At the last possible second, Joe swerved the car to the left, sliding sharply toward the cliff. The pickup sailed by them, barely missing the guardrail, disappearing into the blinding rain. Annie braced her hand against the dashboard as the station wagon swung sickeningly into a spin. Her eyes huge, she saw the guardrail coming at them. The next second, the impact threw her to the right, against the door. As her head struck the window, she heard the grinding metal of the guardrail rip into the car.

In the next few seconds, Annie felt her world tumble out of control. She heard the crack and snap of the wooden guardrail supports. A piece of metal sailed upward, shattering the windshield, sending a shower of glass over them. The station wagon tilted, paused momentarily and then lurched down the rocky cliff with a scream of metal as it tore against the jagged rocks. Annie's head was smashed against the window a second time, and she lost consciousness momentarily. The next thing she felt was the seat belt biting deeply into her body, as if she were sailing through the air. The grating noise halted for a second, then the car plowed nose first into the cliff, flipping over again and again, and once more she lost consciousness.

The first thing Annie noticed as she clawed upward toward awareness was the sound of someone pounding. She was leaning forward, held in place only by the seat belt. The nose of the station wagon, she saw, was buried in the loose rock at the bottom of the cliff. An icy blast of cold air revived her quickly. Hearing a door creak open, she turned her sluggish mind to Gorman. Her eyes blurring, her vision coming and going, Annie fought to become coherent, but her hands and feet wouldn't work. She felt the warmth of blood flowing out of her nostrils and down her chin. Ice pellets whipped through the nonexistent windshield, striking her, chilling her.

Every alarm in her body was going off, screaming out in warning. Annie tried to force her eyes open, tried to move, but she couldn't. Gorman was near. Very near. Opening her mouth, she gasped for air, and felt a jab of pain move up her shoulder and into her neck.

She heard Gorman grab violently for the door handle on her side of the vehicle. Her door was jerked open, making protesting sounds because it was partially jammed. With every ounce of strength she had, Annie forced herself to open her eyes. Gorman's meaty face and leering dark eyes stared back at her as he reached into the car to grab for the shotgun that rested near her left knee. *No!*

Before he could close his hand around the weapon, she swiftly lifted her foot and smashed her boot against his wrist. Gorman let out a howl of pain, stumbling backward, slipping on the icy rocks.

Breathing raggedly, Annie fumbled for and found her pistol. Gorman drunkenly got to his feet, obviously stunned by the crash. He turned, heading rapidly down into the thick pine forest despite the chains that bound him. Too late! Annie made a sound of frustration as she jammed the pistol back in its holster. *Joe?* What about Joe? Her fingers fumbling, she released the seat belt and slowly twisted to the left. Her heart pounding, Annie saw that he was unconscious. Blood dripped from his jaw onto his uniform. His mouth was hanging open, and his body was slack against the harness.

"Oh, no," Annie moaned. She leaned forward, her fingers nerveless partly from the drop in temperature. "Joe? Joe, can you hear me? Wake up! Wake up!" She turned his head slightly, to see a cut along his cheekbone where he'd been struck by flying glass.

Joe groaned. Annie's urgent voice was breaking through the fog that surrounded him. He felt her touch, light and frantic, across his chest, shoulders and, finally, his face. Fighting, he began to regain consciousness. He felt Annie push him back against the seat. Her hands were strong and steadying against his shoulders.

"Joe, you've got to wake up. Gorman escaped! Can you hear me? Gorman's gone!"

Gorman. The word rang hollowly through his brain. With a groan, Joe weakly lifted his hand toward the pain on the left side of his face. *Gorman had escaped.* Suddenly he felt adrenaline shooting through him, propelling him to full consciousness. His lashes fluttering, he opened his eyes. Annie was next to him, her face etched with terror, her eyes huge. He saw blood smeared from her nose across her lips and chin. She was hurt. That more than anything else shocked him into full awareness almost instantly.

"Annie!" He reached out, his hand falling against her cheek.

"I'm okay," she sobbed. "Are you? Are you all right, Joe?" She dug her fingers into his uniform to keep him from falling forward. "Answer me!"

He swallowed against a dry throat, becoming aware of the numbing rain, ice and cold whipping into the car. Her voice was close to hysteria, but he understood why. "Yeah," he croaked, "I'm okay. Annie, call the police. Just call them...now. I'll be okay...."

Shakily, Annie released him. He remained upright. Turning, she automatically scanned the gray wall of rain. Gorman was out there. How far away was he? Was he going to come back? He had no weapons, and he'd need some. Taking the pistol out of her holster, she locked and loaded it. Dividing her attention between the scene outside the car and her next task, Annie perused the broken equipment.

"No go," she rasped. "Those radios are gone, Joe."

"Okay." He unsnapped his harness and sat up. Turning, he looked at Annie, who sat like a tense guard dog, her focus trained outside the vehicle. "How are you?"

"Shaken up, a bloody nose, that's all. Joe, Gorman's near. I can feel him...."

Joe took out his own pistol and put a round in the chamber. "I wish to hell this rain would stop," he growled.

"I do, too. I saw Gorman run to the woods, Joe. The trees are about two hundred feet from us. The car flipped three hundred feet. We're resting at the bottom of the cliff."

"One of us has to get back up to the highway," Joe muttered, moving slowly around in the car, testing his limbs to see if they were injured. He surveyed the damage to the vehicle. It was extensive. The glass between the front seat and the prisoner's section had been shattered. Gorman had escaped because both rear doors had been jolted open by the crash.

"I'll go," Annie said swiftly. "Your eyes don't look right, Joe. Are you sure you don't have a concussion?" She glanced quickly in his direction and then continued to scan the area in front of the car.

"I'm still a little groggy," he admitted.

"Your legs feeling weak?"

"Yeah. Yours?"

"Mine are okay."

Joe glanced at his wristwatch. Ten minutes earlier, they had checked in with the state police. It would be fifty minutes until the next check-in time. When the state police didn't receive their call, they would immediately send out a cruiser following their route, but in this storm, it could be hours before they arrived. "We aren't going to get any help soon," he warned.

"I already figured that." Annie reached for the riot gun and slung it across her shoulder. "If I manage to flag someone down, what do you want me to do?"

"Tell them to drive to the nearest phone booth and make a call to the state police. Write out the instructions to whoever stops, then hightail it back down here." Rubbing away some of the drying blood on his cheek, Joe glanced at her set features. "I've got a feeling Gorman isn't going far in this storm. He could be hurt, too."

"He was staggering, and he had a cut on his face."

"At least he's still in chains and manacles." Joe sighed. "He can't go far too fast."

"That's why I think he's waiting for us just beyond that tree line. He wants our keys to unchain himself. That and a weapon." Her voice wobbled. "Joe, be extra careful down here by yourself. Please." And she reached out and gripped his arm.

Joe saw the unadulterated fear in Annie's eyes and managed a twisted grin, gripping her hand momentarily in his. "Listen, I've got too much to live for to let a slimy bastard like that take me out. *You* be careful climbing up that cliff, you hear me?"

Tears suddenly misted her vision and Annie sniffed. "I'll be careful."

Just as she released him and started to turn away, Joe grabbed her by the arm. "Annie?"

She halted and turned. His face was pale, his eyes a deep, burning blue as he held her startled gaze. "What?"

"Listen, if—if something happens to me, I want you to know how much you mean to me...."

A sob caught in her throat and Joe's face blurred before her eyes. Choking, she whispered, "I—I know. I feel the same about you, too, Joe. Please, be careful...."

Annie was gone. Joe's skin tingled along his jaw where she'd reached out and touched his cold flesh. Grimly, he kept his pistol ready, moving his gaze from right to left, keying his hearing and waiting, just waiting. In those next icy minutes, Joe realized that the crash, the possible threat to their lives, had torn away any doubts about how he really felt about Annie. He was in love with her. The discovery was as exquisite as it was painful. They might not come out of this alive—either of them. Gorman was dangerous and he was intelligent. If Joe were in his shoes, he'd wait just inside the edge of trees until he became coherent enough, then make an attack to get the keys and a weapon.

His numb hand tightened around the pistol. The snow was beginning to lighten, and he could see farther. In the next few minutes, to Joe's amazement, it stopped raining. Above, he could see patches of blue sky intermixed with scudding gray clouds pregnant with more rain. His eyes narrowing, he scanned the forest in front of him. His heart swung to Annie. Was she getting up the cliff safely? Three hundred feet. What if she slipped and fell? She could be killed without ever reaching the road. Oh, God. Angrily, Joe realized he couldn't afford to think about her. His gaze mercilessly probed the thousands of trees before him for any sign of movement, but he saw none. Where had Gorman gone? Not far, that was certain.

His nerves raw and edgy, Joe felt a throbbing pain developing along his injured jaw and the side of his head where he'd been cut. Ignoring it, he decided to get out of the car and move around to the rear. That would give him a far better angle for viewing Gorman, should he try to sneak up on him. Moving slowly, never taking his eyes off the forest in front of him, Joe found that his door was jammed shut. He felt as if every muscle in his body was stretched beyond maximum, and it hurt to move at all. They were lucky to be alive, Joe thought as he forced himself into the passenger seat.

Once there, he leaned over and retrieved his own riot gun. Placing the sling across his shoulder, he eased slowly out of the car. The wind was blustery and sharp, helping him remain completely alert. The surrounding rocks were layered with ice, and he slipped several times as he awkwardly made his way to the rear of the station wagon. Glancing over his shoulder, Joe could see Annie had made it to the top of the cliff. Relief filled him.

His mind was spongy from the crash, and it was difficult to think clearly, much less quickly. Looking up at the roiling clouds that hid the top of Donner Pass, Joe realized that showers could continue on and off throughout the rest of the day. Patches of sunlight appeared and disappeared in the blink of an eye. Shivering, he dug into the rear of the vehicle and retrieved his thick, dark green parka, packed away for just such a purpose.

As he slipped it on, Joe realized that once Annie got back down to the car, they would have to begin tracking Gorman on foot. He knew the police would bring in bloodhounds to try to find their trail, but it was up to the two of them to find Gorman. The task was daunting. Strapping the web belt that held his pistol around his waist outside the parka, Joe felt less vulnerable. Dividing his attention between the forest and getting his M-16 locked and loaded, Joe waited for Annie.

In another half hour she was back, panting from the climb. Joe didn't dare devote his attention to her for fear Gorman might come charging out of the forest at them. A murderer like Gorman had very little fear of someone armed because he understood the value of shock, of his mere presence. Joe knew from bitter experience that shock could cause someone to miss an important shot—just as he'd missed the shot and allowed Jenny to be killed. If he hadn't been so shaken up, the prisoner would be dead, and Jenny would still be alive.

"Okay?" he called to Annie.

"Yes." She watched where she placed her feet as she gingerly made her way to where he stood. "I flagged down a passing motorist and gave her the message. She's a local and said there's a gas station down at the bottom of the pass. It's about twenty miles away, but she'll call the state police for us.''

"Good." Joe nodded, handing her the other parka. "Suit up, we're going to have to go in after him.''

With shaking hands now numb from the cold, Annie nodded. Joe helped her on with her parka, and its warmth was revitalizing. Although they had mitts, Annie didn't wear one on her right hand. The bulky things could cost precious seconds when she was trying to pull a trigger.

"How are you feeling?" she demanded, locking and loading her M-16 and slinging it across her shoulder.

"I've been better, but my head's clear and I'm thinking better with every minute. How about you?'' Hungrily Joe assessed her. The wind and rain had whipped her hair around her face and she was bareheaded, having lost her soft cover somewhere in her climb. Joe noted the stark contrast between Annie's soft features and the equipment she wore. There was no mistaking she was a warrior, however. He was seeing a new side of Annie, the marine and tracker who was at her best in a situation like this one. A gleam showed in the depths of her eyes, and he could see challenge there along with fear. Her mouth, once soft and full, was compressed into a grim line. Just the ease with which she handled her weapons and equipment told Joe she was completely in her element.

"I've got a headache, but that's all,'' she admitted.

Joe watched the forest, his voice lowering with feeling. "I wish like hell you didn't have to go in there with me.''

Startled by the rawness in his tone, Annie looked over at his rugged profile. *Jenny.* He was thinking of Jenny again, and how he thought he'd let her down, gotten her killed. "Listen to me," she said, her voice husky with feeling as she moved over to him and gripped his arm. "I'm not Jenny. It won't happen again, Joe."

He glanced at her, at the fire in her eyes. "I'm trying to believe that," he whispered brokenly. "I'm really trying, Annie. It isn't easy."

For just a moment, she rested her brow against Joe's shoulder. "I know...." Then she stepped back, all-business. "Let me see if I can pick up a trail. You stay a good ten to twenty feet in back of me in case I get jumped. If I see Gorman and he gets the goods on me, I'm hitting the deck so you can fire directly at him. All right?"

Joe felt shaky. It was a stupid reaction to have right now, but he couldn't help himself. Annie's bravery, her professionalism under the circumstances, was heroic in his eyes. "All right. We'll use hand signals to communicate with one another."

"Right." Annie hesitated. She saw the anxiety in Joe's face and felt his concern through every cell of her trembling body. In that moment, whatever fear had been in place between them dissolved. Stunned, she felt an incredible sensation flow through her as the fear left. She saw Joe give her a questioning look. It was as if the crash had shattered her fear, as if the past no longer laid claim to the present, to a possible future—with Joe.

Overwhelmed with the realization, Annie slowly turned away, giving herself a few precious seconds to get back to her center of balance. She didn't dare track when her mind wasn't fully on her job, or on the danger that she knew was very close. Swallowing against a backlash of feelings, Annie bowed her head, trying to come to grips with all of it. Why had it happened now? They were in danger. One of them could be killed—or both of them could be. Her mouth dry, Annie jerked her head up and allowed a cold blast of air to bring her sharply into the present. She had a killer to track.

Chapter Ten

Joe wanted to scream at Annie to not go ahead of him; his years of military procedure warred with his personal fears. Jenny's face appeared in front of him as he watched Annie carefully place each foot on the slippery rocks. Shaking his head violently, he rid himself of the apparition from the past that threatened to overwhelm him with terror for Annie's life. The sky was darkening again, so he knew another rain shower was approaching. Every muscle in his body was rigid with tension and anticipation. Somewhere among those trees, Gorman lay waiting for them. Either waited or was long gone—Joe had no way of knowing which. His fingers were numb around the pistol he carried; the M-16 was slung across his back. A rifle was too unwieldy in a situation like this. The pistol was a much more flexible weapon—especially in a close-range attack.

The forest loomed before them as Annie slowly moved toward it. Joe could sense her searching, probing, feeling her way forward. The rain had washed out any tracks, but somehow she seemed to know where she was going. Looking much closer at the muddy ground, Joe realized very shallow, almost indiscernible indents could still be seen—here and there, Gorman's footprints had faintly survived the rain. Joe wouldn't have seen them, much less realized they were tracks, if not for Annie following them. His admiration for her rose even more.

His throat tight, Joe followed a good twenty feet behind Annie, his gaze swinging like radar from left to right, right to left. His hearing was keyed to an excruciating level. The trees ahead reminded him of fairy tales where some old gnome or evil sorcerer hid in the dark forest depths, ready to grab the unsuspecting, innocent children walking into his clutches. This forest was filled with stately ponderosa pines, rising eighty to a hundred feet into the gray, cloudy skies, their green limbs hanging heavy with a coating of ice. Drips of water slid off the needles, creating a constant icy shower.

The wind began to moan among the trees, and Joe scowled as he inched forward, very conscious of where he placed his feet. He couldn't afford to look down, consequently his feet had to have eyes of their own, sensing each position. No way was he going to turn his attention from Annie and the forest they were entering. In a split second, Gorman could jump out of hiding and kill Annie—or him.

Annie halted just within the line of trees. Her pistol hand was uncovered, though her left hand was gloved and protected from the cold. Swinging her gaze from right to left in the forest's muted gray light, she took in the huge trees, their rough bark and the ice coating their limbs, the moan of the next approaching rain or sleet shower. She felt Joe approaching cautiously behind her. They would never be out of each other's sight from now on. The thought made her feel safe, but she also sensed Joe's trepidation and anxiety over her life being in danger—just as Jenny's had been.

Her eyes narrowed, her ears keyed for the least bit of sound that was out of place, Annie refused to acknowledge Joe. The wind rose and fell, buffeting them, muting the forest sounds till they were nearly impossible to distinguish.

"Why are you stopping?" Joe asked, his voice low as he halted at her shoulder, constantly perusing the forest in front of them.

"The wind. I think we should wait until this rainsquall has passed. It should take about ten minutes."

Joe nodded, respecting Annie's decision to wait. In ten minutes Gorman wasn't going to get much farther ahead of them, not in his cumbersome chains. Snow began to fall—at first a few twirling flakes that managed to make it through the thick canopy of trees above them. The wind rose, and Joe braced himself, on constant alert.

"How are you doing?" he asked without looking at her.

"Shaky."

"Yeah, me too. Damn, the hair on the back of my neck is standing straight up."

"He's near." Annie licked her lips in a nervous gesture. They had moved so that their backs were against each other and touching. It was the best way to maintain a three-hundred-sixty-degree range of vision.

A chill worked its way up Joe's spine. His fingers tightened around the cold metal of the pistol as he held it up against his body, the barrel pointing skyward. "What do you think he'll do?"

"Use this rainsquall to get away from us. He can see us, we don't see him. I sense him somewhere at eleven o'clock from me."

Joe nodded. "Okay...." They'd been trained to talk in terms of twenty-four-hour-clock positions to alert a partner to where danger was coming from. Eleven o'clock meant a little to the left of straight ahead from where Annie stood.

"If you were him, would you run?" Joe asked her.

"Yes. I'd take advantage of the storm. He knows the rain will wash out his tracks. What I'm afraid of is that he'll try to circle back to the car."

"To find weapons?" Joe guessed, respecting her observation.

"You bet."

With a grim smile, Joe said, "We've got all the weapons."

"He doesn't know that, though. He may think we're not as smart as he is."

"A fatal mistake for him," Joe said.

Annie nodded. She liked the solid feel of Joe against her back. A tremendous wave of protection blanketed her, and she smiled a little to herself. Joe was protective, but in a good way. And she appreciated that he was battling not to be overly protective. The wet snow began falling at a heavier rate, driven by a fierce, gusting wind of nearly forty miles an hour. The forest was almost blotted out entirely, and they stood silently, watching and listening, their backs together.

"How far do you want to track him?" Annie asked, constantly shifting her gaze from right to left as the sleet fell thick and heavy around them. The forest was alive with the pinging, chipping sounds of ice pellets striking the ground.

"If we see that he's started to double back, we'll high-tail it to the car, set up an ambush and wait for him," Joe said.

"And if he doesn't?" The woman motorist would alert not only the state police, but the Sacramento air base, which would immediately send military police to help them. Annie was also sure that once Captain Ramsey was notified, he'd help coordinate the search with the Sacramento provost marshal's office.

"We can't leave the police wondering where we are," Joe said, almost thinking out loud. "At some point we're going to have to stop following Gorman and get back to the highway."

Annie nodded. She respected Joe's common sense about the situation. "I was looking at the map earlier," she went on, her voice barely audible above the wail of the wind. "There's a small town south of here, about fifteen miles—a fishing and tourist place called Bradley. I don't know if Gorman knows it or not, but he's heading straight for that little town."

"I'm betting he doesn't know."

Grimly, Annie said, "If he does, and if he makes it there before we can stop him, he could kill civilians or take hostages."

"Or both." Joe was frustrated by the ever-thickening rain. He knew the squall would probably stop within twenty minutes. Still, Gorman could move with reasonable assuredness under cover of the storm without being detected.

Annie glanced at her watch. It was 1400. Within an hour, even with the terrible weather conditions, the state police should arrive. "We've got about an hour before we have to turn back."

"I know," Joe muttered under his breath.

"I could go ahead," Annie suggested, "and leave marks on the trees so you could find me. That way, I could stay hot on Gorman's trail while you wait for the police."

Joe snorted. "Not a chance, Annie. I'm not about to leave you alone with that bastard around. No, either we do this as a team or not at all. What if he jumped you? There'd be no one to back you up." Rain was beginning to leak inside the collar of his parka, and he gave an involuntary shiver.

"I know," Annie said, "but even under the worst weather conditions, if Gorman keeps going south, he'll enter Bradley within the next twenty-four hours. Can we risk that?" Water dripped off her nose and chin, and she kept blinking to keep her vision clear. They couldn't risk taking cover against the rain—Gorman could watch them off guard. Annie tried to ignore the misery of the relentless downpour.

Anger bubbled through Joe. His lips tight, he snapped, "I won't risk your life for any reason."

Annie subsided into silence and continued to wait patiently. Already the curtain of thick sleet was beginning to ease. Sliding her finger around her damp collar, she tried to stop the rain from seeping in, but it was impossible. She was already soaked from her climb up to the highway, and her teeth began to chatter. She could feel Joe's anger and knew it wasn't aimed at her, but at his fear of losing her. Well, what would she do if she were the NCO in charge of this chase? It was a written rule that chasers remained as a team. They were never to split up while chasing an escaped prisoner. No, she'd probably make the same decision Joe just had.

The adrenaline was beginning to drain from her bloodstream and she was feeling more than just a little shaky.

It felt good to lean against Joe's broad back, to feel his breath translate through her, steadying her shredded emotions, which she had so far managed to tuck deep down inside her. The sleet was definitely easing and warming into a steady rain. Her parka had darkened from the soaking it was getting, and Annie thought it offered excellent camouflage, under the circumstances. She was freezing, though, despite its down-filled lining. Living in a desert most of her life had thinned her blood, and she didn't adapt at all well to cold conditions.

"Let's get going," Joe ordered quietly as the rain tapered off into a light drizzle. "We might be able to pick up his trail now."

With a nod, Annie turned. She hungered for a glance at Joe, but denied herself the satisfaction. Her breath came out white and wispy; the temperature was dropping steadily again. One thing in their favor, Annie thought, was that Gorman wasn't wearing much protective clothing—just his one-piece, bright orange prison uniform.

Their black, polished boots squished softly across the floor of brown pine needles. The sound offered a reassuring monotony as they slowly made their way through the silent forest. The wind had ceased, leaving behind the disturbing cracks and pops of ice breaking off the tree limbs and falling. Annie heard the startled call of a raven in the distance, straight ahead in the direction they were walking, as she followed the barely perceptible, random indentations of Gorman's footprints.

Joe jerked to a halt at the raven's raucous caws, though the sound was almost immediately muffled by the thick forest. He saw Annie turn toward him and gesture with her hand toward the noise. Nodding, he held up his hand as a signal that he understood her meaning. Gorman had passed beneath the wary raven and the bird had sounded an alarm for everyone in the forest—including them. He grinned a little. The bird seemed to be a mile or so ahead of them, about the distance he'd estimated that Gorman might have covered while they'd waited out the worst of the rainsquall.

Annie didn't increase her pace, although she was certain Gorman had provoked the raven's cry ahead. By this time the rain and sleet had completely washed out Gorman's tracks. Mentally, she drew a line between her position and the general direction of the raven. Moving at a steady rate, she scanned her surroundings. Suddenly she stopped and crouched down. With numb fingers, she picked up some recently broken-off pine bark. She felt Joe come up behind her.

He leaned over her shoulder. "What is it?" he asked in a low tone.

Smiling, she held up the bark for him to see. "Gorman slipped here and hit the trunk of this tree. This bark is freshly peeled off."

"Nice work," Joe grunted, and straightened, scanning the area.

"He's at least a mile ahead of us," Annie said, standing in turn.

"I know, dammit."

"We have to decide what to do now." She glanced up at Joe's stormy eyes. His cheeks were flushed.

"He's heading straight for Bradley," he muttered unhappily.

Annie nodded. "It's as if he knows...."

"I wouldn't put anything past Gorman." Joe sighed. "Let's head back. I'll bring up the rear and keep guard. We need to meet with the state police and get in touch with everyone, including Captain Ramsey."

Without a word, Annie turned around. Now it was her turn to worry. Joe would be at risk, since he was bringing up the rear. What if Gorman had turned around and was heading back toward them? Her ears were freezing to the point where they were aching, and it hindered her usually keen hearing. Reaching out, she gripped Joe's arm.

"Just be careful...."

Heat flowed through Joe where Annie briefly touched him. He glanced at her, hungrily absorbing her serene features. Despite the hell they'd been through, she looked completely unscathed—as calm and patient as ever. But he wasn't fooled. He could read the anxiety deep in the recesses of her cinnamon eyes, and he'd noticed the way her once full lips had compressed into a single line.

"Always," he promised huskily. "Let's move out...."

By nightfall, everything was in place. Joe sat with Annie in the rear of a heated police cruiser, hot coffee and a welcome sandwich in hand. The weather had worsened again, so the helicopter slated to fly in with heat-sensing equipment to pick up Gorman's whereabouts had to be cancelled. Instead, Annie and Joe were being driven down an icy highway toward Bradley. There they would be taken to a doctor's office to be checked over. All enforcement agencies responsible for finding Gorman would be in place by now. Tiny Bradley didn't have its own police department, so the mayor had been alerted, and phone calls had been made to the three hundred permanent residents of the tourist town, alerting them to Gorman's possible arrival in their area.

Annie leaned back, exhausted. It was 1700 and already dark as the twinkling lights of the town came into view. The coffee and sandwich had tasted fine, but her stomach still longed for some good, hot food. She closed her eyes and sighed softly, attempting to release the tension still gathered in her shoulders and neck.

Joe reached out and slid his hand across hers, squeezing it gently. "We'll be at a motel pretty soon. Just hang in there...." Worriedly, he assessed Annie's deteriorating condition. From the outset, she'd had to be the strong one of their team, because he'd been in worse physical shape from the crash. Now her lashes lay like delicate black fans against her taut, washed-out skin. But as he squeezed her hand, they fluttered open to reveal exhausted eyes. His mouth stretched into an attempt at a smile.

"Buy you dinner tonight? The sheriff says there's a real good steak restaurant near the motel where we're going to be staying."

The warmth of Joe's hand, the inherent strength of it encircling hers, sent a delicious wave of startling new sensations through Annie despite her weariness. "You're on," she whispered, and closed her eyes again. The burning look of care in Joe's eyes had brought Annie to tears, and she didn't want him to see how powerfully he'd touched her. The effects of the earlier crash were impinging on her emotionally. The adrenaline was gone completely, and for the first time today, Annie realized the impact of everything that had happened to them. They could have died.

She didn't want to plug into that realization, not with Joe holding her hand gently in his own, his thumb caressing her skin to a pleasant tingle.

Annie drifted off to sleep, feeling safe enough with Joe nearby to allow herself a quick nap. Sometime later she felt the cruiser draw to a halt, and she opened her eyes. Joe was still holding her hand.

"I told him to take us directly to the motel," he said quietly, releasing her fingers. "We'll get to a doctor after we eat, okay?" He probed her drowsy-looking eyes, wondering hotly what it would be like to touch and taste those full lips, molding them to his own.

"Fine." Annie rubbed her eyes and slowly sat up. She climbed out of the car, freezing cold slapping her full in the face, dissolving her grogginess. They both lifted their hands in thanks to the sheriff's deputy, who waved back, then began to pull away. Joe slid his hand around her elbow.

"I'll check us in," he said, pointing toward the neon Office sign. Gesturing across the icy street toward the restaurant, he added, "Then we'll eat."

"First I want to take a very long, very hot shower," Annie said. She wished for a change of clothes, too, but their personal gear had been left in the station wagon.

Joe nodded and opened the door to the motel office for her. More than anything, he longed to share a room with Annie. But it was a foolish thought, he knew. He'd get them separate rooms. Still, the look in Annie's eyes told him she needed to be held, that she wanted him. Dazed by the swift turn of events between them, Joe signed them in under the startled gaze of the proprietor. Uniformed military personnel didn't normally visit Bradley.

The first thing Annie did when she reached her small, warm room was to strip off her damp uniform and step into a steamy shower. How long she stood there, rivulets of hot water cascading down over her head, she had no idea. Slowly, the water revived her, taking away the small aches and pains from the crash and relaxing her tense muscles. Nearly an hour passed before Joe knocked on her door.

He smiled slightly when Annie emerged from the room. Her black hair was slick against her head, shining and damp beneath the porch light. Joe heaved an inner sigh of relief to see that some color had returned to her face. Without a word, he slipped his hand beneath her elbow and guided her across the street.

Ravenous, Annie ordered a sixteen-ounce steak, complete with a baked potato, a salad and French bread. She sat opposite Joe in a wooden booth, country music playing forlornly in the background. The restaurant was deserted except for a few sheriff's deputies, a state patrolman and themselves. Annie was grateful that the law-enforcement officials left them alone while they ate. Right now she knew that police were watching all the back roads leading into Bradley in case Gorman chose to try an easier, faster route into the small town.

The coffee was strong, hot and good, and she sipped it with relish. Joe looked dangerously handsome with a dark growth of beard shadowing his face. Annie could see the exhaustion in his eyes, but she also saw the constant alertness that overlaid his personal weariness. At heart he was a hunter, and under the circumstances, he was the stronger of them right now.

"I think I'm falling apart," Annie told him wryly, her hands wrapped around the mug.

"It hasn't exactly been a good day for us," Joe agreed. He cocked his head. Annie still looked washed out. He could see a number of scratches on the side of her face and neck where the windshield had shattered, cutting her with flying glass. "How are you feeling?"

"Like death warmed over. How about you?"

"The same." He ached to reach out and slide his hand along the smooth line of her jaw, but he didn't dare. Too many people were watching. "You did one hell of a job today. If you hadn't woken up when you did, Gorman could have killed both of us."

"I know...." Annie shook her head and held his burning gaze. "Joe?"

"Yes?"

Pursing her lips, she looked up at the ceiling above his head. "I—so much happened. The crash affected me a lot more than I first thought." She lowered her gaze and met his tender expression.

"What do you mean, honey?"

Honey. The word flowed sweetly through Annie's terror and tiredness. She dropped her gaze to the coffee mug in her hands. "I... well, I remember coming out of the darkness, and I heard Gorman hitting that door for all it was worth with his foot. I knew we were in big trouble, and I fought so hard to move, to act." She absently drew a design on the coffee mug with her finger. "I was afraid. Not for me, but for you."

"Me?" Joe frowned. He saw that Annie was wrestling with a lot of very real emotions. The word *honey* had escaped him unintentionally. He had no idea where it had come from. He knew it was far from professional, but his heart seemed to be taking control from his weary, benumbed brain.

With a shy little laugh, Annie raised her chin and reveled in the concern she saw in his gaze. "Somehow, the crash ripped away my real feelings for you—or something like that," she admitted. She hitched one shoulder upward. "I don't know...."

Wanting to reach out and grip her hand, Joe kept himself under very tight control. His heart started to pound slowly as he assimilated her words and the soft tremor of her voice. "Annie, what are you trying to say?" he asked, his voice husky.

Leaning back, she held his gaze. "I thought the past was still alive in me, that it hadn't yet been buried."

"Go on...."

Taking an unsteady breath, Annie whispered, "I lay there with that harness cutting into me, and I remember thinking, feeling, that if I didn't wake up soon enough, Gorman was going to kill you. I felt such panic, such a wild rush of feelings, that it snapped me awake." She watched as Joe's dark, unreadable expression changed, vulnerability touching the corners of his mouth. His eyes changed, too, from pointed intensity to banked coals of desire—for her. Annie felt his longing and she swallowed convulsively. No man had made her feel so shaky with need.

"I remember Gorman reaching into the front of the car, reaching for the riot gun, and out of pure instinct, I lifted my boot and smashed his hand against the glove box. I didn't care if he took it out on me, I just didn't want him to hurt you...." Tears flooded into Annie's eyes, and she quickly fought them back, blinking several times. Joe couldn't know just how much she was affected. At least, not yet. Gorman was loose, and tomorrow morning, regardless of the weather, they would be out on the front lines, hunting him down. They still could be killed.

Joe sat very still, watching Annie wrestle with a gamut of emotions. Her head was bowed, her hands clenched in her lap beneath the table. Every fiber in his body screamed at him to get up, go to her and hold her—that that was what she needed right now. And what he needed. Taking a deep ragged breath, he tightened his hands around the coffee mug. Pursing his lips, he watched her from beneath his spiky lashes. His heart was expanding with such joy and such fear that he thought he wouldn't be able to draw in another breath of air. As he nearly strangled on the intensity of his feelings for Annie, the silence grew heavy between them.

Suddenly, he spotted the waitress coming with their meals out of the corner of his eye. "Our food's coming," he muttered, moving his mug to one side. When Annie lifted her head, Joe saw the luminous quality of her dark, haunted eyes, and bitterness flooded him. He understood as few could what she was really feeling, reliving. She had loved a marine and had lost him in a war. And now, if he was correct, her feelings for him had come to the surface, and she was very much afraid of losing him in another kind of war.

"Let's talk later," he urged huskily.

Annie nodded, the huge lump in her throat preventing any attempt to speak. As the waitress smiled and delivered their orders, Annie realized she had lost her appetite. The threat of losing Joe made her gut tighten with such pain that the food no longer even smelled appealing to her. Numbly, she picked up the cutlery, her heart beating painfully with the fear of potential loss. Somehow, she went through the motions of cutting up the succulent steak and putting sour cream and butter on the steaming baked potato. But throughout the meal, she didn't dare meet Joe's gaze.

After dinner they made their way to the only medical office in town and got thoroughly checked over. When the doctor had told them that they were in remarkable shape despite the crash, Joe took Annie back to the motel. The main street in and out of town was now quiet, with a number of sheriff's cars parked here and there. They walked down the sidewalk, which was still icy in spots, bracing themselves against the cold and blustery wind.

At the motel, Joe pulled Annie to a stop in front of his room. "Let's go inside for a moment," he said in a low voice as he opened the door. Annie looked like hell, and he thought he knew why. When she stepped across the threshold into the warm room, he shut the door quietly behind them. Dropping the key on the table, he moved over to Annie and without hesitation placed his hands on her slumped shoulders. Her head was bowed, and he could tell the amount of pain she was carrying by how thin her lips had become.

"Annie," he said in a quiet voice, "look at me, please. . . ."

Steeling herself, Annie forced herself to look into Joe's shadowed blue eyes, which now burned with tenderness and concern. His hands were at once stabilizing and arousing, and she felt heat flowing across her shoulders, moving through her like hot, liquid sunlight, making her aware of just how male he was.

"What were you trying to say in the restaurant earlier?" he asked, his grip tightening slightly on her shoulders. Searching her cinnamon eyes, which were dark with pain, he went on, "I think I know, but I'm not sure, honey. And I sure as hell don't want to assume anything about you—or what might be. Do you understand?"

"Y-yes." Annie closed her eyes and swayed. She caught herself and placed her hands flat against his chest. Feeling his heart beating slow and strong beneath them, she tried to contain her escaping emotions. "Joe . . . this is so hard to say. . . ."

He gave her a small shake. "Then just say it, Annie. Please. . . ."

Tears stung her eyes, and even as she made a valiant attempt to stop them, they escaped, slipping from beneath her lashes. She felt them trickle warmly down her cheeks, and she parted her lips to try to speak. Instead, to her horror, a sob issued forth. Her hand flew to her lips, and she gazed up at Joe. Instantly, she felt his hands draw her forward. It was so easy to take that small half step into his arms. With a little moan, she leaned against him, feeling one of his hands slide from her shoulder along her neck to her hair and press her face against his shoulder.

Joe groaned, burying his face in Annie's soft tresses and inhaling deeply. He was breathing in life, not the tear of death—breathing in her special womanly scent combined with the fragrance of pine and the icy cleanness of the morning air. "Just let me hold you," he rasped unsteadily, sliding his other arm around her waist and drawing her even closer. Annie fit against him perfectly. For every contour of his hard, angular body, she had a soft, answering swell or valley, as if they were matching puzzle pieces that had finally been joined.

Shutting his eyes tightly, Joe allowed his shallow, ragged breathing to synchronize with hers. He felt her long, slim arms slowly wind around his waist as she surrendered to him. The moment was as surprising as it was delicious, and Joe savored it like a starving man too long denied real sustenance in his life. His mouth opened, then closed as he struggled to find words that could match the emotional exchange of their embrace. He felt Annie shudder once and he tightened his arms around her. She was crying, but silently—the kind of crying he'd done in the past when Maria had died. When Jenny had died.

"Let it out, Annie. Just let it go," he whispered brokenly, stroking her hair gently. "I'm here. I'll hold you...." And he did. Joe lost track of time, his exhaustion torn from him, the shock of the crash fading beneath the reality of Annie. All he was aware of—all he ever wanted—was right here in his arms: a woman with incredible strength, intelligence and vulnerability. *Annie.* He opened his mouth to speak, but again couldn't, so overwhelmed was he by a fierce avalanche of protectiveness. Tomorrow, Annie could be killed, just as Jenny had been. Or he could die. Life was so tenuous, such a risk, he realized, that it deserved to be lived only in the present moment.

Finally, her sobs lessened, and Joe led her over to the bed, drawing his handkerchief out of his back pocket. Annie sat down next to him, and he kept one arm around her shoulders as he pressed the cloth into her trembling hands.

"I—I'm sorry," Annie whispered as she blotted her eyes. "I shouldn't have cried...."

Joe absently ran his hand up and down her strong back. "You were in a wreck that could have killed us and you tracked a murderer until dark in freezing rain and snow." He gave her a wry look as she lifted her tear-bathed face to stare up at him. "Is it any wonder you want to cry, honey?"

Again, that one delicious word moved through her like an invisible hand, caressing her heart, freeing her imprisoned soul. "You didn't cry, Joe," she protested, pressing the handkerchief to her eyes again, absorbing his strength and steadiness where she felt none within her.

Leaning over, he dropped a kiss on her hair, the silk of the strands beneath his lips as strong yet as soft as Annie herself. "I wasn't the one who confronted Gorman, either," he reminded her in a roughened tone.

Annie felt Joe slide his hand to her jaw and cup it. Exerting very little pressure, he raised her chin, and she opened her eyes, tears still clinging to her lashes. His eyes were narrowed, burning with a stormy intensity. His large hand cradled her cheek, and Annie released a tremulous sigh, her lips parting. He was going to kiss her, and nothing had ever felt more right to her in her life. As he leaned down, her lashes fluttered closed and Annie strained upward—upward to meet his mouth, which molded hotly against her own.

Her world tilted and caught on fire. She burned beneath his fiery kiss, which stole her breath, started her heart pounding and heated her blood until she felt like so much molten rock beneath his slow, exploring hands. His breathing was ragged, punctuated against her flesh, and she opened her mouth, returning the strength of his kiss with her own strength, love and longing. Lost in the absorption of his firm mouth, matching his hunger with each heartbeat, Annie surrendered completely to Joe's exploration of her.

Their breath mated and became one. Their heartbeats synchronized into a pounding urgency. Their hands slid across each other in blind but sure exploration. Annie floated upon her senses, from the pine fragrance mingling with Joe's very male scent, to the taste of coffee on his lips, to the rough texture of his beard scraping the softness of her face. She remembered once when, as a young woman, she'd stood out on the New Mexico desert after Father Sun had disappeared, marveling at the fiery red, orange and pink sunset. Those colors, each vibrant, living entities in themselves, had seemed to reach out, to touch her and flow through her body until she became those scintillating hues, breathing in the approaching night sky and knowing she was one with the universe.

As Joe's mouth worshipped her lips, Annie realized that those wild, brilliant colors were once again inhabiting her. She had tapped into the pulse beat of Mother Earth, feeling it within the core of herself as a woman. She tasted the texture of Joe's lips, relishing their pressure and male-

ness against her softer, more giving skin, and absorbing
his barely controlled desire to take her and make her his
in every way.

Ever so gradually, Joe eased back from her lips, his eyes
hooded, burning with a fire that scorched the very fiber
of Annie's being. She slid her hands along the rough
stubble of his cheeks, still melting beneath his azure gaze.
She was the fire of the sunset; he was the darkening evening sky—dangerous, mysterious and beckoning.

As Joe grazed her brow with trembling fingers, pushing her mussed hair aside, Annie lost herself in his eyes,
his face, his touch. Never had she been moved like this,
made to feel as if she were of one breath, one heart, one
soul with another. And all he had done was kiss her! His
roving hands had stroked hungrily across her shoulders,
back and arms, inciting such a fierce ache deep within her
that all Annie could do now was stare up at him, still
caught in the splendor of their shared kiss.

Joe caressed Annie's cheek, relishing the soft pliancy of
her skin. Her cheeks burned with a deep pink color and
her eyes had gone nearly gold, her natural radiance re-
minding him of the iridescent, fragile beauty of a rainbow. He wanted to kiss her again, but he didn't dare. This
time, he knew, there would be no holding back, and that
wasn't fair to Annie—or to him. No, if he were to love her,
it would be when they were past this crisis, this terrible
danger that hung like a death sentence over their heads.

"You're so soft, so strong," he whispered hoarsely, and
placed his lips against her temple. He couldn't stand not
touching Annie one more time, but it had to be chaste, not
molten, to keep his wild desires in check.

Closing her eyes, Annie leaned against Joe, her head
coming to rest in the crook of his shoulder, his arms
wrapping around her once more. Placing her hand on his

chest, she sighed. "The way you kissed me," she whispered, "was so beautiful.... It was like Father Sky kissing Mother Earth."

Smiling gently, Joe rested his brow against her hair, content with simply holding Annie and knowing that she cared just as powerfully for him as he did for her. "Sounds beautiful," he mumbled.

Sliding her hand slowly up his arm, his shirt fabric offering a rough texture beneath her fingers, she said, "You are beautiful. There's so much of the earth in you."

Chuckling, Joe pressed a kiss to her hair. "I'm assuming those are all compliments."

Lifting her head, Annie eased away from him enough to see the smile in his eyes. For the first time she was getting to see him without any of the hard, tough walls that all marines erected to protect themselves. She took his hand and held it in hers. "They are. Somehow, I knew that about you, though."

Joe nodded, simply enjoying the feel of her hand caressing his. Annie's fingers were long, expressive and gentle as she stroked him. "I haven't been able to hide much from you from the beginning, have I?"

Her lips lifted tenderly in a smile and she held his gaze, feeling as if warm honey was being poured through her, awakening her and making her yearn fiercely for him in all ways. "No. But I understand why you had to be that way with me."

His fingers wrapped strongly around Annie's hands, and he frowned. "Tomorrow," he rasped, "we're going to have to be very careful, honey. *Very* careful."

Swallowing painfully, she whispered, "Both of us, Joe."

He wanted so badly to tell her so much. His heart was brimming over, threatening to burst with such joy that he didn't know how to contain it or express it. Instead, he brought her fingers to his lips and kissed them. In his heart, he knew he was in love with Annie. There was no denying it now, nor did Joe want to. But time wasn't on their side right now. He closed his eyes and moved her hand against his cheek, soaking up her softness, her womanliness.

Annie sat in Joe's arms, tears coming to her eyes as she saw peace descend over his rugged, bearded face. They had gone through so much so quickly together. The prickly roughness of his beard chafed pleasantly against her fingers and a gnawing ache filled her as never before. His hair was mussed, strands of it falling across his broad brow. Right now, as an answering peace filled her, Annie knew it was Joe's spirit that gave her strength. The spirit of his heart and soul were one with hers. She leaned her head against his shoulder and closed her eyes.

Tomorrow was an unknown. A deadly time in their lives. Who would live? Who would die? She had no way of knowing. And neither did Joe.

Chapter Eleven

Annie saw the police cars, military-police vehicles and sheriff's cruisers gathering outside their motel. It was 0600, and the search was slated to begin in less than half an hour. She had just finished putting on her uniform, noticing while she had that her hands trembled as she buckled on the web belt that carried her holster and pistol. Her heart was bleeding with the fear of possibly losing Joe today as they tried to locate and recapture Gorman.

Her mouth still tingled in memory of that branding kiss that had made her breath, her heartbeat, one with his. Afterward, she had returned to her room and slept deeply—a healing sleep. Annie knew why. She was beginning to open up her heart again to the possibility that love could come into her life. Maybe brig chasing was as dangerous—or more so—than going to war, but the power of her feelings for Joe were simply too strong to be cast aside. Instead, they bubbled like brilliant sunlight dancing across the western horizon, awakening the world—and her own dormant senses, which she'd thought had died with Jeff.

A knock sounded on the connecting door between her room and Joe's. She hesitated fractionally, then swung around to open it. Never had she needed to see Joe more than now. Once they stepped outside that door, she knew they had to be utterly professional, part of the huge manhunt being initiated to locate Gorman. They wouldn't dare give each other soft looks, touch hands or allow the wealth of their feelings to spill over in any way. No, all that must now be set aside. It had to be that way, because Annie knew that if either of them allowed their emotions and growing love for each other to take precedence, it could ruin their focus and distract their attention. And they could end up wounded or dead. Gorman was the type to take advantage of any small lapse of concentration and turn it to his benefit.

Opening the door, Annie stepped aside. Joe looked so strong and confident as he stood there, freshly shaven, his hair recently washed and combed. Her heart fluttered as his gaze met and gently snared hers. Her lips parting, Annie felt the powerful blanket of his love spilling over her, warming and protecting her and making her feel more hopeful.

Joe moved into Annie's room and glanced down at her. "We've only got a few minutes," he said quietly, "and I wanted to see how you were feeling before we have to go out there." He didn't want to touch Annie, but the bereft look on her face made him reach out for her. His hand settled on her arm and, to his surprise and pleasure, she moved into his arms, swiftly fitting against him as he'd always expected the woman he loved would do.

With a groan, he wrapped his arms around her and simply held her. Her arms were around his waist and her head rested in the hollow of his shoulder. He inhaled deeply, aware of the fragrance of the soap she'd used for her shower, aware of her sweet, feminine scent that always drove him crazy with need. Moving his hand slowly up and down her back, Joe marveled at the strength of Annie's limber body. She was strong in so many ways.

Annie drew in a ragged breath, her eyes tightly closed as she savored Joe's strong presence. The fabric beneath her cheek was rough against her skin, but she didn't care. Moments like this were few, and like a greedy miser, she wanted to hoard each one Joe offered. When his hand moved gently up and down her back, she felt some of the tension she carried miraculously dissolve. He was healing for her, and Annie stood in his arms, amazed at the discovery. Jeff's touch had never evoked that kind of feeling.

"Joe," she quavered in a low voice, "I'm scared. More scared than I've ever been."

"I know. So am I," he rasped, and pressed a kiss to Annie's temple, the damp strands of her hair silky beneath his lips.

Easing away just enough to meet and hold his dark, stormy gaze, which was filled with desire, Annie admitted, "I've never felt like this—not even with Jeff." Looking toward the door that would lead out to the gathering of law-enforcement officials, Annie added, "I was never this afraid." Twisting to look up at Joe, she felt his hands move in a soothing motion across her tense shoulders.

"It won't be easy for either of us out there this morning," he told her, "but we've got to do it, Annie. We care too much for each other to do any less."

Bowing her head, she nodded. "You're right...."

"I wish we didn't have to," he added unhappily as he lightly stroked her cheek, wanting so badly to love her, to share what he felt with her on every level. He saw her lips curve upward slightly and drowned in her understanding eyes. "I want to be anywhere but here, honey. I want— God, I want to tell you so much, share so much with you, but I can't. At least not yet."

And maybe never. The icy awareness made Annie shiver.

A sharp, authoritative knock at Annie's door made her jump, her fingers closing convulsively on Joe's jacket. Uttering a gasp, she felt her heart begin to beat erratically. Their time together was over. Perhaps forever.

Joe glared at the door, then looked down at Annie, his expression growing tender. "Listen to me," he rasped, framing her face, "you stick close to me today and concentrate on your work. We'll be a team out there. I'm not going to let them separate us. Understand?"

She closed her eyes, the heat of tears filling them. "Y-yes. Joe..."

Whispering her name like a reverent prayer, Joe bent down and captured her parted lips with his mouth. It was a swift, molten kiss meant to indelibly communicate to Annie just how much he cared for her. He was afraid to say the word *love* because the awareness of it had dawned on him so suddenly. But Joe honored his feelings by sharing them with Annie the best way he knew how. They had to get through today, and maybe tomorrow, in one piece and alive. Then and only then would he be able to come to Annie and lay his feelings fully before her.

Annie's mouth was soft, pliant and hot beneath his. He felt her moan, a fine, vibrating sound that moved through her and translated like sunlight into his body and heart.

There was nothing shy or retiring about her returning kiss, and Joe languished in Annie's own honesty and ability to share her feelings with him in this most delicious and silent language. He wanted more of her. Starved, he captured her face with his hands, framing it and tilting her head back a little farther beneath his shameless exploration. Like a beggar who knew that at any moment the food would be snatched away from him, he kissed her hard and long, taking as well as giving.

Annie swayed and reached out to grip Joe's arm as he finally tore his mouth from hers. They were both breathing erratically, and she saw the glitter of need deep in his stormy blue eyes, felt it in the way he placed his hands on her shoulders. She was his. There was no mistaking the fact. As much as Annie applauded men and women being equals in all ways, she understood for the first time the primitive link between mates. Joe's look was protective, claiming her as his own, and the expression on his face was daunting. The realization shook her, even as it made her feel steadier within herself, and she took in a long, deep breath to reorient herself to the present. Back to the job at hand.

"Let's go," Joe rasped, his voice unsteady. His mouth tingled wildly after their kiss. He wanted to devour Annie with all of this volcanic power that was surging through him. The feelings combined the physical and the emotional in a molten mix, and Joe didn't know how to contain any of it. He tried to rearrange his face in its usual merciless, brig-chaser expression. But inside he was like liquid lava, mingling such desire and tenderness that he felt helpless in a way he never had before.

It was Annie, Joe humbly realized as he opened the door of his motel room and entered the fray of law-enforcement vehicles and personnel. She was like the warm, yielding, fertile earth and he was like a dormant seed just waiting to be showered with her care, the moistness of her mouth, the coaxing of her lips and nurturing of her hands, which had roved across his body with such reverent adoration and need.

The cold morning air slapped him in the face, providing just the jolt he needed to cap his roiling emotions and desires. He glanced down to see Annie walking at his side.

Joe was amazed at how serene she looked. Moments ago, he'd seen the gold dancing in her cinnamon eyes. A man could go crazy with desire simply from staring into her rich brown eyes. But now her entire face was carefully arranged in a stoic nonexpression, designed to hide her real feelings. Still, Joe felt as if he were walking on air, as if he'd been released from some dark prison that had fallen around him from the day Jenny died.

Annie had helped him achieve his freedom, and for that he was more than grateful. As he moved toward the sheriff's car where all the main parties who would take part in the manhunt were gathering, Joe savored their last kiss. Silently, he promised Annie that no matter what happened today, he would never place her in jeopardy as he had Jenny. He would die himself or take the bullet, but he would not allow her to become a target. He loved her. He wanted a life with her after this manhunt too much to do less.

The sky was a clear, deep blue, with scudding white-and-gray clouds just barely showing on the eastern horizon. The front had passed, and with its passing came warmer temperatures. Joe was surprised how fast the cold fled as he and Annie tracked their way north of Bradley. Two hours earlier, Annie had picked up barely perceptible footprints that could only belong to Gorman. Worse, they'd discovered before the search started this morning that the chains he'd been wearing had been found earlier by a sheriff's deputy. Evidently, Gorman had broken into a farmer's barn and used a pair of wire cutters to free himself.

To their left, about half a mile away, a team from the sheriff's department searched. To their right was a state-police team. Coming from the direction of Bradley was another team with several bloodhounds, trying to pick up a fresh scent on Gorman. No one could tell for sure where he might be. For all Joe knew as he walked slowly and quietly, his gaze moving steadily from side to side as Annie tracked ahead of him, Gorman could have frozen to death last night. They just didn't know.

The helicopter armed with heat-sensing equipment had developed engine problems overnight, and another one from Sacramento had been needed in the search for a little girl lost during the unexpected snowstorm in the Siskiyou Mountains north of the city. They were on their own, though Joe wished fervently that the infrared equipment had been available so all these search parties wouldn't be necessary. Instead, they had to find Gorman the old-fashioned way.

The canopy of trees kept most of the sunlight at bay, so a gloomy light surrounded them. Last night's ice had nearly melted, and the forest was eerily quiet. As Annie tracked, hunched over and looking for telltale signs of Gorman's footprints, Joe wondered if she would be able to continue to follow him if the ice melted completely. Then he remembered how easily she'd seen those prints in the sandy soil of Reed.

The trees opened up to reveal a small stream gurgling happily over rocks. Joe stopped when Annie stopped, about twenty feet ahead of him. The stream was nearly a hundred feet wide and very shallow. Ten-foot-high bushes lined the banks, so thick they were almost impenetrable. Under any other circumstance, it would be a breathtaking winter scene worthy of a picture postcard, with the ice glittering like diamonds on the branches. Joe stood alert, pistol in hand, as Annie slowly moved her gaze downstream. What was she sensing? Today they all had small radios attached to the left epaulets of their uniforms. With just the push of a button they could be in contact with everyone else, should something go wrong.

Slowly approaching her, Joe kept alert. His heart was pounding more than usual, and he felt danger. As Annie turned toward him, her eyes were narrowed and questioning. Her pistol was holstered, and both her hands were gloved to keep her fingers warm, though she'd often removed the gloves to lean down and touch the mud or pine needles as she searched for a print.

"What is it?" Joe asked, his voice barely above a whisper.

"I don't know...." She frowned and moved to the right a few steps, sensing, feeling. The hair on the back of her neck was standing on end. Instinctively, she unsnapped the holster, took off her gloves and pulled out the pistol. She locked and loaded it, the snap of the bullet going into the chamber sounding like a small shot.

Joe stood patiently, in tune with the way Annie worked. He realized that part of her skill was actually finding physical footprints, a bent twig, a piece of bark recently fallen from a tree; but the other part, the intangible part that had made her a legendary tracker, was a sixth sense capable of feeling the presence of danger or the direction an escaped prisoner had gone. He saw her eyes narrow to mere slits as she moved to the edge of the stream, near the heavy bush still covered with a coating of ice. Earlier, the sheriff had warned them that this was black-bear country, and that thickets of berry bushes afforded bears food during the late-summer months. For Joe, the thick brush was dangerous because they couldn't see through it. Anything, even Gorman, could be hiding there.

The midafternoon sun was bright overhead, and Joe welcomed the surprising warmth that followed the storm. The sky had completely cleared to a deep blue, and the overwhelming fragrance of pine encircled him. In the distance, he could hear the baying of the bloodhounds. Had they picked up a recent scent on Gorman? He hoped so. Though he stepped carefully, Joe slid a little, the ground muddy beneath his boots. The gurgling of the stream was dangerous despite his heightened alertness because the sound drowned out other, perhaps more important noises. Ice covered the shore at the edge of the stream, and the black rocks were shiny where water raced over them.

Annie crouched down, reaching out with her left hand to touch something on the ground. Joe waited, making a quarter turn to the left, watching the thickets and still sensing that something was wrong. But what?

The hair on Annie's neck stood straight up, and a chill shot down her spine. Automatically, she straightened, sensing danger behind her. Whirling around, her mouth open to shout a warning, she saw Dutch Gorman leap from the thickets—onto Joe! Stunned, she watched the convict attack from behind, Joe's pistol flying from his hand. The two men landed with a heavy thud on the ground, mud and ice flying in all directions.

Shocked, Annie stood frozen for a second. She saw Gorman cock his fist and jerk Joe onto his back. The sickening sound of bone connecting with bone startled her into action. Everything seemed to be happening in slow motion. Digging her heels into the mud, Annie slipped, landing sprawled out across the wet ground. The pistol remained in her hand.

To her horror, she saw Gorman leap off Joe and lunge for the fallen pistol.

"No!" she shrieked, scrambling to her knees to draw a bead on Gorman before he could reach it. Too late!

Joe had gotten up and, seeing what Gorman was doing, threw himself onto the convict just as the other man grabbed the pistol.

Annie sobbed, getting to her feet, both hands on her pistol as Joe and Gorman rolled around on the ground once again, locked in a deadly embrace. Gorman had the pistol. He could use it against Joe! Breathing raggedly, Annie tried to steady herself, steady her hands as she followed the tumbling men through her sights. It was impossible to get a clear shot at Gorman without endangering Joe. Torn, she wanted to race toward them, but what good would that do? She had to stay back, poised and ready to take whatever advantage appeared.

The hardest seconds of Annie's life passed as she listened to the two men's fists landing on each other. Blood spouted from Gorman's nose as Joe delivered a right cross that knocked the convict to one side. Joe got to his knees, but not in time. Gorman lunged upward, swinging the butt of the pistol in a sharp arc. Annie cried out as she saw it connect solidly with Joe's jaw. She saw him stagger and fall backward, blood spouting from a gash on the right side of his chin.

"Hold it!" Annie shrieked, pointing the pistol, her feet planted far apart to brace herself. Her finger brushed the trigger just as Gorman lunged for Joe. His abrupt move made her wait. To her horror, she saw Gorman jerk Joe into a sitting position, the barrel of the gun pressed to his temple.

"Put it down, bitch!" the convict roared. He clamped his hand on Joe's shoulder and jerked him to his feet, the barrel pressed against his temple. "Put it down or I'll kill him!"

Gorman's voice rolled through the area like thunder. Annie gulped, her breathing hard and erratic. Joe seemed to be semiconscious, leaning against Gorman, his eyes barely open, blood dripping down the side of his jaw onto his uniform.

Joe frantically tried to clear his mind. He felt Gorman's hand like a talon sinking into his shoulder, keeping him upright on his rubbery knees. His head whirled with darkness then light, stars dancing before his barely opened eyes. Gorman's voice was like a deep report of a cannon going off beside him. He felt the cold gun barrel digging into his temple, felt the pain as Gorman jammed it against his head. *Annie!* Oh, God, Annie! Fighting for clarity, Joe steadied himself. Gorman shoved him upright and forced him to stand.

"Drop it!" Gorman roared again. "Or your buddy here is gonna buy the farm."

His vision clearing, Joe blinked rapidly. His right eye was swelling shut from the blow Gorman had given him, but he could see Annie fifty feet away, her legs spread apart, arms extended, aiming her pistol at them. He saw the terror in her eyes and in the single line of her tortured mouth. Gorman was breathing harshly, cursing and jamming the barrel against Joe's temple.

"Tell the bitch to put her gun down," Gorman rasped in his ear.

"Go to hell." Joe braced himself. Gorman cursed and jerked him back, nearly off his feet. No matter what happened, Annie mustn't put down her pistol, Joe thought groggily. She couldn't. He regained his balance, his mind still gyrating and stunned. He had to think clearly!

"You put that pistol down or I'm gonna blow your partner away, bitch!"

What should he do? Joe blinked rapidly, scrambling to think. He felt warm liquid dripping off his jaw, felt the pain starting to move upward. But the pain cleared his head, and that was good. For a brief second out of time, Joe realized that Annie was in the exact position he'd been in when Jenny had been taken hostage. And in that moment he understood exactly what Jenny must have felt. So many plans raced through his mind and were rapidly discarded.

Joe knew that, according to regulations, Annie could never drop her gun. He saw the slitted look of her eyes, saw the terror for him in them, but knew that no matter what happened, she must not capitulate to Gorman's request. Knowing karate, Joe wondered if he had a chance to connect a swift, hard blow. But out of the corner of his eye, he could see Gorman's finger brushing the trigger. There was every risk Gorman could accidentally shoot him even if he was jostled. Helplessly, Joe looked at Annie. He felt Gorman's fingers dig hard into his shoulder.

"Tell her to drop her weapon!" the man roared in his ear. Jerking Joe hard, he yelled, "Now!"

Anger funneled through Joe, hot and nearly uncontrollable. "Annie," he called out, "don't drop your pistol!"

Joe's cry echoed eerily through the forest around her. Annie saw Gorman's face turn purple with fury, saw him cock the pistol against Joe's temple. What should she do? Her hands damp and sweaty, she worked hard to draw a bead on Gorman's bobbing, constantly moving head. But Gorman wasn't stupid. He knew that if he remained still, she'd get a clear shot and fire.

Gorman had two choices—whip the gun away from Joc's temple and shoot her, or shoot Joe and use his body as shelter against the bullet she'd fire at him. What would he do? Her throat threatened to close with terror. Her mouth was dry. Her heart rate skyrocketed. If she missed Gorman, she might kill Joe. It was that easy, that terrible. Her fingers were becoming cramped, her arms heavy from holding her outstretched position far too long. Annie felt a fine tremor begin along them, warning her that her strength was fading.

Joe had made the decision to act. It would probably cost him his life, but he was damned if Annie was going to die. Jenny had died because of his indecision at the wrong moment. He loved Annie too much to allow that to happen to her. He met and held her terrified gaze for a split second, wanting that look to convey everything he felt for her—all the dreams they'd probably never have together, all the hopes dashed and destroyed. His lips parted and he wanted to cry out, *I love you. God, I love you so much!* But no words passed through his flattened lips, only harsh breathing strangled with rage, hatred and grief.

Annie was breathing hard, aware of every pounding beat of her heart as she lifted her arms just a fraction of an inch more. She prayed for steadiness, for accuracy. There was no choice left as she saw the hatred glaze Gorman's small, black eyes. She saw his finger begin to twitch and knew he was going to kill Joe. She couldn't let it happen. She had to take the greatest risk of all. In that split second before she squeezed the trigger, pointing at

Gorman's bobbing head, she knew unequivocally that she loved Joe.

The pistol jerked, barked, and Annie felt the reverberation all the way up her stiff arms to her shoulders. Her eyes widened and she saw Joe fall to the left and Gorman to the right. Had Gorman shot him? She had no idea as she watched both men fall to the ground. Holding the pistol in position, she kept her eyes on Gorman. When he rolled onto his back, she saw a faint bloodstain on the side of his head, the pistol he'd held falling nervelessly from his fingers. Had she killed him? She'd never wanted to kill anyone. And Joe! What about Joe? Annie didn't dare devote attention to him. Not yet.

With one swift kick, she sent the pistol sailing out of range of Gorman's reach. He lay unconscious on the ground, arms and legs spread out from his body. Breathing raggedly, Annie got close enough to realize that the shot she'd fired had creased the line of Gorman's skull, knocking him unconscious. Thank God, she hadn't killed him. Relief zigzagged through her. Leaning down with one hand, she jerked the cuffs she carried out of her web belt. With a shaking hand, she snapped them closed over one of Gorman's thick wrists.

Assured that their prisoner was really unconscious and not faking the condition, Annie holstered her pistol, rolled him over onto his stomach and brought both arms behind him. Snapping the second cuff into position, she took a quick breath. Gorman was no longer a threat. Wiping her mouth shakily, Annie turned, afraid of what she might see. Joe . . .

Joe sat up with a groan, his hand automatically moving to the cut on his jaw where Gorman had hit him with the butt of the pistol. He saw Annie turn, her face taut and pale, her gaze pinned anxiously on his as she moved quickly to where he sat. She knelt down, a trembling hand falling on his shoulder.

"A-are you all right?" Her voice was terribly off-key.

Joe gave her a long look filled with relief. "Yeah, just a little shook up." He reached up, touching her cheek. "And you? Are you okay?"

Her mouth stretching into a half smile, Annie whispered, "I'm going to be okay." Joe's hand felt so steadying, so alive and filled with promise against her cheek. He kept touching her, as if he didn't believe this was real, that they were real. *Safe. They were safe.* The words spun in her head, and she gulped for air, grateful just to have survived along with Joe.

Trying to get a handle on his raw emotions, Joe looked around. "Have you contacted the others?"

"Not yet. Let's get you someplace dry. Come on, I'll help you up," Annie offered, stretching out her hand. His fingers, muddied and bloody, wrapped around hers, and she planted her feet in the mud, bracing herself against his weight. Annie saw that he was still a little wobbly. "Come on over here to this log. I'll make the call as soon as you sit back down."

Joe sat heavily, his head spinning, his ears still ringing from the blows Gorman had given him. "You did one hell of a job," he rasped, looking up at her.

Annie divided her attention between Gorman and Joe. Never had adrenaline flowed so powerfully through her, and her own knees felt terribly wobbly in the aftermath. "I was lucky," she said, but her voice cracked. Choking back a sob, she pressed the button and called both nearby search parties, giving their location. After that, she called for a rescue helicopter. Joe was looking very pale, and she was worried about him. Gorman was still unconscious, but even in that state he scared the hell out of her.

Moving back to Joe's side, she took out a dressing from a small first-aid pack she carried on her web belt. As she sat down next to him on the large, fallen log, he turned to her.

"It's over, isn't it?"

Numbly, she nodded and gently pressed the dressing to the bloody cut on his jaw. "Y-yes."

Joe held his hand on the dressing to keep it in place. He searched Annie's upturned face minutely, as if memorizing it for the rest of his life. Reaching over, he gripped the hand that she clenched tensely on her thigh. There was so much he wanted to say. So much. Instead, he gave her a lopsided smile, hoping she would understand just how much he loved her. She offered a wobbly smile in return, her fingers strong around his.

"That was some shooting you did," Joe said finally, hearing a helicopter approaching rapidly from the south.

"I was so afraid of hitting you." Choking back the tears, Annie rasped, "He was starting to pull the trigger to kill you, Joe. I saw him doing it. I didn't have a choice." She buried her face in her hands and hunched over.

"You *didn't* have a choice, honey," Joe agreed. "It's okay," he whispered raggedly, placing his arm around her bent shoulders and drawing her against him. To hell with it. He didn't care if the law-enforcement officials found him holding Annie. Some things were more important than damned protocol. Burying his face in her thick black hair, he felt tears leaking into his eyes. Annie was sobbing loudly, clinging to him, her face pressed against his chest.

As he sat holding her tightly in his arms, Joe realized that his life had changed forever. Last time, it had been him at the other end of the gun. Now he'd been in Jenny's place, and Annie in his. Thank God she hadn't pan-icked, hadn't missed the shot as he had. Bitterness coated Joe's mouth, but he finally accepted his responsibility in Jenny's death. They had each done what they thought right. He hadn't tried to escape from the prisoner as Jenny had. Maybe that's what had made the diffcrence: Gor-man had been less of a moving target. Joe didn't have any final answers, knowing only that the woman he held in his arms was someone he wanted at his side for the rest of his life.

Looking up, blinking away the tears, Joe saw the heli-copter approaching. He eased Annie from his arms.

"We need to release the smoke so the chopper can land," he told her thickly.

Brushing the last of her tears away, Annie nodded and quickly snapped back into her expected marine de-meanor. Six years in the corps, training in some way every day of those years, made her able to move through the motions to bring the helicopter to a safe landing not far from where they stood. She released the canister that sent dark yellow smoke skyward, telling the helicopter pilot where to land and which way the wind was blowing.

Joe, too, snapped back into his professional mode as both search parties converged at the same time on their position. While Annie brought the helicopter in for a landing, he conversed with the law-enforcement offi-cials. He was proud of Annie and told them what had happened. Covered with mud, his uniform filthy, all Joe wanted was a hot bath, clean clothes and some time alone with Annie. But he knew that wouldn't happen soon, be-cause they would both have to fly back to Sacramento and place Gorman in the sheriff's facility there until the Ne-vada brig-chasing team could transport him on to Fort Leavenworth.

The wash of the rotor blades blasted the assembled group of figures huddled around Gorman, who was now becoming conscious. Joe took great pleasure in pulling the convict to his feet, glaring into his eyes and pushing him toward the helicopter. There, Gorman was again shackled and put in the rear seat between Joe and Annie. Judging from the way Gorman looked, he wasn't going to put up any fight, dazed as he was from the crease in his skull. Joe noticed that as Annie came on board the helicopter, Gorman's eyes went wide with respect. At least now the convict knew that her being a woman didn't mean she couldn't handle men like him. A bit of a grin leaked out the corners of Joe's mouth as the helicopter gained speed and took off toward Sacramento.

Chapter Twelve

The last place Joe wanted to be was in a bed at the Camp Reed hospital—but it was the first place Captain Ramsey ordered him upon their return from Sacramento. Unhappily, Joe picked at the light blue spread across the bed. Though he was in a room large enough for four patients, he was the only one in it. Out the window, he could see bright desert sunlight, the blue sky marked by high, wispy clouds. Normal marine activities were being carried on.

Dr. Karen David had been firm, as she'd sewed up the six-inch cut on his jaw, about Joe spending at least twenty-four hours in the hospital under observation. Captain Ramsey had been there, too, and had grimly agreed with the doctor. Of course, all of Joe's attention, his heart, was focused on Annie, who had been taken to another cubicle for examination. He hadn't seen her since, and that had been last evening. Damn, but he missed her. Where was she? Joe had already bugged the corpswave on the floor nearly to death about finding out if Annie was at the hospital, and she wasn't. She'd been released after being examined.

Joe was fuming when he heard his door open. He quickly looked toward it in time to see Annie slip through, a shy smile on her face. To his delight, she was out of uniform and in civilian clothes, wearing a pale pink blouse and a soft denim skirt that fell to her ankles. Simple light brown sandals encased her feet. Meeting and holding her warm gaze, Joe felt his heart begin a slow, hard pounding in his chest. He grinned crookedly and sat up.

"You're a sight for sore eyes," he said in way of greeting.

Annie laughed softly and put her white purse on the table. "And I hear you're like a caged lion up here, raising all kinds of ruckus." Melting beneath his hot, hungry look, she moved forward, her hand outstretched. Instantly, Joe grasped it and pulled her to the side of his bed. His right eye was still swollen shut in shades of black and purple. The side of his jaw was hidden under a clean white dressing.

"Sort of," Joe admitted. "I lost track of you last night. That doctor had me wheeled from X-ray to the lab and all over the damned place. When they took me back to emergency, you were gone."

"I know." Annie liked the feel of Joe's hand around hers. She touched her hair a little nervously. "I wanted to stick around, but Captain Ramsey was pacing back and forth with worry for you. I—" she compressed her lips and looked down at Joe "—I didn't want him to know—about us, I mean...."

Lifting her hand, Joe kissed the back of it. Annie smelled of sunshine and her own special womanly scent. Her cinnamon eyes danced with joy, and she was radiant. He saw her lips part as he kissed her hand again, then grasped it in both of his.

"There was so much I wanted to say to you yesterday," he growled, "but we were always busy with either law-enforcement types or the damned reporters up in Sacramento."

"It's okay, Joe. We were tired and overwhelmed." Annie reached over and gently touched the dressing. "How are you doing?"

"I'm going to do fine now that you're here," he muttered. Picking up her captive hand, Joe smiled up at her, even though it hurt to move his facial muscles. "And you were right: yesterday was a special hell all its own. I'm just glad we're home—safe and almost sound."

Sobering, Annie nodded. She sat on the edge of the bed and faced him. "I'm still reeling from it all," she admitted quietly, and touched her blouse above her heart. "I was glad when Captain Ramsey told me to take the next two days off. I feel shattered, Joe."

He ran his hand down her arm and laced his fingers through hers. "A lot did happen yesterday." His voice became deep and thoughtful. "And we need time to sort it all out, Annie." As he held her luminous gaze, he felt that all his life he'd been starving, and now he was being fed by her mere presence.

"Yes," Annie whispered. Looking away for a moment, she turned and faced Joe's serious expression. "Remember how afraid I was before? That I didn't have whatever it took to reach out to you the way you were reaching out to me?"

"I remember." He saw the pain in Annie's face and realized she was close to tears.

"Well," she began, clearing her throat, "when I had to face Gorman with that pistol to your head, the past sort of dissolved. I realized as I stood there how much I cared for you, how awful life would be without you around." Shrugging, Annie gave him a shy look. "After you kissed me that night, Joe, I sort of went into a crazy spin with my feelings. When I thought Gorman was going to kill you, I knew. I just knew...."

Joe didn't have the courage to ask what Annie knew. He simply continued to hold her hand, grazing the back of it slowly with his thumb. "We've been through an awful lot in a compressed amount of time," he agreed. "But what we discovered through it all, honey, was each other. I want to be real clear about my intentions toward you. This didn't happen overnight."

Annie gulped back tears. "I—I realize that now. I think from the first moment I met you, Joe, something happened here—in my heart. You were so angry and upset when we first met, and I took the blame for it."

"I know," he confessed, "and I'm sorry, Annie. I really am. I had no right to take my anger out on you. It wasn't your fault Captain Ramsey had you transferred here." He smiled slightly. "I'm glad he did, though."

Annie got up and moved quietly to the window, her hands resting behind her back. The silence deepened, but it wasn't a harsh silence, rather one that promised more serenity as time went on. Finally she turned back toward Joe, her voice husky with feeling. "The last two days have upended my orderly life. When you kissed me, nothing had ever felt so right to me. But then I had to wonder if it felt right to you, too." Looking up, she held his dark gaze. "I'm afraid, Joe. Afraid of my feelings, because this is something new, something different this time. I—I thought I loved Jeff, and I'm sure I did, but..." She opened her palms and gave him a helpless look.

Joe's mouth tightened. "Come here," he entreated, and held out his hand to her.

Annie came forward and slid her hand into his. She allowed Joe to guide her to his bed and help her sit down, so that she faced him again.

"I don't have all the answers, Annie. I just know that life isn't worth a damn without you being part of it. Maybe things will settle down at Reed so we have time to get over the shock of what's happened to us with Gorman."

"We are still in shock," Annie agreed. She ached to lean over and kiss Joe, to feel all that heat, strength and tenderness again being shared with her. But now was not the time or place.

"Captain Ramsey said he'd drop by sometime today. I'm going to ask him for a couple days of leave." Joe raised his eyes to hers. "I want to get away from this place in order to heal, Annie, and I want you to come with me."

Startled, she stared at him. "But...where?"

"There's a great place along the coast, a bed and breakfast near Monterey Bay where I'd like to take you. We'll get separate rooms, if that's what you want, and we'll spend the time walking the beach, holding hands and talking—without interruption or worry about Camp Reed people watching us or starting gossip."

Annie knew only too well how gossip could hurt both their careers. She smiled softly. "I like the idea, Joe. But Captain Ramsey will know."

"I don't care if he knows."

"He'll split us up as a team, and I'll be put in another section."

"Yes, and I don't like it any more than you do, but that's the breaks," Joe said unhappily. He reached out and slid his hand along the clean line of her jaw. There was such beauty combined with sadness in Annie's eyes. Without a doubt, if they became close personally—and Joe knew they were heading that direction—that kind of fraternization wasn't allowed. Annie would have to be sent to another section, unless maybe, just maybe, he could convince Captain Ramsey to leave things as is. That was the future, however. Right now, all Joe wanted was some quality time, a few uninterrupted days with Annie. They both deserved it.

"When the captain visits, I'm going to ask for both of us," Joe counseled, wanting to do more than hold Annie's soft, strong hand. "Let's just take this a day at a time, okay?"

A day at a time. Annie nodded. "I'll be at home resting up. I didn't get much sleep last night because of all the excitement, the worry...." Worry for Joe and his condition. She saw the look in his eyes as they turned stormy, signaling a raw hunger for her that made Annie feel weak and shaky inside.

Forcing himself not to reach up and kiss her, Joe rasped, "Why don't you go home and rest? I'll call you this evening."

The phone was ringing. Annie jerked up from where she was sleeping on the couch in the living room. The picture window showed that darkness had already fallen, the marsh was no longer visible. Fumbling for the phone, she sat up.

"Hello?" she said breathlessly.

"Annie? It's Joe. You sound like I woke you up."

She smiled a little and rubbed her face with her hand. "I was sleeping. What time is it?"

"Twenty-one-hundred hours."

"I slept a long time," she murmured in surprise. Tucking her legs beneath her, she smiled. "You sound better. Did Captain Ramsey come by?"

"Yes, that's why I'm calling. He's cutting orders tomorrow morning to give us three days of leave—together."

Annie blinked away the remnants of sleep. "He knows?"

"Everything."

Annie didn't know what "everything" meant, and she was afraid to ask. Resting her elbow on the curve of the couch, she said, "How did he take it?"

"I think he was a little surprised, but he's head over heels in love with Libby Tyler, so he was pretty understanding about our situation."

"I'm so glad...."

"He's a decent officer," Joe said. "Look, I already made reservations for us at the Sandpiper Inn up at Monterey Bay."

"You did?"

He laughed deeply. "You don't think a man can handle a reservation?" he teased.

There was such joy in Joe's laugh that Annie laughed with him. "Of course! It's just so sudden...."

"Ever since we've met, that's been the operative word with us, Annie. Why should it be any different this time?"

He was right, Annie realized. "So what have you planned?"

"Tomorrow morning I get released from the hospital at 0800. I'm going to go home, put on some civilian clothes, pack and then pick you up around 0930. Then we're off for three days of heaven. Are you game?"

Was she? Excitement thrummed through Annie and she smiled softly. "I'm game, Joe. I'll see you at 0930...."

* * *

The Sandpiper Inn was a large Victorian house half a mile from the coast, surrounded by gnarled, grotesque-looking pines that seemed like huge bonsai trees gone awry. Annie stood out on her room's small wooden balcony, deeply inhaling the salt air. It was evening, and the sun was shining brightly on the western horizon. The Pacific Ocean had turned a glittering, shimmering gold color as the rays of the sun caressed the smooth surface. White sea gulls with black-tipped wings endlessly patrolled the beach, looking for morsels.

An incredible peace blanketed Annie as she stood there, her hands on the white rail. Joe had been the epitome of a gentleman, and had gotten them two rooms. On the way up, they had traded off driving his vehicle, because neither of them was completely recovered from the trauma of the past few days. She knew that Joe's jaw was hurting him because he took aspirin several times, but he refused to take stronger painkillers to alleviate the discomfort.

"Annie?"

His voice drifted through her room and out to the balcony. She turned. "Come on in." A smile tugged at her mouth as she saw Joe move tentatively through her bedroom suite. He looked around, then focused on her. She felt a delicious warmth ripple through her.

"Well," he said, coming to her side, "what do you think? Did I do great or what?"

Chuckling, Annie said, "Go ahead and preen a little, Joe. This *is* a beautiful place, so quiet and peaceful."

Trying to keep his hands off Annie, to give her the time she deserved and needed, Joe placed his arm behind her where they leaned against the rail, looking back into her bedroom. "This place is really Victorian. Your bed looks like it came out of some fairy tale."

Indeed, it did. All the furniture was from the Victorian era, and Annie loved the sculpted cherry and oak. Her bed had a canopy of gossamer fabric, giving it a very feminine look. A flowery rose pattern covered all of the upholstered furniture and a matching bedspread. Pale pink walls were hung with an array of old Victorian photos and paintings. Fresh flowers, mostly golden California poppies, blue lupine and dark pink rosebuds, filled two vases.

Annie looked up at Joe's satisfied features. "To tell you the truth, I feel like a fairy-tale princess." The rooms must have cost him a small fortune, but after what they'd gone through, they deserved something wonderful.

"You're my princess," he agreed. And then he grimaced. "Not that I'm a prince."

With a laugh, Annie turned and gave him a hug. She wasn't disappointed. Joe's arms came around her, his large hands resting on her waist and hips. "You've very much a man of a bygone era," she told him seriously. "I think all marines see themselves as knights coming to the rescue of those who can't protect themselves."

Sliding his hands up Annie's rib cage, Joe felt her tremble. He cupped her shoulders, caressing them gently. A throbbing ache had centered in the lower part of his body, but his heart was equally involved on another level. "The lady standing in front of me is the most heroic person I've ever met. They might not have given you a suit of armor and a horse from the Middle Ages, but you sure outclass most of us here in the twentieth century, honey. You're a blend of strength and softness." With a shake of his head, Joe whispered, "Maybe silk is a better way to describe you—beautiful and strong."

Lifting her hands, Annie slid them along Joe's arms, feeling the thick, silky hair on them. His skin was warm and firm, belying the physical strength she knew he possessed. "I've never seen myself like that," she said wonderingly as she drowned in the blue of his gaze.

"You wouldn't," he said with a slight smile. "You seem to be completely unaware of how much you affect people—and what you can do when the chips are down."

With a shrug, Annie said, "The Navajo are a matriarchal people. Our women are as strong as any man, and we're expected to be that way. We weren't put in little boxes and told that women can be only this or that."

"Your world allowed you to grow toward your natural strengths," Joe agreed.

With a sigh, she leaned against him as his arms slid slowly around her again. Pressing her head against his shoulder, she reveled in the scent of him as a man, his overwhelming physical presence and the low tone of his voice, which seemed to vibrate through every pore of her sensitized body. "All I want," Annie told him softly, sliding her hand across his chest, "is you. I want to explore you, Joe. I want to look inside your head, your heart. When Father Sky brings the Thunder Beings across Mother Earth, he loves her by sending not only the life-giving rain, but the wild, beautiful lightning bolts." She felt the tension in him as she slowly moved her hand back and forth across his chest. The thud of his heart was like a deep drum being played against her ear, and she closed her eyes, her lips parting with need.

A fine trembling stole through Joe as he held Annie in his arms. The gold of the sunset turned a fiery red-orange in the sky above the glassy Pacific. Annie might appear quiet like that ocean, but underneath he knew she was as molten as that red-hued sunset. Moving his mouth against her hair, he whispered, "I want to go for a walk with you . . . now, on the beach. What do you say?"

With a nod, Annie drew away. Joe's eyes mirrored the turbulence, desire and heat in her own, making her long for him even more. "I'd like that."

"I had them make us a picnic basket," Joe said, gesturing toward the beach. "After driving all day, I thought a long walk to stretch the kinks out of our legs, with some sandwiches to eat as we watch the moon come up, might be just what the doctor ordered." How badly he wanted to kiss Annie, but that could wait. As Joe slid his arm around her waist and led her out of the room, he actually savored the waiting.

Night had fallen long ago, and the tide was incoming. Annie sat in the circle of Joe's arm, a small driftwood fire dancing joyfully about ten feet away from them. The air had turned cool but not cold, and the cotton blanket they sat on kept the chill away. The crash of the breakers, foaming and bubbling upward over the slightly sloped beach, was like music. The moon, a thin slice in the east, shed just enough light to make the water dance with dappled coins of silvery illumination.

The fire was warm, but not as warm as Joe's arms, Annie thought, leaning back against him. She sighed and closed her eyes, her head resting against his shoulder.

"I didn't realize how much I needed this until now. . . ."

"I know." Joe pressed a small kiss to her brow. "Your forehead isn't lined anymore, and I don't see that constant alertness in your eyes."

"Me? What about you?" Annie opened her eyes and smiled up into his. She felt the caress of Joe's hand along her arm and she trembled.

"All I need is you."

Sobering, Annie felt drawn into his darkened, hooded gaze. "Two days ago," she said suddenly, her voice choking, "I didn't think I'd ever see you again. When Gorman's finger brushed that trigger mechanism, I thought you were dead. I thought the worst."

His mouth moved into a wry line. "I did, too." He leaned over and set the picnic basket aside. The blanket was large and he wanted to lie down with Annie in his arms. They had spent nearly three hours simply talking, munching on the food provided and allowing the worries of the world to float away.

Annie surrendered to Joe's strength as he lay down against her and she found herself beside him, her head nestled in the crook of his arm, looking up into his darkly shadowed face, lightly touched by firelight. The gleam in his eyes reminded her of the cougar that had faced her so long ago. Joe was dangerous in a thrilling new way Annie had never experienced. A quiver moved through her as he lifted his hand slowly and began to unbutton her blouse, one button at a time. Each time his fingers grazed her flesh, a small fire leapt to life in that spot. Annie lost herself in the stormy blue-and-black depths of his eyes, feeling as if she were being drawn upward into the embrace of the churning, roiling thunderclouds that as a child she'd so often seen scudding across the reservation.

The blouse fell aside. Annie had never worn a bra because of her tall, skinny frame. Now she saw Joe's eyes grow darker and more intense, felt his inspection of her, although he hadn't yet touched her. The ragged breath he released flowed across her like a warm caress. Her skin tingled under his gaze, and Annie responded from the core of herself as a woman, as an equal to the man who held her protectively in his arms.

Reaching up in turn, she began to unbutton Joe's shirt. The corners of his mouth moved upward, and she smiled at him with her eyes. He liked her boldness, encouraged it, and she felt a fine tremor course through him like a bolt of lightning. In those suspended moments, Annie understood what Father Sky must feel for Mother Earth. As Joe's shirt fell open to expose the dark hair spread across his massive chest, she slid her hand through that curly silk, relishing the texture of him, reveling in the tightening of his skin in her path of discovery of him as a man.

When she had completed her exploration of his chest, Joe slid his hand across her shoulder with a very male smile, coaxing the blouse off of her. Annie lay in his arms, open to his inspection, and it was like lightning dancing across the night sky wherever he grazed her with his callused fingers. She tensed as his hand moved in a lazy, caressing circle over one breast and she surrendered entirely, her fingers digging convulsively into his warm, hard chest. She felt a frenzied, wild expectation as he leaned over her. Then his lips drew her boldly into him, and the suckling motion sent heated waves of light and fire through her until she moaned his name and pressed herself urgently against him.

The crashing of the ocean reverberated through her as he suckled her other nipple in turn, his hand moving in a provocative motion of small circles spiraling down, down beneath the soft fabric of her slacks to her rounded belly. The heartbeat of the ocean became her heartbeat. Nothing else mattered but to enjoy, savor and return the pleasure Joe was giving her. Annie felt her slacks being unbuttoned, then pushed downward until they slid from her feet. Joe's touch was reaffirming, teasing and inciting at the same time, and she felt like the wild, restless ocean, desperately needing to be satisfied.

As her silken lingerie slipped from her feet, she lay naked in his arms. With trembling fingers, Annie unsnapped his jeans and shakily tugged them downward until they, too, were pushed aside. She drowned in his male look, his eyes narrowed to predator intensity as he divested himself of his boxer shorts. Her mouth was dry, her heart pounding like a frantic drum in her breast.

"Come here," Joe rasped, and reached for her.

All her dreams, all her reality melted together as Joe drew her onto him. He lay on his back and she straddled him as she might a horse—only this was no horse. It was a man who made her realize how primal he was, connecting at a deep level with her rich, inner longing. A small gasp escaped her as she settled against him, her blood pulsing throughout her lower body. Her hands came to rest against his flat, hard belly, and his hands fell upon her hips. Lost in the blazing depths of his eyes, she felt him begin to move her slowly forward, then back against him, teasing her, beckoning her. Slick heat purled and flowed from her, touching him like the life-giving rains shared by Father Sky with Mother Earth.

Tipping her head back, her eyes fluttering closed, Annie gave herself to him: her body, her heart, her spirit, which loved him with a fierceness that could never be matched. Knowing this, she moved against him with a wanton sureness that told him how much she wanted him to enter her, to take her and allow her to enfold him like a molten lightning bolt. His groan reverberated through her, exciting her, making her mouth part and the corners move upward, her hands grasping his narrow hips.

For a second out of time, Annie felt herself hesitate fractionally, not out of fear, but out of savoring the coupling that was to come. Never had she wanted to love a man as much as Joe. Never had she wanted to give so much as now. She felt his hands tighten almost painfully against her hips as she slid down, down upon him, pulling him into her, joy racing side by side with the fire that blazed through her. Every inch of her was like lightning dancing against the fertile, moist earth. His hips surged upward, and she gave a cry of triumph—more a growl shared with her mate, telling him how much he pleasured her.

The ceaseless, pounding tide moved in time with them, and Annie felt herself expand to become the sandy, granular beach, the rhythmic, cool ocean. She was like the blackness of the sky, with thousands of shimmering stars exploding through her as Joe brought her to a series of climaxes that shattered her, put her back together again and shattered her once more. The pleasure came in wave after wave, just as the thrashing of the ocean waves repeatedly caressed the beach. Her world was one with all of nature, with Joe, with his heart, which beat in unison with her own as she collapsed against him, their bodies slick with the heat of passion.

The roar of the ocean became the roar of his heart against her ear, and his groan of surrender made her smile with joy as she felt him arch, tense and release himself deep within her. Her senses were spinning, the ocean drowned out by Joe's ragged breathing. As his hand slid upward to cup her chin and guide her lips to his, Annie whispered his name, a reverent prayer.

Heat and tenderness and power combined as his mouth slid across her lips, capturing her, making her his in every conceivable way. His uneven breath grazed her, heightening her tactile sense as she returned his fiery exploration in equal, rhythmic measure. All she was aware of was Joe's hard, slick body against hers, their thighs touching, their arms tangled, holding each other as closely as possible.

Gradually, ever so gradually, Annie returned to the present. The sensation of unity slowly dissolved, just as their shared heartbeats began to separate. But their quiet breathing was still synchronous, and it brought tears to her eyes. The tears formed and beaded on her lashes, and she felt Joe's lips come to rest lightly against her, kissing them away. Her mouth lifted in a tender smile, and she opened her eyes. He lay propped on one elbow, his other arm around her waist, holding her protectively against him. His black hair shone in the moonlight, damp and curled against his smooth, broad brow. The hunger in his eyes had been sated to banked coals of desire, and Annie purred like a happy cougar beneath his continuing touch.

"You're as wild as that cougar you met," Joe rasped. He leaned down, capturing her wanton mouth once more, drowning in her fullness, the life that she offered him like the fertile earth. "Wild and beautiful..." Joe ran his hand across Annie's damp hip and thigh. "Untamed." And she was. Annie had such harmony within herself—she was a woman able to unleash all her femininity without shame or prejudice and give to him fully, without reserve. Joe shook his head, amazed. She wasn't like any other woman, he'd discovered. Her tender smile, the luster in her eyes, moved through him like sun melting the cold wall that had held his heart captive for so long, removing the last of his grief until only good memories remained.

"You sure you aren't a medicine woman?" he teased, brushing several strands of damp hair from her cheek.

"Very sure...."

"I'm not," he growled, and lay down, bringing Annie back on top of him. The night air was growing cooler, but the heat of their bodies and the loving act they'd shared kept them warm. Annie's smile was languorous, tempting and sated. Sliding his hands upward, he framed her oval face, her high cheekbones, and absorbed the beauty of her as a woman.

"You're one of a kind, honey," he told her in a low, off-key voice.

"Your kind," she whispered and closed her eyes, reveling in his touch, languishing in his tenderness.

"Look at me, Annie...."

She opened her eyes slightly and met his intense gaze, loving the hard lines of his face, formed by a very tough life. Joe hadn't ever been given much, Annie realized. And no one wanted to give back to him more than she did. It was a fair trade. "What?"

"My heart feels like it's going to explode," he rasped, "but it's a good feeling, honey. You put it there. I want so much for us...."

Annie understood and laid her head down on his bare, warm shoulder, content to have his arms enfold her. "I do, too."

"Maybe we'll have the time now," he said, running his hand lightly across her long, deeply indented spine.

"Yes...." Annie embraced him with all her female strength, and she felt Joe absorbing her as rain was assimilated by the earth. They fed each other in a positive, joyous way. It was too soon to say I love you, but it was there in her heart, waiting to be said at the right time. She knew Joe loved her, too, but they needed time to grow together.

The words mattered little to Annie, anyway. She'd grown up in a household where loving touches, smiling eyes and laughter conveyed the fierce love that bound her family together. As the waves continued to crash onto the beach, their roar a wild lullaby, she closed her eyes and breathed in sync with Joe. Their lives were lived on the edge, a sword they walked daily. One slip, and one or both of them could die. Still, Annie understood as few people ever would about having a dangerous career and loving a man who was in equal danger.

In her heart, as she snuggled more deeply against Joe's shoulder, her face pressed against his jaw, Annie knew that they were a special breed of human beings who liked living on life's raw edge. From the day she had met the cougar and taken his medicine, she, too, had been destined for such a future, for a cougar always lived in danger. Their love, although new, was strong—like the silk Joe had spoken about on the balcony. And with time, Annie knew it would only grow stronger. Just as the storms of Father Sky inevitably danced across the surface of Mother Earth, she would live her life in communion with Joe—forever.

* * * * *

Silhouette

SPECIAL EDITION™

THE Jones GANG

by Christine Rimmer

**Three rapscallion brothers. Their main talent: making trouble.
Their only hope: three uncommon women who knew the way to
heal a wounded heart! Meet them in these books:**

Jared Jones

hadn't had it easy with women. Retreating to his mountain cabin, he found willful
Eden Parker waiting to show him a good woman's love in MAN OF THE MOUNTAIN
(May, SE #886).

Patrick Jones

was determined to show Regina Black that a wild Jones boy was *not* husband
material. But that wouldn't stop her from trying to nab him in SWEETBRIAR SUMMIT
(July, SE #896)

Jack Roper

came to town looking for the wayward and beautiful Olivia Larrabee. He never
suspected he'd uncover a long-buried Jones family secret in A HOME FOR THE HUNTER
(September, SE #908)....

**Meet these rascal men and the women who'll tame them,
only from Silhouette Books and Special Edition!**

Rugged and lean...and the best-looking,
sweetest-talking men to be found in the
entire Lone Star state!

Diana Palmer

LONG, TALL TEXANS

In July 1994, Silhouette is very proud to bring you
Diana Palmer's first three LONG, TALL TEXANS.
CALHOUN, JUSTIN and TYLER—the three cowboys
who started the legend. Now they're back by popular
demand in one classic volume—and they're ready to
lasso your heart! Beautifully repackaged for this
special event, this collection is sure to be a
longtime keepsake!

"Diana Palmer makes a reader want to find a Texan
of her own to love!"   —*Affaire de Coeur*

**LONG, TALL TEXANS—the first three—
reunited in this special roundup!**

**Available in July,
wherever Silhouette books are sold.**

Take 4 bestselling love stories FREE

Plus get a FREE surprise gift!

CAN YOU STAND THE HEAT?

Silhouette

SUMMER

Sizzlers '94

You're in for a serious heat wave with
Silhouette's latest selection of sizzling
summer reading. This sensuous collection
of three short stories provides the perfect
vacation escape! And what better authors
to relax with than

ANNETTE BROADRICK
JACKIE MERRITT
JUSTINE DAVIS

And that's not all....

With the purchase of *Silhouette Summer
Sizzlers '94*, you can send in for a FREE
Summer Sizzlers beach bag!

SUMMER JUST GOT HOTTER—
WITH SILHOUETTE BOOKS!

MONTANA MAVERICKS

Stories that capture living and loving beneath the Big Sky, where legends live on...and the mystery is just beginning.

Watch for the sizzling debut of
MONTANA MAVERICKS in August with

ROGUE STALLION

by Diana Palmer

A powerful tale of simmering desire and mystery!

"The powerful intensity of Diana Palmer's storyline is exceeded only by the sizzling tension between her protagonists." —*Affaire de Coeur*

And don't miss a minute of the loving as the mystery continues with many more of your favorite authors!

Only from  *Silhouette*®

where passion lives.

MAVT

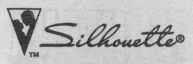

WILD RIVER

by
Laurie Paige

Maddening men…winsome women…and the untamed land they live in—
all add up to love! Meet them in these books from Silhouette Special Edition
and Silhouette Romance:

WILD IS THE WIND (Silhouette Special Edition #887, May)
Rafe Barrett retreated to his mountain resort to escape his dangerous feelings
for Genny McBride…but when she returned, ready to pick up where they
left off, would Rafe throw caution to the wind?

A ROGUE'S HEART (Silhouette Romance #1013, June)
Returning to his boyhood home brought Gabe Deveraux face-to-face
with ghosts of the past—and directly into the arms of sweet and loving
Whitney Campbell.…

A RIVER TO CROSS (Silhouette Special Edition #910, September)
Sheriff Shane Macklin knew there was more to "town outsider"
Tina Henderson than met the eye. He saw a generous and selfless woman
whose true colors held the promise of love.…

Don't miss these latest Wild River tales from Silhouette Special Edition
and Silhouette Romance!

SEWR-4